SKY HIGH STAKES

Ted Clifton

Sky High Stakes
Ted Clifton
ISBN 978-1-927967-73-7

Produced by IndieBookLauncher.com
www.IndieBookLauncher.com
Editing: Nassau Hedron
Cover Design: Saul Bottcher
Interior Design and Typesetting: Saul Bottcher

The body text of this book is set in Adobe Caslon.

Also Available
EPUB edition, ISBN 978-1-927967-74-4
Kindle edition, ISBN 978-1-927967-75-1

CONTENTS

❄

Free Preview:
Four Corners War

❄

1

Billy the Kid Rides Again

1989 marked the end of the Cold War, the fall of the Berlin Wall, and the Exxon Valdez oil spill. George H.W. Bush became President of the United States. Margaret Thatcher was Prime Minister of Great Britain. The first version of Microsoft Office was released and Nintendo debuted one of its legacy products, the Game Boy. The Internet and cell phones existed, but were very limited. The World Wide Web was only an idea, and the first satellite in the GPS system was launched.

Ruidoso, New Mexico

"Just shut up and let me think. *Why the hell did you try to shoot me?*" Deputy Samson screamed at Charles Jackson, a big son-of-a-bitch, who at that moment was crying and begging the Deputy not to kill him. Jackson owned a small auto body repair shop just on the outskirts of Ruidoso, New Mexico. He was also a bookie, mostly taking bets on the horse racing at Ruidoso Downs. He was supposed to pay the acting Sheriff a cut of his action every week. Deputy Samson had been sent to collect an envelope from Jackson. Simple enough—just an errand. Samson didn't even know what was in the envelope he was supposed to pick up. Then Jackson pulled a gun on him—not smart—and Samson shot him.

The deputy began pacing and rubbing his hands together. He'd fired the shot more as a reflex than anything else, and now he didn't know what to do. Samson was honest—not a saint by any means, but unlike many who worked as deputies in Lincoln County he still clung to his basic values. A primitive part of his brain said to kill this dumb piece of shit so he could leave and forget about the whole thing. Erase the whole ugly mess. He wouldn't do it—he knew this even as he thought about it—but he was going to have to deal with acting Sheriff Marino over the shooting and that had him sweating.

"I send you to do one simple thing and you screw it up—maybe I should come up there and shoot both of you assholes." Martin Marino had a bad temper and was in a perpetually foul mood. Marino had left Miami some years ago to visit a cousin in Ruidoso, New Mexico, in order to avoid embarrassing questions about the $300,000 or so that had gone missing from his father-in-law's trucking business. After a few months in Ruidoso, Martin had heard that the father-in-law considered it money well spent and arranged for his daughter to divorce Martin, enthusiastically cursing his name as he did. He let it be known that if Martin ever showed up on the east coast again he'd be dead, but that he didn't give a shit if he stayed in fucking Mexico. Like many people, Marino's father-in-law got New Mexico, the state, and Mexico, the country, confused.

Now feeling safe, Martin had begun a new career as a corrupt, even evil, deputy sheriff. Being a thug doesn't usually lead to advancement, but in a lucky twist for Martin it turned out that thugs shared many attributes with a certain kind of lawman. When Sheriff Rodriguez got sick, Deputy Marino acted like he was the logical choice to step in and no one objected-- at least to his face. As the Sheriff became increasingly ill and was eventually put in the hospital, Marino gradually took over, threatening anyone who got in his way. Being an especially vile creature made his threats credible—everyone believed he meant them.

Deputy Marino headed to the body shop where Samson was holding Jackson. As he drove, he became increasingly angry. His deal with Jackson had been for a twenty percent cut of Jackson's net take. Marino thought that was fair, and now the bastard tried to stiff him—not a good decision. Jackson wasn't the brightest guy in the world, but everybody knew him. He was a fixture at the racetrack. He always had an opinion on what horse was going to win and after a few beers would share it with anyone who walked by. Marino thought he was a scumbag.

"Sorry Martin. I just saw him pull his gun and I shot."

That bit of news earned Samson a hard blow to the side of his head from Marino. He fell to the ground and—for just a second—thought about reaching for his gun. Marino gave Samson a look that said *I'd love to shoot you today—just reach for that gun, you moron*. Marino turned his attention to Jackson.

"Okay you idiot, tell me exactly why you shot my deputy—and it better be good or you're dead." Marino's calm monotone was more frightening than if he'd been yelling.

"Look, Mr. Marino, I didn't know who he was and I thought he was going to rob me. When he walked in, the light was behind him and I couldn't tell he was in uniform—all I saw was that he had a gun. Man, I'm bleeding here, I need an ambulance."

In a fit of temper, Marino kicked the bookie very hard several times, one blow landing on his head. The man howled and turned pale, his face contorted in obvious pain. In an amazingly short time he was dead.

"Fuck, fuck, fuck. Now look what you've done you dumb shit—he's dead." Marino directed his words at Samson, ignoring the fact that he'd been the one to kick the bookie, which was without question the blow that had killed him.

Samson knew that his could be the next body on the ground and put his hand on his revolver.

"What the fuck, Samson, you going to shoot me? You really are an idiot. You shot this bastard and he's dead, and you think the best solution is to shoot the sheriff. Get your hand off of your gun and call for an ambulance, now!"

"Jeez, Martin, he's already dead."

"I know that, but the ambulance people won't. You tell them that he pulled a gun on you for no reason and you had to shoot him. Now give me your gun, do what I say, and this'll all go away."

Samson hesitated. No one in their right mind would trust Martin Marino—the little shit was just plain evil—but the deputy was in a bad spot. If he didn't do what Marino wanted, it could get real ugly for him. How the hell had all of this happened? The Lincoln County sheriff's department had once been an honest place to work, but now it was more like a crime family. Samson made his decision, taking off his gun belt and handing it to Marino. Then he called for an ambulance. He hoped he'd still be alive the next day.

Lincoln County is best known as the location of some of the west's worst open range conflicts, The Lincoln County Wars, featuring the likes of Billy the Kid. Martin Marino was short in stature, just like the Kid—he was also crazy, just like the Kid. Lincoln County had survived Billy the Kid—Martin Marino might be a different matter.

2

Beginnings

Some weeks later—Truth or Consequences, New Mexico

Ray Pacheco had been the sheriff of Dona Ana County for many years before retiring. He'd bought an old abandoned cabin with an infamous past and settled into a relaxing life of doing nothing—at least for a few months. He soon realized that when you're working and busy all you want is some free time to relax, but when every day is full of nothing but leisure time, you quickly come to want something else. The days became tedious, contributing to a feeling of isolation.

The cabin Ray had purchased was located on Elephant Butte Lake just outside of Truth or Consequences, New Mexico—locally known as T or C. He looked the part of a rural western sheriff, with his cowboy hat, boots, western shirt, and jeans, but he wasn't actually the outdoorsman type. This strange contradiction was the result of having always devoted his life to his work in law enforcement, never taking time to try hunting or fishing. It seemed clear to Ray that despite his lack of knowledge, the solution to his inactivity was to become a fisherman. He was retired, lived on a lake, and bored out of his mind, so it was a natural: *take up fishing*.

To facilitate his move into the world of fishing, Ray had gone to the largest bait shop on the lake—Jack's Bait, Boats and Beer. It was an act of courage simply to enter the store. He remembered the off-putting odor and was still unsure, even now, of what its source had been. Now as he thought back with fondness, he realized that he actually missed the smell, which had disappeared after recent renovations.

That had been the beginning of Ray's venture into fishing—and, more importantly, the beginning of his friendships with Big Jack and Tyee Chino. Big Jack owned the bait shop and dispensed advice on almost everything to anyone who would listen. Ray recalled how Big Jack had recommended that Ray learn to fish before buying any fishing gear from his store—honest advice from the dispenser of numerous tall tales, related to fishing and to life in general. Big Jack was a contradiction. By all appearances he seemed to be a man with little ambition who had experienced little success in his life, but Ray discovered over time, not much was what it seemed when it came to Big Jack.

During their first meeting, Big Jack had advised Ray to seek out Tyee Chino, one of several fishing guides on Elephant Butte Lake, who was known for his extensive skills in the art of catching fish—and also for his frequent drunkenness. Big Jack had insisted that there was no one who knew more about all things fishing than Tyee Chino, and advised that Ray ignore any first impression and simply hire him. Tyee Chino was an Apache Indian who, Big Jack said, used a tourist-baiting dumb Indian schtick as part of his professional persona. The fishing guide business was surprisingly competitive, and Chino was going to use any gimmick that would attract paying customers.

But as Big Jack said, "no one else knows half the shit Chino does about fishing."

Once Ray spent time with Chino he found out that Big Jack had been right. Most of the Indian guide routine was an act, although the drinking was real. Chino was recovering from a failed marriage and had taken up drinking as his primary pastime. The Indian act had some truth to it—after all, he was Apache—but his stereotypical way of speaking, like a Native American in an old western movie, was bogus. Tyee had a double degree from the University of New Mexico in Albuquerque in Computer Science and English Lit. He had needed to make a living after his marriage collapsed and he began drinking, so he'd become a fishing guide. The Hollywood Indian act seemed to work well with tourists, and it also suited Chino's whimsical personality.

Beginning with that encounter, Big Jack and Tyee Chino had become Ray's friends and eventual business partners. The journey to friendship involved some adventures tied to murder and intrigue. As they became more involved in solving the strange disappearance of a guest from the Hot Springs Inn, they realized the talents they collectively had at their disposal. Maybe so that he wouldn't have to fish *all* the time, Ray had suggested that they open a private investigation business operated from the outbuildings on his property at the lake.

Through an unusual set of circumstances they had ended up with two primary sources of cases: the FBI and the AG's office for the State of New Mexico. The FBI was supporting *Pacheco & Chino, PIs* because the agency had been negligent in a case involving Ray, Big Jack, and Tyee, which had put Ray in harm's way. In order to make amends, the FBI had agreed to provide the new firm with consulting work and also to provide computer training and access. This had mostly involved Tyee, with his background in computer science.

The other source of revenue was assignments from Tony Garcia, the Attorney General of New Mexico. Tony and Ray's history went back to their Dona Ana County days in Las Cruces, New Mexico. Tony had recently been given the new responsibility of looking into the functioning of county sheriff's offices. The Governor and many other officials had expressed concern that some of the sheriff's offices were not being properly monitored. Tony had reached out to Ray—as a past Sheriff—to assist him in getting a better handle on some of the less-than-cooperative Sheriff's departments in the state.

Completing Ray's transition from lonely retiree to this new world was his recent marriage to Sue Lewis. Sue had been the waitress at the Lone Post Café in T or C. Her history was troubled, with a bad marriage followed by a deep depression when her ex-husband killed himself. Sue couldn't help feeling responsibility for his suicide. She'd been a physician's assistant, and even had experience in forensics, but her emotional state had driven her to abandon most opportunities and to hit the road—repeatedly—at the first sign of personal involvement with anyone. Until she met Ray. She was younger than he was, but the match seemed to be just what they both needed.

Ray had been married for many years until his wife's death almost eight years before. He had thought that he'd never be involved with anyone again, much less get married. His son, Michael, who had become an attorney and moved to Boston prior to his mother's death, wasn't pleased with his father's marrying again. Ray was disappointed that his son seemed upset, but decided that he had to really live what was left of his life, not just wait alone to die just to please his absent son.

Another addition to Ray's household came as a result of his first investigation case. He'd inherited a pedigree show dog, who he'd named Happy. Happy was smart, loyal, wagged his tail a lot and—according to Ray—had a great smile.

On a bright, sunny New Mexico day Ray, Tyee, and Happy were headed to Ruidoso. This was located more or less due east of T or C, and up into the mountains, but between T or C and Ruidoso was the White Sands Missile Range. This was a huge military installation covering thousands of square miles, and had been the location of the first atomic bomb blast. All access to this vast area was prohibited, a rule enforced by the military. As a result, the trip involved either going north to US Highway 380 and dropping down, or going south to Las Cruces and over to Alamogordo, then north through Mescalero. Either route added many hours of driving to what would otherwise have been a fairly direct shot, but there were no roads through White Sands and, even if there were, you'd be dodging missiles. Ray and Tyee decided to go south first and then north. One advantage to this path was the chance to drive through Mescalero, Tyee Chino's home town.

"When was the last time you were in Mescalero?"

"Many years. I had trouble adapting to the tribal ways when I was a teenager. I was sent to live with my aunt who lived in Albuquerque when I was in high school. I only came back once, for my mother's funeral."

"Guess you still have lots of relatives in this area."

"Old white man suddenly nosy old woman."

"Yeah. Sorry. Guess you don't want to talk about it."

"No, my fault, Ray. It's just not a good memory. As far as relatives, the Apaches are a small tribe and everyone's related. In your world there are millions of people in your tribe—in my world there are just a few thousand. It makes it hard when you're not a part of your clan, and doubly hard that you're shunned by your closest kin. I guess I was a rebel—I rejected the life and the people and it hurt my mother a lot. It's something I regret to this day."

There was stillness in the old Jeep—even Happy seemed subdued. Ray had always thought of Tyee as someone who had left the old ways behind and ventured out into the "real world" to find a better life. Now he was beginning to understand how much Tyee had given up to escape the reservation life he couldn't live in, only to enter a white man's world that was not very accommodating.

"Better watch your speed though this area, Ray. One of the primary sources of revenue for the Apache Tribe is speeding tickets."

Ray had already noticed that the speed limit had decreased significantly as they entered the city limits. Going from fifty-five to thirty-five that quickly was bound to create a lot of opportunity for ticket revenue. Just as he was thinking about it, they saw an Apache Police vehicle by the side of the road ahead of them. They kept an eye on the rear view mirror in case he should decide to get closer to them.

As they continued, the elevation began to increase rapidly. Soon the pine trees were huge and the air was much cooler. At several points there were scenic turnouts where you could see for many miles down to the desert floor—White Sands was visible off in the distance and thousands of feet below. The gleaming white sand made it seem like an unconnected, far-off world. Ray's old Jeep—dog-ugly, as it was often called—had some trouble with elevation, but always made it to the top. At least it had so far. Tyee had volunteered to drive his newer Ford F-150 pickup, but with two grown men and Happy it would have been more than a little crowded.

"Tell me, Ray, why do you think the AG wants us to look into the Lincoln County Sheriff's office?"

"Well, not a hundred percent sure. Tony wasn't real forthcoming about his concerns other than to say that the Sheriff has taken ill and in his absence a deputy has stepped in and apparently is turning Ruidoso into some kind of little Chicago or something. I've talked to some people I know in the area and they say this guy, Deputy Marino, is running roughshod over everyone. One of my contacts says the rumors are that the guy is getting kickbacks off of almost all the activities in the area where he can force his way in—and if the businesspeople or crooks don't agree, it gets ugly. There's talk that the recent death of a racetrack bookie wasn't the accident that the deputy is claiming it was."

"Why don't they just send in the State Police and take the department over?"

"Indian very wise. I'm not sure why he's asking us to look at this. If it's as blatant as I'm hearing, I don't understand why they're hesitating. Tony and I have been friends since our days in Las Cruces. He was the County Attorney when I was the Sheriff and we worked together very well. He was smart, and aggressive on crime prosecutions, and one of the most honest men I've known. The other day when I talked to him about this assignment, I got an uneasy feeling he was holding back something."

"Sounds like we could be riding into big pile of horse shit."

"Is that an old Indian saying?"

"No, that's just stating the obvious."

3

The Village of Ruidoso

Ruidoso is a mountain resort town, sustained mostly by skiing and horse racing. The ski resort, Ski Apache, is owned by the Mescalero Apache Tribe. It's located on Sierra Blanca, a 12,000-foot mountain. The other major attraction is the Ruidoso Downs racetrack.

Long before Ray reached the town limits he pulled off the highway at a sign indicating the turn for The Inn of the Mountain Gods. This is a resort located just outside Ruidoso, also owned by the Apache Tribe.

"Hope this is okay, I made arrangements to stay here before I realized it was owned by your tribe."

"Sure, I always liked this place. Sometimes the tribe employs a lot of members and sometimes they just contract out the operation to professionals—not real sure how they're running it now. Even if I see someone I know, generally they just ignore me—sort of like I'm dead."

"I had some relatives that did that to me after I went into law enforcement."

As they entered the grounds of the Inn it became obvious that this was a world-class resort. The landscaping was amazing. The backdrop of Sierra Blanca was like a living postcard.

The main building had an impressive entrance that managed to capture the intimate feel of a log cabin, but on a grand scale.

Out of respect for the upscale surroundings, Ray found an out of the way parking spot for his reliable but ugly Jeep. Letting Happy out released a burst of energy from the dog, who'd been cooped up for longer than was normal for him. He sprinted around the lush grounds, inspecting everything in sight. He seemed to approve.

Attaching Happy's leash, they entered the beautiful, massive lobby. There was an abundance of huge windows, which framed the mountains in such a way as to make them resemble a painting. Check-in was simple and quick. There were a few special instructions related to Happy, but he was welcome, as the staff had said he would be when Ray had called to make arrangements. There were rules about his activities, but none of them seemed unreasonable. The staff was very accommodating and made them feel like honored guests. They had two rooms, one for Ray and Happy and one for Tyee. They quickly unloaded the Jeep and inspected their rooms, Happy smelling every inch. Ray got Happy some food from his bags and some water in a bowl, resulting in much slurping and tail wagging. Soon they were all back in the Jeep, headed to the sheriff's department in Ruidoso.

The drive into Ruidoso was only about ten minutes. They entered a resort mountain community with a main drag filled with tourist shops, bars, and restaurants. There were also ski rental outlets and various hotels, motels, and lodges. There was a busy quality to the downtown area, with a lot of tourists driving the streets and quite a few pedestrians. The sheriff's department was not far from the main downtown area, just north of town.

"Hello, my name is Ray Pacheco and if possible I'd like to see Deputy Marino."

"Sorry, Mr. Pacheco, Deputy Marino's out of the office today. Would you like to make an appointment or maybe see someone else?"

"Hum, I guess I thought I had an appointment with the deputy this afternoon. Guess he forgot."

"Maybe so, sir. He didn't say anything to me about an appointment and I don't show anything on the calendar." This exchange was with a very serious looking young woman, probably in her first job. To Ray she seemed nervous, but that might just be her normal office manner. Ray told her he could be reached at the Inn of the Mountain Gods and asked if she'd have the deputy give him a call, then he and Tyee headed back outside.

"Sounds like Deputy Marino decided he didn't want to talk to you."

"Yeah. I just called out of the blue and made the appointment—told him I was the retired Sheriff from Dona Ana and was going to be in town and wanted to drop by. He seemed friendly enough—but something must have changed."

"Well, what's the plan now?"

"Some weeks ago a bookie from the racetrack was killed by a deputy in what was described as an accidental shooting in this guy's auto body shop. The input I'm getting from a couple of people I've talked to is that it doesn't smell right. The gossip is that Deputy Marino was getting some kind of kickback from this bookie and maybe they had a falling out, leading to this guy being shot. Thought I might let you out at the track and have you check out what people are saying about the guy's death."

"A day at the racetrack with an Apache Indian, sounds like some kind of strange tourist attraction."

"Yeah, sounds strange alright. Don't get too nosy and stir up anything until we can figure out what's really going on. While you're doing that, Happy and I'll run over and talk to the police chief."

"Do you think the chief's involved in any of this strong-arm stuff?"

"Nah. I know this guy, Chief Nelson. He hasn't done much of anything in fifteen years. It's only a four man department and mostly takes care of parking and traffic issues in the downtown area. Any criminal activity gets turned over to the Sheriff's department. But he's a notorious gossip, so more than likely he knows everything that's going on—whether or not he'll share with me is another question."

Ray drove down to the racetrack area and let Tyee out. "Remember, ask questions but be careful. Don't get yourself shot."

"White man leader offer good advice." Tyee waved and headed into the track.

Police Chief Larry Nelson was older than Ray and should have retired ten years before. When he was hired as a Police Chief he was the only member of the Ruidoso Police Force. It was created by the town council because the downtown business leaders insisted that they needed a police presence to stop the hippies from smoking pot out in the open, right in front of their stores.

Chief Nelson had handled the hippie-shooing duties himself for a couple of years, but after one rather rowdy weekend he'd requested an additional officer to assist him. After a few years the department had grown to four, and then it stayed that size. Chief Nelson was diligent about having his men give enough tickets to cover most of the department's overhead. The Chief was happy and the downtown merchants felt protected.

Ray parked his Jeep in front of the downtown storefront police department. He made sure Happy had air and was comfortable, with plenty of water.

"Sheriff Pacheco, son of a bitch. I thought you had died." Chief Nelson enjoyed a good laugh at his own wiseass remark. The Chief had to be at least a hundred pounds overweight and puffed on an old cigar—if anyone in the room was going to die that day it was likely going to be him.

"Chief Nelson, good to see you too."

"What brings you to my fair city?"

"An old friend asked me to look into the recent shooting death of Charles Jackson, who I believe owned an auto body shop and was also a part-time bookie."

"Yeah, I'd heard you were now a private investigator. Matter of fact, I heard you had partnered up with an Indian and a disbarred attorney. Sounds like quite a group."

"Well one of my partners *is* an Apache. He's also my friend. You should meet him, he's a great guy and a much better person than either one of us. He's with me on this trip." Ray was starting to remember why he had never liked the police chief.

"Yeah, whatever you say. I was a little surprised when I heard that you were back in the game—figured you would have had enough of law enforcement."

"No question I was tired of dealing with the local politics of running a sheriff's department, but after a while of doing nothing but fishing I decided I better do something or I was going to rot." They both nodded, with knowing chuckles.

"I know what you're saying, Ray. Not sure I'd live long if I quit."

"What do you know about the death of Charles Jackson?"

"Don't quote me, but there's no question that asshole Martin Marino had something to do with it. My guess would be that the piece of shit was the one who shot Charles and the deputy took the fall."

"Are you saying it was an accident or something else?"

"Ray, this is the most evil person who ever lived. I'm saying he killed Charles Jackson and he's getting away with it. Martin Marino needs to be dead!"

"I'd guess you don't have any proof that he did it?"

"Right, he's the goddamn sheriff. He's the one who would investigate, and he's saying it was an accident—bullshit. I'd also guess he has something to do with Sheriff Rodriguez being in the hospital. I can't prove a goddamn thing, but let me tell you one thing: this man will continue to cause harm and create havoc in this town until he's dead."

"What do you know about Charles Jackson?"

"Not the brightest guy in town, but everybody liked him. He was big and friendly, liked to drink too much, and he'd occasionally run a few illegal games of chance—but he was born here and well liked. He didn't deserve to die no matter what bullshit he was involved in with that bastard Marino."

Ray thanked the chief and told him he'd stay in touch. The man had been very open about his hatred for Marino, and if Marino ever showed up dead the chief would be a prime suspect. Ray thought that his bluster was mostly show, with no substance, but he wasn't real sure. And after all, the guy did carry a gun.

Ray decided to head back to the racetrack and locate Tyee. Something about his conversation with the chief was making him nervous. He sure the hell didn't want to ignore the fact that there could be real danger in poking around asking about Jackson's death.

The racetrack was impressive—its double-decker grandstand was the tallest structure you could see as you drove up. Ray parked and made sure that Happy was comfortable, then entered the general seating area, which was free. He looked around for Tyee. The man's six-foot-four-inch frame should have stood out, but Ray didn't see him. He wandered over to a snack bar and bought a hot dog—the perfect diet for an old man out in the sun without a hat.

"Hey, if Sue finds out you were eating a hot dog you won't be allowed out on any more field trips."

"You Indians sure know how to sneak up on people."

They headed over to a quiet corner and took a seat. Ray continued to consume his tasty treat.

"Saw the Police Chief. He claims Deputy Marino is the devil himself."

"Well he's not the only one. Seems as though this guy has alienated half the town. I ran into a cousin of mine who's still talking to me—he said the deputy acted like he owned the town. He also said that he was forcing almost every businessperson to pay him some kind of protection money. This Marino guy is apparently living in an old 1930s black and white crime movie taking place in New York City. The guy must be nuts to be doing what he's doing—it's going to get him killed or arrested."

"Yeah, I know. It just seems so strange that the AG or governor hasn't done something."

"I know—it's very weird. You'd think there'd be all kinds of state or federal law enforcement here putting a stop to this. By the way, I know the racetrack manager. His name's Dick Franklin. I went to school with him at UNM. I'm sure he'd see us—you want to do that?"

"Sure."

They headed off to find the track's administrative offices.

"Tyee, it's great to see you. I'd heard some pretty scary stuff about you after your divorce—I was worried about you. This is just great. You don't know this but you were one of my heroes at school. You just seemed to have your act together about what you were going to do and everyone assumed you'd be a big success."

"Well it's good to see you too, Dick. And yeah, I kind of took a tumble after my divorce—fell into a whisky bottle for a few years. But now I'm working with Ray and we've started a PI business—everything's a lot better for me."

"I'm pleased. So what brings you to the track today—not just to look me up I'd assume?"

"We're looking into the death of Charles Jackson."

"Well, Tyee, if you can eliminate the scum who did this it would be a great service to mankind."

"Are you saying you know who killed Charles Jackson?"

"That lowlife Deputy Marino is saying his deputy shot Jackson by mistake—that's bullshit. Marino killed him or had him killed. I'm being robbed every day by that thug and I can't get anyone to do anything about it. I talked to the Police Chief—what a joke he is. I've called the State Police and they said it's not their jurisdiction. My god, the jurisdiction is the county sheriff's and he's the asshole robbing me—why they can't see that as a problem beats the shit out of me."

"Mr. Franklin, how is Marino robbing you?" This came from Ray.

"Please, call me Dick. He's stealing a percentage of the net take every day. He's threatened me in no uncertain terms that if I don't pay his 'fee' *I'll suffer consequences.* He's saying it's a surcharge for additional services from the sheriff's department—just complete bullshit. It's robbery. I decided this morning I was going to contact the Feds and ask for help. If the state government won't do something about this then I'll move up the ladder until I find someone who will."

"What are the other town officials saying?" Ray asked.

"Mostly they're afraid of this goon. He's evil—meaning he'll kill you without hesitation. I have no idea how he thought he could carry on this way without some repercussions, but it's quite possible that besides being evil he's completely stupid."

"Dick, Tyee and I have been asked by the AG's office to look into what's going on with the sheriff's department. I don't know why they've been slow to respond, but as of today the AG will be informed that crimes are potentially being committed by the sheriff's department and that he needs to get enough state police officers up here to take over until it can be straightened out."

"Well, that'd be great news. I just hope they listen to you, because if something isn't done then someone will take action to stop this bastard."

They thanked Dick Franklin for his time and headed back to the Inn. After letting Happy romp around a bit and take care of his business they headed towards Ray's room to discuss what they knew and to make calls.

Ray called Tony Garcia, Attorney General of New Mexico, and got his voice mail. "Tony, you should know that there's an explosion up here ready to happen. The acting Sheriff is running a crime syndicate or something, and half of the town is ready to start shooting. This is very serious. Unless you act at once by sending in a small fucking army to shut down the sheriff's operation, you're going to have another Lincoln County war on your hands—and trust me Tony, I'm not exaggerating." Ray left his contact info at the Inn and hung up.

They agreed they'd meet for dinner in about an hour. Tyee went to his room to rest a bit and make a few calls. Ray lay down for just a while and tried to collect his thoughts. He'd never seen anything like what was going on in this little town. The bad guys had moved in and taken over—it was more like a B-grade western movie than anything else. The question was where in the hell were the good guys?

Ray left Happy asleep in the room and went to meet Tyee for dinner. They had a few beers and two of the best steaks either had ever tasted. Ray asked the waiter to ask the Chef what seasonings he had used on the steaks—he'd been handling much of the cooking at home and was becoming a skilled amateur cook. The waiter returned with a written note that described the various ingredients the Chef used. Ray was pleased.

After dinner Ray decided to turn in—it had been a long day. They said their goodnights and agreed to meet in the morning for breakfast.

Sometime in the middle of the night the phone rang in Ray's room.

"Yes."

"Well, the bastard is dead. I mean really fucking dead—shot eight times, mostly in the head. He was in his patrol car parked in front of Tito's Bar on Main Street. No one heard or saw anything. Do you and your Indian want to come down and take a look?"

"Yes. We'll be there in ten minutes."

Ray called Tyee and gave him the news. They met at the Jeep and headed to town. Happy was sound asleep and Ray decided to leave him in the room.

4

A Killing

"Yep, really fucking dead."

They were on the main drag through town. All the lights and patrol cars had attracted a lot of attention. Most of the officers present, both police and deputies, were busy with crowd control. The situation felt close to being out of control. The police chief was there but not really doing anything.

"Chief, I'm taking charge of this crime scene. I'm acting on the authority of the Attorney General of New Mexico with the knowledge of the Governor. If you are anyone else has a problem with that they need to contact those gentlemen."

Well fuck, he'd done it now. He was supposed to be an observer not a participant. But Ray couldn't stand by and watch these morons screw up the investigation, especially since one of the logical suspects was the police chief himself.

The chief gave Ray a dirty look and told him he didn't really give a fuck what Ray did and he didn't give a fuck what the Governor or the moron AG did either—then he walked off.

Ray pulled Tyee aside. "We need some help up here. Call the Sheriff of Dona Ana and ask him if he can send some men. Also, do you think the Apache police would spare a couple of officers and vehicles, just until we can get the state police involved?"

"I can sure call. I know the guy who runs the police department—he's a good man and I think he'll want to help. I'll call him and the sheriff in Las Cruces."

"Good. Also, I want you to call Sue and Big Jack. Ask them both to come up here as soon as they can. We are going to need some help and we need people we can trust."

"I'm on it." Tyee left to find a phone.

Ray instructed two of the deputies from the sheriff's department to cordon off the area with yellow police tape. He had them cover the windshield of the patrol car, partially concealing Marino's body. They had one side of the street completely blocked, which was creating a traffic problem and contributing to the sense of chaos. Ray grabbed one of the sheriff's deputies.

"My name is Pacheco and I've taken charge of this crime scene under the authority..."

"Yeah, we've all heard you're in charge, Sheriff Pacheco. Every man here will do what you ask. We're all embarrassed about what's happened to the department since Marino took over. We'll cooperate fully and do whatever you tell us."

"Great. We need to get this car removed to a secure location. I don't want the body moved from the car yet. But if we could get a careful tow truck driver in here and move the whole mess somewhere else, it will help restore order."

"I know who to call—he'll be here in minutes."

"What's your name?"

"Deputy Samson, sir." Samson left to make his call.

Another possible suspect making crime scene arrangements. Ray needed his own crew as soon as possible. Before he could do much more, the tow truck showed up. The driver was neat and articulate—obviously a tow truck driver imposter—and within a very short time he had the patrol car secured and was ready to head out. The driver said they had enough space at his shop to put everything inside for the night. Ray agreed and followed the driver down the street about three blocks, and then turned off of Main and traveled about four more blocks to a large junk yard and shop building. The driver skillfully maneuvered the car with the body inside into the shop and detached it. Ray had brought one of the police officers from the scene and told him to stay with the car until someone came to relieve him. Then he went back to find Tyee.

"Thought you'd run off with some young female police officer never to be seen again."

"Young female police officers could do a whole hell of a lot worse—but I was dealing with the car. It's in storage—just need to arrange to have someone watch it to make sure it isn't tampered with."

"Oh, shit. This sounds like cheap labor—in other words Indian work."

"Bingo!"

"I talked to Big Jack and Sue. They're planning on leaving first thing in the morning. Should be here before noon tomorrow."

"Great. I'm going back to the Inn and get Happy. We'll both stay here tonight and then decide on what to do tomorrow morning. Be back in about thirty minutes or so."

Ray returned with Happy without incident. Tyee reported that the towing company owner had come by and said it was fine to stay there with the patrol car and body and that they could use the phone if they needed to. Happy seemed less than pleased to be so near a dead body, but he settled into a corner in the office and went to sleep.

Somewhere around three in the morning two state patrol cars with three officers each showed up at the tow company building.

"We were instructed to report to you, Mr. Pacheco, and do what you say."

"Two of you should stay here and make sure no one messes with any evidence. We'll have forensic people in here by the morning. The rest of you should go to the sheriff's department building and take charge. You'll be acting on my authority to give out assignments and keep the department functioning. I hope that by tomorrow afternoon we'll have a more developed plan about how to proceed, but our first duty is to make sure the citizens are assured that someone's in charge." Ray provided his contact information at the Inn and then he, Tyee, and Happy headed back to their rooms.

When Ray got to his room he saw he had a message. "Ray, this is Tony. I flew up this evening. I know you're busy, but I'd like to meet first thing in the morning for breakfast. I'm also staying at the Inn. If you can, let's meet at about seven thirty in the main dining room. See you then."

Great, that was only a few hours away. Ray decided to lie down and try to get a couple hours sleep. He had been used to this kind of schedule once upon a time—it had happened a lot when he was Sheriff—but he was getting a little old to pull all-nighters.

"Wow, Ray, you look like shit."

"Good morning to you too, Tony."

"Sorry, guess you had a long night?"

"Yeah, there's a real mess here. Martin Marino was acting out some mobster fantasy or something. The guy seemed to think he could run roughshod over almost everybody in the county and no one would do anything. And now he's dead."

"I know Ray. I should have acted quicker. This is partially my fault—or fuck maybe it's all my fault. I'm sorry."

"What's going on, Tony?"

"First, fill me in on what you think happened yesterday."

"Well, we're a long way from knowing anything for sure. I'll need the forensics and we'll need to question witnesses and anyone we believe wanted Marino dead—which by the way is a very long list. At this point we know for sure that he was shot multiple times late last night while he was in his patrol car. Looks like he was shot through an open driver's side window eight times in the head and neck with a small caliber hand gun—my guess would be a .22. We have yet to find anyone who heard a shot—the gun could have had a silencer, or with all of the noise inside the club I'm not sure that anyone could have heard a small caliber gun like a .22. Probably he was dead from the first shot. The other seven looked like someone with a lot of hate for Marino."

"If you hated him that much it'd seem like a shotgun would make more sense."

"Yeah, in a way. I'd guess the small gun was easy to hide. Also that size gun is often a woman's weapon of choice. And of course, the smaller caliber makes a lot less noise than a 44 magnum or a shotgun, which probably would have alerted the whole town. I would also guess it was someone he knew. The window was down like he was talking to someone or getting ready to—there were no defensive wounds to his hands or arms from a struggle. We could speculate at this point that he was meeting someone at that location and rolled the window down as they walked up. Maybe they exchanged words or maybe not, but at some point the assailant pulled out the weapon and shot him in the face. Once again, I only had a brief look at the body, but my guess is that he was shot at very close range—almost point blank. Then the assailant quickly discharged the additional bullets and left. The whole exchange could have been only a few seconds."

"You said you had a long list of suspects."

"In a way almost everybody in town is a suspect. This guy was terrorizing the town—mostly the businesspeople, but he was making new enemies every day. Now, you tell me why this is your fault."

"I delayed taking action because of my wife. There's a family connection with this bastard Marino. Her half-sister used to be married to him. I know we'll need to talk about that at length—for right now let me say that it was a mistake for me to have delayed taking more decisive action to stop Marino. My wife can be difficult for me to deal with at times, and I guess I let her push me in the wrong direction. The governor has asked me to appoint you the special authority for Lincoln County with all of the power and responsibility as you'd have as a sheriff. You'd have the title of sheriff, too, with an appointment for one month. After that the Governor would name someone for a longer term until a special election can be held. That's legal, and I'll have the papers filed in court in Santa Fe this morning. Ray, I know this isn't what you signed up to do, but we need your help."

"Tony, I'll do this because someone needs to be in charge immediately. I'll only do it for one month, and it'll be at my regular hourly rates including all of my support people. Also, I'll only do this if I'm working directly for the Governor. Not sure what you're trying to tell me about your wife, but there's an issue here related to the slow response and I don't want to be in the middle. I'll follow the facts wherever they lead me. You and I have been friends for a lot of years and I want to stay friends, but if someone wasn't doing what they should have done I won't cover that up."

"Understood and agreed."

Tony seemed distant, like he was thinking about something else. Ray was concerned that his friend was involved in something that could cause him big problems. Ray said he had to go to start getting the department reorganized so that the normal operations of the sheriff's office could resume. They said their goodbyes.

Ray, Tyee, and Happy headed out to the Sheriff's office. It was a quick drive. They pulled into a parking spot in front of the office and went in. Ray asked the young woman at the front desk to have everyone gather at the office as soon as possible. She told Ray that about half the deputies weren't on duty due to the late night the night before. Ray thought about it, but decided that he needed everyone there. He told her to call them and have them show up, but they could be in civilian clothes and it'd only be for a meeting that'd probably last about thirty minutes. She began calling.

It took a few hours to get everyone into the office. Ray could tell there were a lot of nervous people waiting to find out what was going to happen.

"I know this isn't what you want to be doing right now, but I think it's important that you should be the first people who know what's going on. As of this morning the governor has enacted, under his authority, a provision in state law that allows him to name a temporary sheriff for this county. That person is me. Some of you may know me, some not. I used to be the sheriff of Dona Ana County, so I have some idea about what needs to happen operationally. We're hoping that Sheriff Rodriguez will recover quickly and return to duty. If that hasn't happened within a month, the governor will call a special election to fill the sheriff's position. We have joining us today state patrol officers, who will remain on duty here for a few days until we can get back to normal, and we have two patrol cars and officers from the Apache tribe here to also assist as well. I'll be your boss for the next month. What has happened in the past will not affect your employment with this department unless you're subject to an investigation based on your actions. I'm not sure what that means, but if there's any sign that you participated in illegal activity, you'll be relieved of duty. I know this could be difficult in that you'd feel you were only following orders, but no one will remain active on this force if there's reason to believe they could be charged with a crime."

Ray paused to let them absorb what he was saying and how it might affect them. There was some murmuring, but nobody said a word.

"Acting as my second in command will be Tyee Chino. You'll obey orders from Mr. Chino as if they came from me. Our primary focus will be to investigate the death of Martin Marino and the claims that he was running a rogue operation out of the sheriff's office, which included some kind of protection racket. This means that we will be talking to you about those activities. Some of you may feel you'll need legal counsel—we encourage you to do that if you're concerned. At some point we will have a better idea if any of you'd be subject to charges for what has happened—at that point you'll be placed on paid leave until a special prosecutor can determine if you were complicit, or if you were forced into your actions. This is going to be very trying for everyone. I'll start on a work schedule this morning that will incorporate the state patrol, and one unit each from the Dona Ana Sheriff's Department and the Apache Tribe Police, so we can give many of you some time away from the job to be able to assess where you are and what you want to do. Please contact me or Mr. Chino if you have special requests or private concerns that you think we need to hear. For the time being we'll try as best we can to return to some kind of normal operation. Thank you. For anyone not currently on duty, you may leave and we will contact you sometime today with a new schedule."

Most of the deputies left quickly. It was apparent that many of them were eager to get out of the building rather than discuss any matters related to the past.

"What's the second in command to the sheriff called?" Tyee seemed unfazed by his new duties.

"Chief deputy."

"I think we may be approaching destiny territory."

"Yeah, I guess we could all see that coming—chief deputy."

"Does this mean I get a gun?"

"No."

5

Visiting Kate

A Month Prior—Miami, Florida

"What do you mean the little shit stole from you? When? What the fuck did he steal? Jeez, I'm going to kill the bastard no matter what you say—you understand me?"

"Dad, please, calm down. I don't know when he took it—must have been before he ran off. The stuff isn't worth anything, he just took it because he was pissed. I hadn't even looked in that lock box since he left."

"What a bastard."

"I didn't tell you this to make you mad. I'm over the guy. I was the one who made a mistake—you don't need to be involved. I've grown up a lot since my insanity with Martin. It's just that I know where he is and I want to contact my half-sister and see if she can help me get my stuff back."

"What does she have to do with anything?"

"Dad, Martin is working as a deputy sheriff in Ruidoso, New Mexico, and Kate's husband is the Attorney General for New Mexico."

"New Mexico? I thought the bastard had gone to Mexico—the country."

"No, not Mexico. Look, dad, I want you to agree to not interfere with this, okay? What he took has no value, except to me. It's some things grandma left to me, and he took it just to be a shit. He may not even have them any longer—who knows? But if I can get them back without starting World War III, then I want to. The reason I'm telling you this is that I want to go to Santa Fe and ask Kate for her help—and I didn't want you to go ballistic."

Lisa Collins loved her father. He was loud. And without question he was violent, although never with her. And was probably involved in the mob. She didn't care—he was a great father. Her mother was a slut who married Ricardo Collins because he was rich and could provide the life she wanted. She didn't believe her mother had ever loved her father, and on most days probably didn't even like him. But Rick doted on his daughter. He was always kind, generous, and thoughtful to her, from the first time she could remember. Her mother was usually drunk from morning to night—yelling and demanding to be noticed. When Lisa was only four years old her mother drove her car into a bridge in a drunken stupor and ended her painful existence. From that moment on her father became her whole universe.

It was about five years before that Lisa, in a teenage fit of rebellion, had started seeing Martin Marino. She did this to let her dad know that she was now a grown woman. She knew Martin worked for her dad and that that would drive her dad nuts. One thing led to another, and the more her father demanded that she stop seeing the little shit the more Lisa was attracted to the little shit. Reflecting back on that time now made Lisa a little sick—to think that she was ever involved with Martin Marino, the little shit. Teenage hormones have led to worse things, but her father seemed sure that this was the worst. In a fit of mindless rage at him she had run off with Martin and married him. Her father had gone completely berserk. It was clear that her dad was going to kill Martin and spread his parts from Miami to Jersey. Martin decided to leave town, so he stole money from Ricardo's trucking business and left.

Lisa reacted calmly, telling her dad that she now hated Martin and wanted a divorce or an annulment. She told her father that she must have been going through some kind of chemical imbalance to ever believe that she'd loved the creep. Rick made a strategic decision. All he cared about was having his daughter back. He put out word that as long as Martin stayed far away, he wouldn't kill him. Both Lisa and her dad then forgot about the evil little man named Martin Marino.

Then, about six months ago, Liza had been reminded that she and Martin had opened a private lock box at a storefront operation. Martin told her he'd inherited some money and needed a place to keep it, and he wasn't sure he could arrange it himself because his driver's license wasn't valid due to some issue that he was in the process of straightening out. Most of the things Martin told her during their time together were bullshit—no doubt the money was some that he'd stolen from her dad. But at the time she'd been enamored of Martin's rough ways, so she'd opened the lock box with his name added as a co-owner. She had some things her paternal grandmother had given her just before she died that she kept in a shoe box, so to show her faith in her new boyfriend she'd taken her stuff and put it in the shared lock box. When Martin left, she'd forgotten everything connected with him. The lock box fee was covered by a credit card that her dad paid for, so she never saw the bill. Then one day her dad's bookkeeper had asked her if the charge was for her. She'd gone to the lock box store and found the box empty. The little bastard had not only taken the money, but also her worthless-but-priceless keepsakes. In that moment, all she'd wanted was to kill Martin Marino so he couldn't continue to hurt people—but at that point she hadn't known where he was.

Lisa had worked in the human resources area of her dad's trucking company for the last several years. She enjoyed it, and she knew that her presence created a much friendlier work environment than when her dad was left unchecked. As far as she knew, the trucking business was legitimate and a huge success—if some portion of that success had to do with her dad's murky past she wasn't aware of it. She just knew that she was proud to work there and proud to be his daughter. It was this job that led to her knowing where Martin was. The company had received a request for a background check on Martin in relation to his job as a deputy sheriff in Lincoln County, New Mexico. When she saw it she almost laughed out loud—who could be so dumb as to hire that thug to be a deputy sheriff?

Now that she knew where Martin was, she began to create a plan to confront the scumbag and get her things back— and if he wouldn't give them to her, she'd make him pay a steep price.

Lisa flew into Albuquerque and took a shuttle to Santa Fe. She'd talked to Kate the day before, giving her a rundown of her travel plans. She was going to be staying at the La Fonda on the Plaza. Lisa hadn't been to Santa Fe before and she was excited to see the sights and try some of the wonderful food. On the other hand she was somewhat apprehensive about seeing her half-sister.

Lisa had talked to Kate over the years maybe a couple of dozen times. Their contact was polite, but not warm, and they'd never met. Kate was much older than Lisa, and had grown up living with her wealthy father in New England. It was Lisa's impression that Kate was something of a snob, and reluctant to have anything to do with her lower status half-sister. But to Kate's credit, when Lisa called and said she was going to be in Santa Fe and would like to meet, Kate readily agreed.

The shuttle ride from the Albuquerque airport took about an hour, delivering her straight to the La Fonda entrance on the famous Santa Fe Plaza. Lisa was struck by the colors and the feeling of joy that seemed to permeate the lobby—it reminded her in a way of some of the small hotels in Miami. The smells, colors, and festive music created a cheerful atmosphere, and she liked the place immediately. Contributing to the feeling of activity was the number of people milling about. There was a sense of things happening and people headed towards some exciting activity. Lisa thought she remembered reading that the population of metro Santa Fe was about 100,000, but that on any given day there could be 100,000 or more visitors as well, which creates a vibrant, big city feeling in the space of a small town, especially since so much activity is centered on the historical plaza.

She had a few hours before meeting her sister in the lobby bar, so Lisa decided to lie down for just a minute and release some of the travel tension. She went to sleep quickly and dreamed of wonderful colors, beautiful music, and ringing—ringing? She woke quickly and realized that she'd been asleep for some time.

"Hello."

"Lisa, this is Kate, did I get the time wrong?"

"Oh, Kate I'm so embarrassed. I was just going to close my eyes for a minute and I went to sleep. Give me ten minutes and I'll be there."

"Don't worry, Lisa. I'm sure it was a tiring day. I'll just get a drink and find a quiet place for us to talk. No hurry. Take your time."

Lisa couldn't believe it. Maybe scheduling a meeting right after you arrive from an airplane ride of many hours and a shuttle van ride for over an hour wasn't the smartest thing to have done. She quickly pushed her hair into place. She thought about redoing her make-up, but decided what the fuck, after all it was her sister—sort of. She headed to the lobby.

As Lisa entered the lobby, she looked around for someone who might be Kate—and immediately she knew. Kate looked just like their mother. She was taller, but there was no question about who she was. Lisa's memory of her mother was based mostly on photos, but she had been the most beautiful woman Lisa had ever seen. Now Kate was standing in front of Lisa, even more beautiful than their mother had been.

"Kate, I'd know you anywhere .You look just like mom."

Kate smiled and gave Lisa a small hug. She returned to the table and smiled sweetly as Lisa sat down.

"We share a family resemblance. I'd think most people would say we look like sisters—but of course, we are sisters.

I'm sorry this is the first time we've ever met—there's no excuse for that. Time and distance just worked against us. So, what brings you to Santa Fe?"

Lisa sensed a coolness. Her instincts told her that this person was almost always standoffish. She needed to go slow and get to know her a little before she jumped into her need to track down her scumbag ex-husband.

"I just love this hotel. It feels exotic but very comfortable. How long have you lived in Santa Fe?"

"Yes, the La Fonda is very nice—it's incredibly old. Not sure, but maybe a hundred years old. We've been in Santa Fe about five years now. My husband was a county attorney in southern New Mexico when the AG resigned to take a private job. Tony, my husband, was appointed by the Governor to finish out the remainder of the term. Then he ran for the office and won, which was about two years ago. We're still considered newcomers at this point. Tony enjoys his work and has a great reputation, so I think he'll run again—if he wins, I guess we'll be around for a while. You haven't told me why you're in Santa Fe."

"Kate, I was going to try and avoid that until we had some more time to get to know one another, but I get the feeling that you're a no-nonsense kind of person so I'll just spit it out. I'm looking for some help getting back some things my ex-husband took from me. They're things with sentimental value that my paternal grandmother gave me before she died. My ex is a useless, rotten SOB who took them just to hurt me—for all I know he threw them away a long time ago. I only just found out that they were missing in the last few months, but he took them some years ago so this could be a wild goose chase. I'm here because he's working in Ruidoso. Anyway, I thought it'd be a good time to stop by and meet you and also to see if there was any way you could help."

"Well, I'm sorry to hear about your stuff. At the same time, though, I'm glad that it brought us together. About help from my husband, I'm not sure there's much he can do. He's basically the state's attorney and handles legal matters where the state has to take a position in court. There are other duties, but none of them directly involve him in law enforcement. The best thing would be to contact the law enforcement agency in the town where your husband lives."

"Yeah, but that's part of the problem. Apparently he's working at the sheriff's department in Lincoln County as a deputy. It probably wouldn't get much of a response if his ex-wife called from Florida saying that her jerk of an ex-husband stole some useless sentimental items from her years ago and she wants him shot."

"Especially that shooting part." Kate had a playful smile that softened her words and gave Lisa hope. "Let me talk to Tony and see if he can help in some way. How long are you going to be in Santa Fe?"

"I was planning on just a couple of days. But I'd like to see you again and maybe meet your husband—if you've got the time."

"Sure. I'll call you tomorrow and we'll make plans. By the way what's your ex-husband's name?"

"Martin Marino."

6

Field Work

Present Day, 1989—Ruidoso, New Mexico

Sue and Big Jack arrived a little after one. They went to the Inn first, where Sue was escorted to Ray's room and took a little time to freshen up. Big Jack was shown to the room Ray had arranged for him. He glanced around the room, deposited his bags, and headed to the bar, where he was enjoying a cold beer when Sue arrived.

"Let me guess, that's lunch?"

"It was a long drive and I'm thirsty. It's just this kind of attitude that caused me problems with both my wives."

Sue smiled and ordered a glass of iced tea. It definitely had been a long, hot drive from T or C, and she sympathized with Big Jack's desire for a cold beer. She looked around, admiring the resort. She'd heard of the Inn of the Mountain Gods, but had never been there before.

"Guess we might as well head out and see if we can find your husband. I never signed up for field work, and I need to get back to my business before Chester runs it into the ground."

The business in question was "Jack's Bait, Boats & Beer." Chester was Tyee's cousin, who'd started working for Big Jack recently and had turned the business into a smoothly run enterprise, making more money than Jack could have imagined before Chester had signed on. Jack's idea of running the business was drinking beer with the customers and sleeping on the dock in the afternoon—Chester, meanwhile, was something of a merchandising genius. Having Jack out of Chester's way for a while would double the store's operational efficiency, but the place wasn't the same without Big Jack around.

"Hey, it's really great to see you." Ray gave Sue a hug. It had only been a day, but he'd missed her—their marriage was still new and exciting. He was glad to see Big Jack, too, but shook his hand rather than hugging him.

They spent the next hour laying out a plan of action for Sue and Big Jack. Sue would coordinate the forensics and lab work to make sure all of the evidence was properly documented. Big Jack would visit with the owner of the bar where Martin had been found. Big Jack liked bars.

Jack's "real" name was Jack Parker, at least that was the one he now had courtesy of the FBI. Prior to that he'd been Philip Duncan, a successful defense attorney in L.A., but he'd gotten into some trouble with the Mexican Mafia and had had to disappear. He also had a couple of ex-wives looking for him. While traveling through New Mexico avoiding most hot spots, he'd stumbled upon Jack's Bait, Boats & Beer, right next to Elephant Butte Lake, and had bought it from the original Big Jack, thus becoming the new Big Jack. At about 300 pounds, the name was in sync with his stature, but it also suited his outsized personality. Big Jack was an equal partner in *Pacheco & Chino, PIs*, but chose to remain a silent partner.

"Tito Annoya, what can I do for you?"

"My name's Jack Parker. I'm helping Ray Pacheco look into the shooting of Martin Marino. Did you or any of your customers hear any shots that night?"

"Nah. This place is usually pretty loud. If somebody heard something, they didn't say anything to me. Probably a good thing. Lots of people carry arms around here—if they knew that little shit was being shot they might have joined in."

"Not a popular guy, Marino?"

"The only people who didn't hate the bastard were people who didn't know him. I'll tell you right now that two nights before he was shot I threatened to kill him in front of a bunch of witnesses. He was robbing me every week with his protection fees. I was done with that shit. When he came in to collect I told him to fuck off and said that if I saw him in my club again I'd shoot the bastard."

"Did you shoot him?"

"No."

"Where were you when he was shot?"

"Well I don't know when he was shot, but I was in my office in the back of the club all night until the cops showed up and started questioning my customers about it."

"What do you think he was doing in front of your club that night?"

"Beats the hell out of me. I can't believe he'd be coming in here after our discussion—unless he had a small fucking army. I think he understood that I was done with his nonsense and that if he wanted to go to war, I was ready. Maybe the little dirtbag was waiting on me to leave so he could ambush me or something. All I can tell you for sure is that I'm happy as hell that he's dead and so are a lot of other people."

"Thanks for your information Mr. Annoya. Why don't I settle in at your bar and sample one of your beers while I ponder what you've said."

"Smart move big man."

Big Jack always enjoyed beer, and free beer was especially delicious. He was a born cop.

"You know, Ray, I think the biggest question here is why Martin Marino was hired in the first place to be a deputy. What I'm getting from people is that he reeked of badness, like a terrible cologne—I can't imagine someone in law enforcement not knowing immediately that this guy was bad news."

Ray and Big Jack were sitting on a sofa in the waiting area at the Sheriff's department. "Good point. No way they could have run a background check on him and still hired him. I think maybe we need to see how Sheriff Rodriguez is doing. If he can talk, he should be able to tell us why Marino was hired."

Ray found Happy asleep in the small alcove where the receptionist, who doubled as the dispatcher, sat. This was the attractive young woman Ray had seen before. Happy seemed to be attracted to nice-looking women—after all, he was a smart dog.

They headed to the hospital, a small, two-story building located close to the center of town, to see the sheriff. Ray made sure Happy was comfortable, then he and Big Jack entered the building. At the receptionist's desk he asked to see Rodriguez.

"I'm sorry, sir. He left this morning."

"I thought he was deathly ill or something?"

"You'll have to talk to a doctor for any patient information. All I can tell you is that he checked out this morning."

"Is a doctor available?"

"No, sir. If you'd like to leave your name and a contact number I'll have someone call you."

"Thanks." Ray gave her the information, leaving the number at the sheriff's department.

"What does that mean?"

"No idea. Some kind of miracle recovery, maybe. Or maybe with Marino dead the sheriff had no further need to be ill."

"This thing is smelling worse all the time. Reminds me of some of the stuff I saw in L.A."

Ray suggested that they needed to contact Sue and Tyee about meeting up at the Inn for a few drinks and a debriefing. Big Jack thought that was an excellent idea. They headed back to the sheriff's department to find Sue and Tyee.

"Ray, before we go back to the Inn I want you to meet Officer James. He's with the state police and has been running things today with a lot of skill. I think he's a guy you can give some authority to without him letting you down. He's waiting for us in the Sheriff's office." Tyee liked having the title of Chief Deputy, but wasn't interested in handling the day-to-day bullshit that went on in a law enforcement agency.

"Hello, Officer James. Tyee says you've done some good work today. Thanks—we sure need the help at the moment."

"Well, I was just trying to keep things running. The biggest issue to resolve is who's going to be let go or put on leave and who can be used in patrols. We have some of my men, a couple of guys from the Apache police, and two teams from the sheriff's office in Dona Ana, but it's going to be hard to schedule until we know who we can use among the local officers."

"Of course. I'll conduct interviews tomorrow. Maybe you could help by setting those up. Let's start around eight in the morning and schedule each deputy for about fifteen minutes. If you could have someone pull their personnel files and leave them in that small conference room, I'll go through them fairly quick. Based on what Tyee has said and talking to you now, I'd like to appoint you as my assistant—that okay with you?"

"I'll do whatever's needed."

"Good. I'll make sure the AG and the Governor are made aware of your contribution."

"That isn't necessary, but good reports are always welcome."

Ray liked the guy immediately. He seemed to be focused on what needed to be done without any dramatics—a let's-just-get-the-job-done approach. Ray shook his hand and they agreed they'd make some decisions by the next afternoon so the department could get back into a routine.

"Before leaving, I wanted to let you know that Sheriff Rodriguez checked out of the hospital this morning. Until I can meet with Rodriguez, I want to make it clear he has no authority in this department."

The team loaded up and headed back to the Inn. They all went to their rooms to freshen up a little—except Big Jack, who said he was fresh enough and headed to the bar. They agreed to meet in a while for drinks and discussion before dinner.

Once Sue and Ray got to their room, other priorities surfaced. They were going to be a little late for the drinks and discussion.

"Sorry I'm late. Sue'll be down in a minute." Ray took a seat and ordered a beer.

Big Jack and Tyee just grinned.

"I guess at this point, Tyee, you've got this all wrapped up?"

"Half of the county sheriffs in New Mexico are crooks and half aren't. My guess is that Rodriguez is in the bad half and hired Marino because he was a thug and he needed him to run roughshod over somebody. Then, somewhere along the way, Marino got out of control and started doing very stupid things. I'm sure we'll find out that Marino has always done some very stupid things—it's his nature."

"Well, Tyee, I agree with you. There has to be some reason to hire a thug to be a deputy, so it starts with Rodriguez, and if I was guessing, I'd say he's disappeared. So we need to look for connections to Rodriguez that can help us discover why he hired Marino."

"Got to be drugs, Ray. What else has that kind of power over people? There's just too much money involved."

"Yeah. Almost has to be. What a curse on this part of the country. Good people tempted by all that easy money. Well, I think we have a good idea of how to start. Maybe it turns out to be something else, but the logical answer is illegal drugs."

Big Jack jumped in to the conversation. "Another thing, Ray, some of those deputies had to have been on board with this stuff. Probably some were intimated by Marino and just didn't do anything to stop him, but I think some of them almost have to be dirty."

"Yeah, I was thinking the same thing. This is going to hurt a lot of people before we get it cleaned up. I'm going to go call the AG and see if he'll sit in on those interviews tomorrow. Be back in a minute." He left to find a house phone.

Ray came back. "Tony wasn't real thrilled but he agreed to sit in on the interviews. Something I haven't mentioned to either of you yet is that Tony told me he dragged his feet on taking action against Marino because his wife's half-sister used to be married to the guy. I still get an uneasy feeling that Tony isn't telling us everything he knows—which is presenting a problem. I'm not sure I can trust him."

The process of interviewing the twenty-two deputies was shortened when eight resigned and six didn't respond to the request to come in to the office. That meant that only eight committed to showing up. Ray decided that since they'd have time to conduct the eight interviews with room to spare, he and Tony would first talk to the administrative staff, beginning with the receptionist.

"Tina, you should be aware that it's possible there have been criminal acts committed by members of this department. This is an official investigation and if you're uncomfortable with the process we can delay this meeting until you've contacted legal counsel. Do you understand what we're doing and how this might affect you?"

"Yes."

"Good. Do you want to continue this interview at this time?"

"I do. Mr. Pacheco, I've been wanting to talk to someone for a long time. I'm the lowest person on the totem pole around here, and mostly I'm ignored like I'm invisible. The only exception to that is if one of the morons who works here wants to make some inappropriate remark about my looks or my boobs, or just in general be offensive. I went to school at New Mexico State and graduated with honors with a degree in law enforcement, and I've been working here for almost a year. This place is a complete one hundred percent fucked up mess. I should have told someone a long time ago, but it seemed to me that everyone in authority was right in the middle of the mess."

Ray looked at Tony but didn't say anything.

"At least half of the deputies are crooks, just plain old-fashioned hoodlums. These people ran errands for Sheriff Rodriguez more than anything else. There's no question in my mind that they were involved in selling drugs, or looking the other way when one of their gang was selling drugs—like Tito Annoya. When Rodriguez got sick, or whatever happened to him, the amazingly offensive Marino took over like it was some kind of gang operation where the meanest and dumbest gets to be in charge. I couldn't believe it. I know I should have called someone, but to tell you the truth I was afraid."

"It's okay, Tina. We understand. Do you have any documentation or evidence that could help us with our investigation?"

"I do. I kept notes and copies of lots of things over the last three months. I recorded some phone conversations—maybe even illegally, I'm not sure—and I have other files that I took after Rodriguez went into the hospital."

Ray had always believed it only took one good person to undo the damage of many; and sitting in front of him was that person—the lowest one on the totem pole—Tina.

7

Wrap-Up

One Month Later—Truth or Consequences, New Mexico

"Just talked to Tony. He says I'm officially no longer the acting Sheriff of Lincoln County. He gave me a run-down on what's happened and where they see things headed over the next year or so." Ray was addressing everyone—Sue, Tyee, and Big Jack—sitting at the conference table in the company offices in T or C, located in the outbuildings on Ray's remote cabin property.

"Right now they've charged six deputies with criminal violations related to drug distribution. Eight others are still under investigation and have been fired from the department. That leaves eight of the existing deputies who've been cleared of any wrongdoing. Officer James has done such an excellent job that the Governor has appointed him the new Sheriff—he'll be in office for fourteen months, when a new election will be held. They wanted to have enough time to clean things up and get back to some kind of normalcy before holding an open election."

"What about Deputy Samson—the guy who shot the bookie. Was he charged or cleared?"

"Tony mentioned him and said he's done an excellent job over the last month and he was cleared both of the drug charges and also the shooting death of the bookie. But what hasn't happened is that no one's been charged with the killing of Martin Marino. Also the only people charged with drug violations are Rodriguez, who has yet to be located, and the six deputies. All of the deputies say that the person running everything was either Rodriguez or Marino. Tito Annoya, the guy who owned bars in Ruidoso, was implicated by the deputies and by some of Tina's information, but there wasn't enough to charge him."

"Indians get axed, Chiefs smoke victory pipe."

"Your Apache wisdom hits home again. I'm afraid we still don't know what happened in Ruidoso. Rodriguez wasn't an idiot, but he was lazy. He never would have put that operation together without someone telling him what to do. I told Tony that he was letting this one go because it was politically expedient. He said I'd turned into an asshole and hung up."

"Well that's not very satisfying, letting the murder of someone go just because the guy was such a creep. I'm really surprised that Tony would do that." Sue wanted justice in every one of life's interactions, even though in much of her own life there'd been very little justice.

Big Jack hadn't said much, sitting and listening, and sipping his beer, but now he piped up. "I think what isn't being said is that maybe Tony doesn't want to know what happened to Marino. We don't know anything about what his wife or her half-sister did with regard to Marino—did they contact him or not?"

"I agree that this is for shit, but we have no way to pursue it unless we're asked. On the plus side, we made a lot of money with this latest assignment. I believe that calls for a celebration dinner with steaks and lots of beer—how does that sound Big Jack?"

"As Tyee would say, White man is very wise."

Over the following days things started to wind down and there was a quietness that seemed to settle over everyone. Ray and Tyee started fishing again. Ray was still a novice, but he seemed to be lucky—an important quality in many pursuits, including fishing.

Big Jack started campaigning again for the position of Mayor of T or C. The election was about two months out, and it was a two-man race between Big Jack and the former mayor, Martinez. The two men were more than opponents— they really hated one another. Martinez held Big Jack partially responsible for his son's downfall as sheriff of Sierra County. The ex-sheriff was now serving time, and his father definitely held a grudge since Ray and his team had been instrumental in proving the Sheriff was involved in criminal activity, for which he was convicted.

After his son's arrest Martinez had resigned as mayor and gone to Las Cruces to stay with his brother. Many people had thought that he'd never return to T or C, but he had. After licking his wounds—some said that his brother had kicked him out—he'd come back to live in his old house in T or C and had entered the race for mayor. There was a complication, though, since in a technical sense he was still mayor. While he had resigned, the county commissioners, demonstrating their usual incompetence, had never officially accepted his resignation. Rather than fight a legal battle with the rotund demon, they'd declared his resignation invalid and he'd resumed his duties as Mayor. Now back in office, and fueled by his hatred of Big Jack, the Mayor had come out swinging, accusing Big Jack of almost every bad thing a person could do.

The mayoral race's nastiest phase officially began when Martinez accused Big Jack of being a crook himself, saying he had evidence that Big Jack was in reality a disbarred lawyer from Texas. Ironically, Big Jack really was a disbarred lawyer, but from L.A. The information Martinez had was close to the truth, but contained many inaccuracies. At their first debate, Big Jack tore into Martinez for making up stuff about him and laid out the actual story of his past in great detail. This detailed past was bullshit, a fabrication by the FBI in support of the new identity they'd created for him, but with the bureau involved the new identity appeared as solid as if it were true. Before the episode was over, Mayor Martinez had to apologize for getting bad information from someone. Ray guessed that it had actually come from Big Jack himself.

Another odd twist was that the mobile home in which Big Jack lived was parked next to his store on Elephant Butte, which was almost three miles from T or C. Any sensible person would have thought that Big Jack didn't live in T or C and, therefore, couldn't run for the Mayor's job. But in his constant conniving, Mayor Martinez had been instrumental in getting the town to annex a small strip of land out to the lake and along the north shore, so that things were not what they seemed at first glance. At the time it had made many of the lake people angry, though the Mayor didn't give a shit. His goal was to collect taxes on what he anticipated would be huge growth along this edge of the lake. It didn't turn out that way due to a host of factors, ranging from economic circumstance to a long dry spell that caused the lake's water level to drop almost ten feet, exposing an ugly shoreline right on the land the city had annexed. That had been years before and the city largely forgot about the annexation. Nonetheless, it meant that Big Jack was a T or C resident.

"Who owns this pile of shit?"

"Who the fuck are you?"

"Inspector Morris with codes enforcement, if you must know fat man."

Big Jack stared at the man for a long moment, as if making up his mind about something. In a single quick, smooth motion, he picked up his favorite Johnny Bench signature baseball bat and headed toward the offensive asshole who had just walked into his store. Chester stepped in front of Big Jack and held up his hands.

"Not sure you should kill this asshole until we know what he wants."

The matter-of-fact way Chester said 'kill this asshole' seemed to alarm Inspector Morris. He had a police radio attached to his uniform, and he pressed the button, asking for the sheriff's department to send backup.

"Once the Sheriff's deputies have arrived, I'll beat your brains into the floor. You got that Morris? If your ass is still standing here when they get here, I'll kill you. I'm going to wait until they're here just to make sure I get the proper credit for eliminating your sorry inspector butt from all existence." Big Jack had lost any semblance of control and may have been foaming a little around the corners of his mouth.

Morris wasn't used to this kind of response, and now looked confused about what he should do.

"Look buddy," Chester said, "I'm sure you're here to write a ticket about some code violation or something—probably at the urging of the mayor. My suggestion to you is to get the fuck out of here while you can, and when the sheriff's deputies arrive we'll tell them what happened: that you threatened Big Jack with violence and he defended himself. You can, of course, dispute that, but it'll be your word against Big Jack's word and the testimony of an eyewitness, which is me." Chester wasn't only a great shopkeeper, he also was a natural-born negotiator.

Inspector Morris turned and headed for the parking lot. He didn't leave, he seemed to be waiting for reinforcements.

The election was getting ready to turn nasty.

8

Tony's Story

1963—Midwest City, Oklahoma

There are times in life when all things seem possible. Today was one of those times: October first, Tony's birthday, the best day of the year. Not sure why he liked his birthdays. Most times there hadn't been much fuss—a few gifts, a couple of hugs, and maybe five bucks—but something about the day of his birth made it seem like a day of promise.

Tony's perception was very likely distorted by the fact that *any* day in October in Oklahoma held promise. The place had the worst fucking weather in the world—tornados, ice storms, monsoon rains, snow—shit, it was just bad. But along comes October and for a few days it all seems like heaven. The state fair was in October, which meant it would rain some, but that was a small price to pay for mostly pleasant, gentle weather—not often seen in God's country.

Tony had graduated from high school after a less-than-glorious educational experience. The whole system was screwed up, and his experience was exacerbated by his own not-so-stellar contributions. Maybe some people just were not meant to be educated. Stewart Bellman, whom Tony had known since grade school, was destined to be a doctor or something else

that would demonstrate his superiority in a socially accept-
able way, but Tony knew he didn't know shit. How does that
happen? What he knew was how to do school. He was the
absolute best student there had ever been—but a doctor, not
so sure.

Success in school was something you were either good at
achieving or not. The ones who were good at school might or
might not be good at anything else. They had learned how to
study—big fucking deal. They had learned how to suck up—
actually a quite valuable skill. They had often learned how to
cheat—best goddamn educational tool of all—and with some
exceptions those who were the best at cheating became political leaders.

Life had given Tony, in a fairly short period of time, many
opportunities to poke fun at the smarter, more studious achiev-
ers who seemed to surround him, and he took the opportunity
with great relish, shaking his rattles like some strange witch
doctor, and proclaiming that normal standards of achievement
were a big fucking crock. The spectacle he created was real, but
there wasn't much of an audience.

His goal was to seek truth—take that Mister Asshole
Bellman. Tony's biggest challenge in this quest was his to-
tal lack of knowledge about what actual truth was. Living as
a protected child in a protected world meant that truth was
based more on what he saw on television than much of anything else.

At the ripe old age of eighteen he determined that the
only way to seek truth was to head to the most foreign land
that existed in his world: California. You might wonder about
Nepal, or maybe fucking Timbuktu—but no, those weren't real

to Tony. What was real and represented all the knowledge that anyone might ever have was Los Angeles, California. Truth was somewhere on the beach, or in the Hollywood Hills.

As a precursor to his trip he left a note for his doting parents, basically saying that they had screwed up and that as a result he was leaving to find out who he was. So long Ma and Pa, I'm headed to the bright lights of another world.

Tony had an old beat up car, thanks to his long-suffering parents, which might or might not get him to California. He had about $250, also thanks to his parents. The car and the limited money seemed adequate to reach California—what would happen after he ran out of gas and money didn't deter him, but there were other issues.

Tony's girlfriend's name was Vickie. He had been dating off and on for over five years, but she was still not the person for him—he was sure it was true, Vickie thought he was wrong. What complicated things was that Vickie and he were having sex. There had been many a day over the last few months when he'd actually given thanks to the almighty for Vickie—what a wonderful, sexual being she was. It was difficult for him to imagine giving up sex with her, which was going to be a real problem if he was in the promised land of California and Vickie was still in God's country, Oklahoma.

While not on anyone's list for valedictorian, even he could figure out that the only solution was to take Vickie to California with him. He was pretty sure that bringing her along didn't violate any of those crossing-state-lines-for-illicit-purposes acts that he'd seen on the FBI shows, but he also was pretty damn sure that her parents would be looking for his head on a stick once they found out she was gone. Her father scared the shit out of him, and he wanted nothing to do with her less-than-bright brothers—but sex was a powerful force. At eighteen the idea that you only live once had almost no real meaning for him—nonetheless, it was the mantra that settled him on a plan of action.

Vickie, of course, thought that going to California with an unemployable near-juvenile, with $250, in an unreliable piece of shit car, was an absolutely brilliant idea. The failure of the educational system wasn't gender-biased.

The plan was to leave at night and make it as far as possible before anyone noticed they were gone. The flaw in the plan was that the 1953 Ford Victoria's right headlight wasn't working, so the strategy was changed to leaving first thing in the morning. And since they were no longer leaving that night, they went to Potter's, which was the place to be in the town of Midwest City. The headlight didn't matter in Tony's hometown—everybody knew Tony Garcia, even the cops.

Tony wasn't a star athlete, he wasn't an academic super star—he wasn't really much of anything, except maybe known. Tony had lived in the night realm for several years. With an aplomb not often seen in young men, he'd established a reputation for being a stand-up guy in a night-time world. He was young, almost childlike, but was accepted by mature, grown men in the little town's nightlife.

"Tony, I love you so much."

There were times when he found Vickie a little too much. He was still not sure what love was—he had a better understanding of lust, and Vickie definitely fit into his idea of lust.

"Hey Vickie, you know I'm not sure what I know about love. You and I, I think, are having a good time—maybe that's love. Shit I don't know."

"Tony, how can I love you so much and also think you're such an asshole?"

Vickie had big tits but she wasn't stupid. You had to like both qualities.

"Sorry, Vickie. Maybe you should stay here with your parents. If going to California is going to cause a bunch of problems."

"Look you asshole. I'm going. You know why I'm going? Because if you go by yourself you'll be dead and then I won't have a boyfriend. You are too fucking stupid to understand that without me you've got no chance of surviving in the real world—so there's no discussion. I'm going."

Goddamn he hated it when she bossed him around. He didn't think she was right, but on the other hand he sure enjoyed sex, and if she didn't go it might be a long time before his next lay. Fuck, life was so complicated.

"You know, your goddamn family will chase me to hell and string me up to a tree if you go with me."

"You should watch you language Tony Garcia. And listen, my family will be pissed, but at the same time they'll be overjoyed that I have a boyfriend, maybe a husband? They won't kill you—just mess you up a little."

Jeez, she was probably right. They both knew the realities of life in 1963—if you had a daughter or sister who had graduated from high school and wasn't some egghead going to college, she needed to get married at once. It was like an unwritten law—otherwise she could be sponging off of the family for years.

They might bust him up a bit, her moron brothers, but there was no logic in killing him. They could care less about her virtue—they wanted her gone, married.

Potter's was the local drive-in, car hops and everything. There were maybe fifty parking spaces, and on most nights at least that many cars circling, waiting to pull in. This created a dynamic that often ended in some kind of male chest-beating to try and clear out the weak so you could park—and it often ended in an ugly mess.

While smugly observing the losers going round and round, Tony noticed his buddy, Bill Mason, circling. He gave him a wave and told him to park down the street at the elementary school and join them. Bill did as directed. Once in a while the cops would ticket, and eventually impound, cars parked at the school, but that was usually after some nasty fight or damaged property brought in citizen complaints. Most times the cops didn't give a shit. From their point of view, having all of these lowlifes in one place made their job easier.

"Hey, Tony, Vickie. What's going on?"

"We were thinking about heading off to California."

"You and Vickie are going to California?"

"Yep, what do you think?"

"I think her big ugly brothers are going to kill you."

"Yeah, we thought of that, but Vickie thinks they'll just hurt me. In the long run they're better off with me alive, as Vickie's future husband."

"Why do you tell Bill everything? This is none of his business. Maybe I'll ask my brothers to kill you as a special favor to me."

"Jeez, Vickie, we're just horsing around here—calm down."

"Vickie's right—you need to develop some manners before you leave mama."

"Well, isn't this just great the two of you ganging up on me. You know this is my piece of shit car and my spot at Potter's. Maybe you both should go get in Bill's junk car and start circling again."

At this, Vickie began to pout and Bill began to laugh.

"Look, Tony, I came to find you to talk to you about something. My uncle's offered me a job in Dallas and he said he could use another worker in his warehouse—thought you might be interested."

"What would your job be, Bill?"

"He said I'd start out as an assistant buyer. Not sure what that is, but I'm sure it would be a flunky."

"So you'd be an office flunky and I would be a warehouse labor guy pushing boxes around, is that right?"

"Tony, if you don't want the job, okay, but don't push on me because he's my uncle not yours."

Bill was right—not his fault Tony had useless relatives. A dead end job in Dallas or a truth-finding, brother-dodging trip to L.A. with no money and no prospects. All of life's decisions should be so easy: California here we come.

"Thanks for thinking about me Bill, but me and my babe are heading to the land of opportunity—California."

Sometimes the best plans don't work out. Tony took Vickie home and then went to Bill's to spend the night, since he'd already left the note telling his parents he was gone. His father, in an unusual fit of anger at the arrogance of his only son, called the police and reported the car stolen. Like everything Tony used he didn't own it—it was in his father's name. The police were reluctant to pursue the matter because they saw it as a family dispute, but by some strange coincidence one of the officers said he knew where the car was: at Bill's. It was a small town, after all. Tony's dad arranged to have the car impounded from Bill's driveway.

Tony went and talked to his dad and mom. He told them he was sorry for making them worry, but he was now eighteen and it was time for him to take responsibility for himself. They agreed. They also gave him $750 so that he could go to Dallas and take the job with Bill's uncle. Also, his father agreed he could take the car. Being responsible for yourself was a lot easier with mom and dad's financial support. Now the hard part: he had to go tell Vickie the California adventure was off.

Tony worked in Dallas and reached a certain level of success. He was quickly promoted out of the warehouse and demonstrated an intelligence and drive that impressed his boss. Over the years Tony had matured, and had even started to think about his future. Vickie had moved into his ratty apartment in Dallas for a few months but quickly decided that Tony wasn't as much fun as he used to be. His friend Bill had decided to go to college and had gone back to Oklahoma to go to school at Central State.

Tony started going to night school at one of the community colleges in Dallas. He had no problem with the classes but everything was moving too slow for him. He had sent letters to several schools in Texas and Oklahoma asking about scholarships and any other financial programs they had that would allow him to attend school. With his Hispanic last name he soon discovered there were, in fact, many programs that he could apply for. Over the next few months he applied at more than a dozen schools for various financial support programs. He eventually selected an offer from the University of Oklahoma for a minority scholarship for pre-law. He hadn't given much thought to being a lawyer—he usually thought of all lawyers as assholes—but this was the best financial deal, and it'd make his parents very proud since they were big OU football fans.

Tony soon discovered that he thrived in the academic environment at college. He'd hated high school, but the university atmosphere was like finding the perfect place to be—and it was just down the street all of the time. He completed his pre-law bachelor's degree in the shortest time possible and became one of the university's acknowledged leaders while in law school.

As he approached graduation, employment offers poured in—he had too many job offers to even assess each one. While he was as anxious as anyone to make some money, what really interested him was working within the justice system for the government. With some nervousness, he eventually accepted a position as an Assistant District Attorney for Harris County, in Texas, working in Houston.

9

Tony's Story, Part 2

Houston, Texas

Tony thrived in the DA's office like he never had before. He became a star, promoted at such a fast pace that it was rumored that he had something on the DA—but it was all based on performance. He'd had found his place in the universe.

It was while working in the DA's office that Tony met his future wife. Kate Martin had been arrested for drug possession. While the offence was routine in Houston, this arrest was unusual. At the time of her arrest she'd been in possession of almost $250,000 in cash. Often the police department would notify the DA's office when an arrest was made that they thought needed their attention because the case was unusual or involved someone other than the lowlifes who were typically brought in.

"Tony, this is Sergeant Nelson. We've got a woman down here who was arrested for drug possession. It was only a small amount, and more than likely she'll only be charged with a misdemeanor. The odd thing is that she's an upper class person and she had a bunch of cash on her, like a quarter of a million dollars. We have her in a holding cell and she hasn't called an attorney. She's just sitting in the cell, not saying anything. I think we need someone other than our normal grab-ass gang to talk to her and find out what's going on. Can you come down and see her?"

"Ms. Martin, my name's Tony Garcia. I'm with the DA's office. You've provided the police with your name, but no other information. Are you from Houston?"

There was no answer. Kate Martin was maybe the most beautiful woman Tony had ever seen, at least up close. She might easily have been a movie star, everything about her was as near to perfect as he'd seen. Her hair, her make-up, and her clothes were suited to a supermodel—but here she was, sitting calmly in the county holding cell, apparently not even very upset about it.

"Ms. Martin, you were in possession of a lot of money at the time of your arrest. I believe $250,000. While that in itself isn't illegal, it raises suspicions about why you'd have that much money and be walking around in an area of town that by most standards would be considered unsafe—even without the money. Can you tell me why you were in that neighborhood?"

"I'd like to have an attorney before I answer any questions."

Well fuck, why hadn't she said that hours ago? Tony didn't understand what was going on—something he didn't like.

"Of course you can have an attorney present—it's your right. Why didn't you ask for one before?"

"I was waiting for you."

Tony looked at her. She looked at Tony. He was feeling uncomfortable.

"I'll have the sergeant provide you with a phone to call an attorney."

Tony left the interrogation room and asked the sergeant to allow Ms. Martin to make a phone call. There was no question that he was terribly attracted to Kate Martin—it was actually making him a little shaky. He found a bench in the lobby and sat for a while. He couldn't figure out what she meant about waiting for him. Maybe she just meant waiting on someone other than the cops. That was probably it, but somewhere in the remaining teenage part of his brain he fantasized that she'd been waiting on Tony Garcia. He was almost embarrassed.

Tony went back to his office and was working on another matter when Sergeant Nelson called. Her attorney had arrived and she was ready to talk.

"Mr. Garcia, my name is Max Ellison—I'm with Ellison, Mathews and Ford. I represent Ms. Martin, and I'm requesting that you release her at once or charge her with a crime."

"Mr. Ellison, good to meet you. I've had dealings with your firm before. Good to see the named partners still visit clients in jail."

"Mr. Garcia, Kate Martin is visiting Houston on a personal matter. She's a well-known resident of Boston and has no criminal record of any kind. The amount of drugs alleged to have been found in her possession is minor and she says that she didn't illegally purchase those drugs. Regarding the money in her possession, that relates to a personal matter and doesn't involve any criminal activity and is therefore no concern of the police. Once again, I request that she be released."

Tony looked at Ellison and then at Kate. She smiled. She could have been mocking him, but it seemed to be a friendly smile—more like: *hey, better luck next time.* However she intended the smile, Tony liked it just fine.

"She's released."

Several days passed, and Tony was very busy with all kinds of bad people causing all kinds of mayhem. He was in his element and quite happy, although he couldn't quite get Kate Martin off of his mind. He knew he couldn't contact her, but he had a feeling that they'd connected in some way. Oh hell, probably every man who saw her felt that way. He needed to forget about her—but he couldn't.

"Mr. Garcia, there's a Kate Martin on line one for you. She says you'll know what it's about. Do you want to take the call?"

"Yes—yes I do, thank you."

Tony's heart began to race. He was actually blushing. Jeez, how embarrassing is this—he needed to calm down.

"Hello, Ms. Martin. What can I do for you?"

"Mr. Garcia, I'd like to meet with you today, is that possible?"

"Sure come on in, be happy to meet with you."

"Do you think we could meet for a drink or something rather than at your office?"

Okay, now new fantasies started to kick in. There also seemed to be an alarm bell going off in Tony's head. The most beautiful woman he'd ever seen—ever, not just in jail—wanted to meet with him over drinks. He knew he should immediately tell her that it wasn't appropriate, but that he'd be pleased to meet with her in his office—with a chaperone.

"Drinks, sure that would be perfect. When and where?" Oh good—he was now on the path to disbarment.

Kate mentioned a downtown bar and restaurant not far from Tony's office and suggested five thirty. Tony agreed and hung up. Now what? Should he call his boss and fill him in? But why? It was only for drinks and she hadn't been charged with anything. He could certainly have a meeting with a woman he met in the course of his work without permission from his boss. He knew he was rationalizing—but he still wasn't going to tell anyone.

The afternoon dragged on like the last hour of high school, except longer. Tony was about ready to leave for the day when he got a call from the DA. He knew he must have been caught, and he was on the verge of being arrested by the fantasy police.

"Tony, just wanted to remind you about our appointment in the morning to discuss the Brewster case. I've asked Mr. Brewster's attorney to sit in on our meeting. I think we can reach a harmonious conclusion on this matter if we will give just a bit. Wanted to give you that heads-up before you walked in here tomorrow. See ya then."

Tony let his breath out. What was happening to him?

He arrived at the restaurant a few minutes early. He asked the hostess if anyone was waiting—she said no. He went to the bar and ordered a gin and tonic. Maybe alcohol would help him calm down. He'd taken a few sips and was actually feeling a little better when Kate slid in beside him.

"I'm not a big drinker, but I do love bars."

If anyone had asked he would have said that he could not have imagined Kate looking any better than she had when he'd first met her—but he'd have been wrong. She was even more stunning, almost jaw-droppingly gorgeous. She ordered a white wine from the very attentive bartender.

"Mr. Garcia, I'm sure you are wondering why I wanted to see you."

"Please, call me Tony. Yes, I was curious—it's a bit unusual to have someone you've met in county lockup give you a call."

"They shouldn't have arrested me. I think they saw me and the way I was dressed, and in that neighborhood they decided I must be doing something wrong. Kind of reverse discrimination against high class white women being in a black neighborhood." This was said with a mischievous grin.

"Well, as I'm sure you can imagine it's not appropriate for me to discuss anything to do with your arrest."

"Of course, Tony. The reason I asked to see you is that I need help. I just mentioned the arrest to explain that there's no crime they can charge me with, because I didn't commit any crime. The officers who arrested me really scared me, but when you walked in I knew you were someone I could talk to. If I misread something just tell me—but I thought there was a connection."

What the fuck. Of course there was a connection. He's in love with her. This makes no sense, he doesn't know her—only that she's beautiful—but he's madly and stupidly in love.

"Look, Ms. Martin—"

"Please Tony, call me Kate."

"Okay, Kate. I'm an assistant DA, that means I have all sorts of ethical issues just talking to you—but if we're talking about me helping you with something that could be handled by the DA's office, there are also legal issues. You need to contact your attorney and let him handle whatever legal matters may arise from your arrest. He's one of the best defense attorneys in town."

"Yes, I know. He'll handle the arrest that has brought us together. I wanted to talk to you because I think I'm going to be charged with murdering my fiancé, Jeffery Peterson."

Tony felt like he was on a slippery slope straight to hell. He wanted desperately to be with this woman for the rest of his life. Now she's telling him she might be a suspect in the death of her fiancé. He should get up, not say another word, and leave. If he did anything else, he'd regret it. He looked at Kate and she smiled a gentle, questioning smile. He just sat there and said nothing. What were the odds that this was just some kind of strange dream?

"Sorry about dropping that on you. By the way I had nothing to do with his death. He died, I think, of a drug overdose, and I have no idea if it was an accident or murder. I arrived in Houston three days ago, and when I went to his penthouse he was already dead."

"Kate, why are you telling me this?"

"I'm a very serious person, so this type of behavior is out of character. I thought we shared a moment, and I was interested in seeing you again. If the next time you heard my name was in connection with someone's death and I was a logical suspect—well, you might run away and never talk to me again. I didn't want that to happen."

Well, at least there was one possible explanation for her behavior other than wanting him to get her off of a murder charge.

"You seem very calm about the death of your fiancé."

"Yes, I know. He and I have not really been engaged. I've cried over Jeffery in private, we were just friends. It was one of those things our families thought made sense, so we went along with it, but it had always just been a front to avoid arguments. As a matter of fact, he was gay—his family didn't know."

"If he wasn't really your fiancé, why were you in Houston to see him?"

"He asked me to bring him the $250,000. He told me to go to a bank in Boston and they would give me the money. He wanted me to fly to Houston and bring the money to him. I asked him what the hell was going on, he only said he was in some trouble and needed the cash and that he'd explain when I got here. Not too bright on my part, but while he wasn't my type of man, he was a great friend and I cared about him a lot."

"He had that kind of money readily available?"

"Oh my goodness, yes. His family is probably worth billions, but Jeffery himself must have been worth over fifty million."

"Wasn't there a problem carrying that much money on a flight?"

"The Boston bank gave me a certified letter from them stating that the money belonged to Jeffery and that I was legally taking the cash to him for non-criminal purposes. There were all sorts of contacts listed, including the bank's attorney. When I boarded in Boston they seemed very comfortable with the letter's authenticity and hardly questioned me at all."

"Did he tell you what kind of trouble he was in?"

"You know, Tony, I think you must be a good prosecutor. You sure know how to ask questions." She gave him a very engaging smile.

"Well yeah, I guess asking questions is sort of a reflexive reaction on my part. Gathering facts about crimes is a big part of what I do—I'm sorry if the questions feel out of line."

"Oh no, I wasn't saying that—please ask whatever you want."

"When he said he was in trouble, did he give you any information about what the trouble was?"

"No. However, knowing Jeffery, my guess would be sex. He was a very active homosexual with way too many partners. I know he'd used money before to buy off boyfriends who became troublesome. I'd guess it had something to do with his love life or his drug habits."

"He had a penthouse in Houston?"

"Yes. He lived at The Montgomery in the River Oaks area—a thirtieth-floor penthouse. He also had a house in Boston, but over the last few years he seemed to favor Houston. He was a principal owner and director of Fox Petroleum and was active in the management of the company. He also enjoyed the social life of Houston more than Boston—plus his parents lived in Boston and never visited Houston, so he didn't have to worry about running into them at some restaurant or other place."

"So you went to his penthouse to give him the money—how did you get in?"

"I had a key. I'd stayed with him some last summer, just to get away for a while, and I still had the key. I let myself in and called out to him. There was no answer, so I went into what had been my bedroom and deposited the small carry-on I'd brought. I went into the kitchen and got a drink of water and just started looking around to see if there was anyone there. I saw him out on the balcony lying on a lounge chair. I was pretty sure immediately that he was dead. I panicked and ran out onto the balcony. As I got closer, there was no question—he was definitely dead. Maybe for a day or so. I felt sick, so I went into a small bathroom off the kitchen. Afterwards I cleaned myself up a bit and washed my face. I was shaking and not sure what to do. I didn't want to see him like that again, so I just left."

"Why didn't you call the police?"

"At first it was just that I was so upset. I had to get out of there. I wasn't thinking clearly. I needed to escape the ugliness. Maybe I was thinking there was something wrong and someone had killed him and if I stayed the police would accuse me, or the killer would kill me—I don't honestly know exactly what was going on in my head. I just wanted to run away."

"So you left your bag in the room?"

"Yes. After I wandered around a while, I remembered that there was another address where I used to send him some of his packages when they came to my apartment in Boston. I'd asked him about why he was receiving mail at my apartment, and why I wasn't mailing it to his address in Houston. He just said in a joking way that it was secret spy stuff—never directly answered my question. I'd assumed it was his boyfriend's address, but I really had no idea. I found a cab and went to the address. As soon as I got out of the cab I knew it wasn't an area of town Jeffery would ever go to. By that point I was dazed and not thinking straight at all. I just sat down on the curb and started crying. After a while some guys came up and started harassing me. Then, out of the blue, some cops came along and gave the guys a rough time. After they'd run them off they started asking me questions, but I wasn't thinking clearly at all. They must have decided I was down there to buy drugs or something—maybe they thought I was on something right then. They asked if they could search my purse and I just handed it to them. I'd forgotten all about the money. There were two stacks of hundred-dollar bills about six inches high. They just stared at the inside of my purse like they couldn't believe what they were seeing. At that point I had no idea what was happening—I was having trouble focusing on what was going on. They put me in their patrol car and took me to a field police station, and that's where I met you."

"Where are you staying?"

"I'm at the Hyatt Regency, just a couple blocks from here."

"Kate, there's some chance that I'm a complete fool, but I believe what you've told me. While you'll probably be a suspect, it won't be for long. If what you've said is correct, you weren't even in town when Jeffery died. You came in that morning and, based on what you saw, it sounds like he might have died the night before. The coroner will be able to establish the time of death within a few hours, and if you were in Boston or on the plane at the time then you couldn't have killed him. I think the investigators will be very interested in learning what you've told me about Jeffery—it suggests that he may have been involved in drug dealing at some level or another—and that's probably what got him killed."

"I hope you are right. I kept waiting for something to happen, for someone to call or something, but as of yet no one has contacted me or my lawyer."

"Any chance the body hasn't been found?"

"No. It's been three days. He had a cleaning service, and someone would have reported him missing after that long anyway."

"Let me make a call. I'll be right back."

Tony left the bar and found a phone. He placed a call to Sergeant Nelson and asked him if there was an investigation in progress related to a body found at the Montgomery in River Oaks. When he got off the phone he returned to the bar area.

"Kate, there's no investigation because the body hasn't been found. I asked the sergeant to send someone over there and see if there is actually a body in the penthouse, but as of right now there's no investigation because nothing's been reported."

"Oh my god. Could he still be on the balcony? That doesn't make any sense. I know he has a cleaning service that comes in at least three times a week. I can't believe this."

"Would you like to have dinner?" It had sounded sensible in his head, but stupid when it came out of his mouth.

"Tony, could you take me back to my hotel. I think I just want to lie down a minute, but could you possibly stay for a while?"

They walked slowly to the Hyatt. Tony commented on the beautiful cool evening, which was unusual for Houston, but mostly they just walked quietly. At the hotel, they went to her room. It was a large suite with an impressive view of Houston and the suburbs. Kate went into the bathroom. Tony found the phone and called Sergeant Nelson. After getting the information he needed, he went over to the small bar and fixed a drink.

Kate was gone for some time and Tony became worried. She came back into the room wearing a robe, barefoot. Tony suddenly felt light-headed.

"Sorry that took so long. I needed a little time to compose myself. Did you find out anything else?"

"Yes. A patrol car went to Jeffery's apartment. A person answered the door and said he was a friend of Jeffery's and that Jeffery had gone to Boston. He let them look around the apartment, but they found nothing."

"Oh my god. What does that mean? He was dead. Fuck. He was dead. What's going on?"

Tony got up and walked over to Kate and held her. She began to cry uncontrollably and he continued to hold her. She looked up at him and he was amazed at how beautiful she was. She kissed him.

10

Tony and Kate

"Tony, what the hell is going on? I told you how important this meeting was and you show up forty-five minutes late? Son-of-a-bitch, Tony." He was getting one of those looks from his boss—the kind that no employee wants to experience.

"Bill, I'm so sorry. I got involved in something last night that made me late this morning. Are they still here? I'm ready for the meeting."

"Well, shit—they left. But it wasn't because of you. Brewster's attorney is an idiot, and I guess I told him so. That's why I needed you here, Tony—you know I have no diplomacy. Shit, what a mess. He called me a moron and I called him an idiot. Maybe you could call him in a little bit and see if you can be the peacemaker and get this back on track. I'm ready for this case to be gone."

"Sure I can, Bill. I'll call him in about an hour and we'll get this fixed."

Bill didn't look happy. He headed back into his office and slammed the door. Tony turned and headed to his own office—he had a silly smile on his face.

Tony had taken Kate down to the sub-station she had been transported to after her arrest. He'd convinced her that she needed to make a statement to the police and file a missing person report. He told her the downtown sub-station would be easiest, and that the statement could be taken by Sergeant Nelson, whom Tony had already called.

After their night together, Tony couldn't take his eyes off of Kate. He was so in love, it hurt. Once she had completed her statement she was supposed to call so he could pick her up and take her back to the hotel. After two hours, he went to find her.

"Hey, Sergeant. Did Ms. Martin leave?"

"Yep, about half hour ago. Said she was walking back to her hotel. Tony, she's kind of a strange lady. One minute everything was fine and then in the middle of her statement she seemed to lose it. Not sure what is going on with you and her but take it from an old fart, be careful."

Just what Tony needed—advice from a dumb sergeant.

"What do you think, Nelson? Has a crime been committed?"

"Well, I can tell you something isn't right. Too much smoke not to be a fire somewhere. Jeffrey Parker isn't exactly a homeless guy—once I put out bulletins with his name, I got numerous calls. Apparently the 'important person' alarms bells went off somewhere. Detective Benson called ten minutes after I finished my paperwork and wanted information. Our resident star cop doesn't deal with any cases except the most important, so my guess right now is this is much bigger than we knew. That could also mean that we've both stepped into a big pile of horseshit."

Tony grimaced. Detective Benson was the police chief's special attack dog—and to be avoided at all costs.

"Son of a bitch, Tony. Is this your week for one fuckup after another? My phone hasn't stopped ringing. The police chief wants to know why one of my Assistant DA's is fucking the top suspect in a murder. What the fuck, Tony? I'm about to have a fucking heart attack here."

The DA's face was turning an alarming shade of red. If Tony hadn't seen it before he'd have been dialing nine-one-one. How had such a high strung person managed to become DA? On the other hand, he had every right to be yelling, spitting, and turning ugly shades of red over Tony's behavior. Just a few days before Tony had thought about the fact that everything was orderly: his life, his work, his brain. Today it was all mush.

"This pushy asshole, Detective Benson, is on his way over here to talk to you. What a piece of shit. He told me—*I'm the goddamned DA*—to have you available in a half an hour. He's bossing me around—what an asshole."

"Bill, please try to calm down. I may have screwed up—if I have, so be it. It has nothing to do with you or your department. All of the shit will fall on my head, nowhere else. I'm sorry you're taking crap for my actions. I'll talk to this guy and it'll be okay. I may have used poor judgement, but Bill, I haven't committed any crime. Worst case for you is that you fire me and I go away. I'm sorry."

Bill seemed to calm down. He and Tony had become friends, and Tony knew that was the real reason he was so upset. The internal politics would be difficult, but Bill was a survivor and he'd come out okay— Tony might not.

"Sir, there's a Detective Benson here demanding to see Mr. Garcia."

"I'm going to tell you right now," Bill said, "it sounds like you've screwed the pooch. At this point I haven't thought too much about what sort of crimes you could be charged with, but there's no question your career just went into the toilet."

Detective Benson entered the room. An old-school cop, part enforcer and part philosopher, he had been on the Houston force for as long as anyone could remember. He did one thing in life and only one thing—enforce the law. No exceptions—everyone was treated the same way, mostly bad. He began demanding answers without preamble, making it clear that this was a serious problem for Tony.

"I understand, Detective Benson. How can I help you?"

"Well, at least your attitude is right. I need to know what's going on. What's happening between you and Kate Martin? I need to know everything you know about Jeffery Peterson. Tell me your story."

Tony obliged. He told the detective everything, including the lovemaking. He'd decided that the only way out of this mess was to tell the whole truth. He hoped that it wouldn't harm Kate, but all he could do was to be candid and then help her in any way he could.

"Well, son, it's been a long time since my dick overrode my brain, but I'm not unsympathetic. My advice to you is to run like hell from Ms. Martin. I'll also tell you that if I find you interfering in my investigation, you're at risk of losing that dick—understand?"

"Yes." Understand? What kind of stupid question was that—he was in the middle of a shit-storm and had no idea how to get out. Of course he understood. But he was in love. He had to find Kate and decide what to do. No doubt he was going to lose his job—everything he'd worked for—but it was strangely okay with him.

Tony went to the Hyatt, but Kate didn't answer his call. He hadn't got a key from her, and he was reluctant to use his authority to get the hotel to open the room. He sure the hell didn't want to have another encounter with Benson. He went back to his office and shut the door, leaned back in his chair, and closed his eyes. He'd always been overly attracted to women. He thought about Vickie. He hoped she was happy. He was starting to feel exhausted—the emotions were taking a toll.

"Mr. Garcia, Ms. Martin is on line two. Do you want to take the call?"

Tony ignored the question, grabbed the phone, and hit line two.

"Where are you?"

"Sorry, Tony. I just had to get away for some time and think."

"We need to talk. Can you meet me at the same bar in about thirty minutes?"

"Yes, I'll be there."

Sitting on the same barstool as his last visit, Tony gulped a gin and tonic and ordered another one. His mood was bouncing all over the place, from joy to anger to fear. He was fairly certain nothing was going to be the same—his nicely ordered life was going to change.

Kate leaned in and gave him a kiss on his cheek. She took the barstool next to his. Her aroma was intoxicating. He looked at her—he wanted to just stare at her.

"You're looking a little pale, Tony. Are you feeling okay?"

He almost wanted to laugh. She seemed so composed and he was falling apart.

"They haven't found a body or any evidence of a crime at Jeffery's apartment. They also didn't find your bag or any evidence that you'd been there. But all hell is breaking loose because he's missing. Apparently your fiancé was a big political supporter—lots of money contributed to campaigns—so all of those politicians are up in arms, trying to figure out if this is something that can hurt them. They've assigned a bulldog homicide detective to the case, and he's in the process of looking for somebody to blame for whatever in the fuck actually happened—starting with me."

"Oh, Tony, I'm so sorry. You need to distance yourself from me right away."

"Will you marry me?"

Kate looked stunned. She looked away, a move the bartender interpreted as wanting to order, so she asked for a white wine. She seemed lost in thought. Tony waited.

"Tony, I'd love nothing more, but I can't do that to you. You know nothing about me. I'm a complete mess. I have been in and out of therapy my whole life, and I'm still screwed up. The last thing in the world you want is to be married to me."

"Kate, I love you. Will you please marry me?"

"Well, since you said please, I guess I will."

Kate was smiling in a wonderful, knee-buckling way. Tony turned and they embraced, to the delight of the sparsely populated bar.

The next few days went by in a whirlwind. Tony resigned, shocking everyone who knew him and creating some wonderfully vile rumors about love and murder. Detective Benson threatened him with all sorts of consequences and Tony told him to bring them on or shut the fuck up. After a few days of this type of exchange it became clear that leaving Dodge—or, in this case, Houston—might be a good idea.

Tony spent several days working the phones with contacts in the legal community and some people he knew from school. One of his professors from OU told him he knew of an opportunity in Las Cruces, New Mexico. Tony had no idea where that was, which made it sound perfect. The professor called his contact and enthusiastically recommended Tony.

The Dona Ana County Administrator reached out to Tony and offered him the job as County Attorney at about half of what he was making in Houston. Tony said yes. Tony Garcia realized that they probably thought he spoke Spanish, which he didn't. They probably thought he'd have top-notch references, which he wouldn't. Tony decided whatever happened, he'd be fine.

Tony and Kate were married in Galveston in a civil ceremony with random passers-by for witnesses—and they couldn't have been happier. Kate told her father, and he gave his blessing. His health kept him from traveling, but he said he was anxious to meet Tony. He had a ridiculous amount of money transferred to their new joint checking account as a wedding present, leaving Tony speechless. Kate said it was actually very small, considering her father's wealth, which left him beyond speechlessness.

Tony's father had died and his mother was suffering from Alzheimer's disease. He talked to her from time to time, but she didn't know him. He felt guilty for not having been a better son.

Tony called his old boss, Bill, and once again apologized for quitting the way he had. Bill said he should do what his heart told him to do and wished the couple great happiness. Tony would miss him.

Only a few months before, Tony could never have imagined that his life would be what it had now become. Married to the most beautiful woman in the world—who it turns out is rich. He felt pretty lucky.

As they settled into Las Cruces, their life became centered on themselves. Kate was naturally a loner, and she loved the house they'd purchased. She spent hours working in the back yard and having projects done on the house. Tony couldn't wait to get home each day and spend time with her. They were happy.

Tony maintained some contacts in Houston. Jeffery Peterson was still missing, but now the police described him as presumed dead. No evidence, especially a body, was ever uncovered. Peterson's parents' attorneys cleaned up all of the legal matters. Kate had written Jeffery's parents a letter telling them what had happened and returning the $250,000. She knew they probably hated her for not staying at the apartment and waiting on the police, or perhaps hated her because they thought she was lying and somehow involved. She didn't reach out to them further and she heard nothing from them. She seemed to put it all behind her.

11

More Killing

Present Day, 1989—Truth or Consequences, New Mexico

"Hello, this is Ray Pacheco."

"Sheriff Pacheco, this is Deputy Samson in Ruidoso."

"Well hello, deputy. I hear you're doing a good job up there. What can I do for you?"

"Thought you might want to know we just got a report out of El Paso that Sheriff Rodriguez was found dead. He had been shot once in the head—with a .22."

Ray got as much information as he could from the deputy. Rodriguez had been missing since he left the Ruidoso hospital months before. Most people assumed he'd gone to Mexico and would never be heard from again. Shot in the head with a .22—just like Marino. The only difference was that it was only one bullet. The Marino shooting had been a hate-driven crime—this sounded more like an execution. There just had to be some kind of connection.

"I don't think so." Tyee was offering his opinion on Marino and Rodriguez murders being connected. "I think he was shot by one of the Mexican cartels—that sounds like their method of execution, and I don't think they had anything to do with Marino. I still think that was personal, not business."

"Good analysis, Tyee. That makes a lot of sense. But still, another loose end in the Marino killing is eliminated. Maybe it's the cartels—but it could also be someone tying up those loose ends."

"Yeah, but who? It's somebody who has no trouble killing people. Is it someone we met in Ruidoso? Or is it more likely tied to drugs and hitmen?"

"I know this isn't our case, but I think maybe we should run up to Ruidoso and poke around a little bit more—what do you think, Tyee?"

"Apaches have long history of riding long and far seeking truth and justice, let's giddyup."

"Let's giddyup?"

"Yeah, let's giddyup."

Ray wasn't sure he wanted to be in the car with anyone who found it reasonable to say giddyup, but they put together plans to leave the next day.

"Just heard from my cousin Beverly. She's taking her two kids to Disneyland and will be driving through in a couple of days. She wants to stop and visit."

Sue looked like she had just been told about an impending alien invasion.

"Uh, is that a good thing?"

"It's a fucking disaster. She's the most annoying person I've ever been around. She lives in Denver with her equally annoying husband, although he isn't going to be with her. The last time I saw her was twenty years ago, when she was a very annoying child. Ray, my family is a complete mess. I'm not kidding when I tell you I'm the only normal person in my whole damn family—and you know I have more problems than sense. I can't imagine how bad her kids must be. She totally caught me off guard and I didn't know what to say."

"How did she even know where you lived?"

"I'd invited her older sister, who was kinda a pal of mine when were younger, to our wedding. I knew she wouldn't come because she still lives in upstate New York. Beverly said she got my information from her sister and was so excited about seeing us."

"Well Sue, my dear, I think the best thing for you to do is to be nice for a short span of time and hope for the best. She'll probably just stay one night—how bad can it be?"

"Wait a minute. You're not going to be here are you?"

"I don't know. I'm going to Ruidoso tomorrow with Tyee to follow up on some things but I don't expect to be gone long. When will she be here?"

"Tomorrow night. How did you know about this?"

"Sue, I didn't know about your cousin. Look, if you want me to be here, I'll stay here and go to Ruidoso the next day."

Sue was frowning but also thinking.

"No, this isn't your burden to bear. She's my crazy relative."

Ray gave Sue a hug. He told her he'd try to be back as soon as possible and was sorry he was going to miss her cousin, but he privately thought that dumb luck had allowed him to dodge a bullet. A crazy cousin with two kids sounded very much like something to avoid at all cost.

The morning was cool and misty, unusual weather for the high desert.

"What's the plan of action once we get to Ruidoso?"

"First we're going to stay in town rather than at the Inn—cheaper and closer. Some place called Mountain Manor. Next, we want to see Deputy Samson and hear what he has to say. We'll check in with the new Sheriff of course, and I thought we should drop in on Dick Franklin and see how the horse racing business is getting along. From there we'll just react to what we learn."

"Well that definitely sounds like a plan. How about the ceremonial police chief?"

"Yeah, Chief Nelson. Not sure he'd be much help, but as I said before he's a world class gossip, so we should probably drop in on him and get all of the latest dirt about the fine citizens of Ruidoso."

"I guess one other unanswered question is about Tony's wife's half-sister. Do we know if she made any attempt to contact Marino when she was visiting her half-sister in Santa Fe?"

"No, and it's starting to piss me off just a little. I have yet to get a straight answer from Tony. He's just stonewalling the whole situation. The small pistol, the viciousness of the shooting—that could fit with an act by an ex-wife fueled by anger. But it's hard to pursue that angle and not step on Tony's toes—not sure I want to do that just yet."

"Of course there are other options. This Marino guy apparently was hated by half of the county—could be we don't have any idea who did it or why."

"Sure, no question. We're working with what we can see, but this could be something that was only known to Marino and the shooter. In that case we may not be able to identify the killer. But something tells me it wasn't a one-time random event—somehow this is all tied together, and Sheriff Rodriguez being shot in El Paso convinces me that the killer is still active in whatever mischief caused these crimes."

Happy stayed with Sue this time, so it was just Ray and Tyee in the old Jeep. The seasons were changing, so as they climbed in altitude there was a noticeable change in temperature. Leaving the desert floor at Alamogordo the temperature was in the mid-eighties, but as they climbed the mountain it dropped into the low sixties. In another month they'd start getting snow in Ruidoso. Ray liked the contrast and found it invigorating to be in the mountains, but he was sure he didn't want to live in a place that often got many feet of snow in a single day.

As they pushed up the mountain, the old Jeep had some trouble keeping their speed close to the limit. One of these days Ray would have to retire the trusty old beast, and it didn't make him happy. Easing over the top of the last pass, they began a long downhill drop into downtown Ruidoso. They found the Mountain Manor on the main drag through town. It was many steps down from their previous stay at the Inn of the Mountain Gods, but it was convenient. They checked in and deposited their gear.

"Tina, how are you doing?"

"Hello Mr. Pacheco, Mr. Chino. I'm doing great. Everything is much better. So much has changed since you were here last. It feels like a real sheriff's department now. Sheriff James is just wonderful and really has everyone working together. I have people telling me every day how much better everything is—I'm proud to work here now."

"That's great Tina. You had a lot to do with getting things cleaned up—you should be proud of what you've done for your town." Tina blushed in a little girl fashion. If she'd had them Ray thought she'd be twirling her curls—it was a very cute reaction to the compliment.

"Is Sheriff James in?"

"No, he's actually out most of the day. He's taking a tour of the northern area of the county and meeting with some city officials. He'll be back this evening."

"How about Deputy Samson?"

"Well he's also out, but just on patrol. Let me call him on the radio and see where he is."

Tina got ahold of the deputy, who agreed to meet Ray and Tyee at a Dairy Queen about two miles north of the administrative building.

Ray pulled in next to the deputy's patrol car. Deputy Samson was standing outside his vehicle, eating a soft-serve ice cream cone.

"Ray, I'm going to have one of those cones you want one?"

"You go ahead Tyee, I'm going to pass for now."

"Good to see you Sheriff."

"Well it's good to see you deputy. I was just visiting with Tina and she was saying everything was much better with the department."

"Completely different. Sheriff James is a real professional. The old sheriff, even before Marino started with his thug tactics, wasn't nothing but a good ol' boy—he didn't know anything about how to run a professional law enforcement agency. But Sheriff James has us involved in training and following procedures. He's teaching all of us what it means to be a professional staff. It's taken some getting used to, but I think everyone feels like we're much better at protecting people and following the rules so we don't have any screwups. I'm proud to be a part of this sheriff's department."

"I'm so glad it's worked out for you and the town. Anything else you can tell me about Sheriff Rodriguez?"

"Not much. The El Paso police said it looked like a professional job. There were no forensics, finger prints—nothing at the scene that could lead to the killer. They've seen a lot of this kind of killing with the cartel drug wars. Their best guess was that it was a cartel-related execution—or someone trying to make it look like a drug execution."

"What did you think about Rodriguez as sheriff?" Ray still couldn't get a good feeling for who Rodriguez really was.

"Well, I hate to bad mouth the dead, but he wasn't very good. Like I said, he was a good ol' boy. He liked to drink beer and hang out. I don't think he was a very dedicated officer of the law. Not sure how he kept getting re-elected—could be it was just that he never really offended anyone, because he did so little."

"Do you think he could have been the one who set up the drug operation?" Tyee interjected between licks off of his ice cream cone.

"Well he obviously had something to do with it, but my impression was that he was not a leader—he was the sort of guy who gets bossed around. While I'd say he wasn't very good at his job, I'm still surprised by the things that went on in the department. He was lazy and probably not the brightest guy on the planet, but I don't think anyone would've said he was an evil person. Everything started going downhill when the new deputies were hired. And the hiring of Marino was just bizarre. Why he'd hire an obvious hoodlum as a deputy never made any sense. Plus Rodriguez seemed just as intimidated by Marino as anyone."

"Do you think Rodriguez could have known Marino before he hired him?"

"I didn't see any indication of that. They sure weren't pals of any sort. The story was that Marino was here from the East Coast visiting a cousin, but I never saw the cousin or even heard his name. If anything I'd have said that Rodriguez didn't like Marino and didn't want to have anything to do with him."

"Guess some of your previous deputies have resigned, and I believe six have been charged with criminal violations. I heard those were mostly related to distribution of illegal drugs. Do you think Rodriguez was the one heading up that group or was it Marino?"

"Those six deputies were the worst guys we had. I think four of them were recent hires, and they seemed more loyal to Marino than Rodriguez. Even with that, though, I'd have to say Rodriguez was right in the middle of the whole mess. What it seemed like to me was that someone else was running the show and Rodriguez and Marino were kind of equal and competing first lieutenants."

"Suppose that was true, any guesses on who was running the operation?"

"No clue at all. If I was going to take a wild stab it would be someone from El Paso or Juarez—nobody local."

"Yeah, that might make sense. Plus that could explain Rodriguez being killed in El Paso."

"One other thing. I got a call this morning from Tito Annoya. Even though the evidence wasn't strong enough to charge Tito, there's no question he was funneling some of the drugs through his clubs. But I think he's just a small part of the big picture. Anyway, he called this morning because he heard about Rodriguez and he wanted protection. I told him I wasn't sure what the sheriff's department could do under the circumstances, but that I'd discuss it with Sheriff James. Then I asked if he was willing to give us inside information about the drug trafficking business and he hung up."

"Interesting. He thinks someone killed Rodriguez because of what was going on here and might want to kill him too. That sounds like he thinks he knows who it is."

They talked further while Tyee had another ice cream cone. Ray told the deputy that he thought they might go by Tito's club to see if he was there and that he'd let him know if anything happened.

"Ya know, Ray, I kind of like that idea that someone in El Paso was behind all of this. And I also think there may be a link with the previous sheriff in Sierra Vista."

"Could be. Not sure what makes sense. Sometimes I think this is just a little scam that got out of hand, and other times I wonder if there isn't something bigger behind all of this."

Heading south down Main Street, they quickly found themselves in front of the Tito Club. Pulling into a parking spot in front, the old Jeep looked right at home—most of the patrons at Tito's were not real status-conscious about their vehicles. Although it appeared imperative to have huge wheels—the cab step up on some of the pickups had to be almost three feet off the ground. Probably not a lot of short guys in the club.

It was late afternoon and most of the customers in the club appeared to be more interested in drinking than anything else—even the music seemed subdued for this mixture of ruffians. The place was dark, so Ray and Tyee took a few moments by the door letting their eyes adjust.

"Hi, my name is Ray Pacheco and this is Tyee Chino. We're working with the Attorney General and would like to have a word with Tito Annoya. Is he in?"

The bartender gave them a stare that suggested he'd just as soon shoot them as serve them a beer. After a while, thinking maybe he was deaf, Ray started to repeat his question.

"I heard you the first time. I don't know where in the fuck he is and I don't care, and you can go to hell along with the Attorney General. And by the way, we don't allow no fuckin' Indians in this bar." The man turned slightly to glance at his audience sitting along the bar. He had a smug look on his face, as if he'd just scored some sort of victory for his team.

In a move that will probably be passed down in bar lore, Tyee jumped flat-footed over the bar and swiftly secured the bartender, placing him on the floor—dislocating his shoulder in the process.

"Don't kill him, Tyee." This got everyone's attention. Most headed towards the door, although some hung back to see what was going to happen. The bartender screamed in pain and ill-advisedly cursed the huge Indian sitting on his back.

"Let me ask you again. You answer real nice and I'll call an ambulance for you. If you don't, who knows what happens next. Where's Tito?"

"He left about an hour ago and said he was going out of town for a few days. Told me to tell anyone looking for him to go to hell."

In a move that took Ray by surprise, Tyee bent down and forced the bartender's shoulder back into place. The man screamed, then fainted. Tyee got a wet towel and placed it over the unconscious man's face.

"He'll be fine. I've had my shoulder separated playing football a half a dozen times—hurts like hell, but usually no major damage. Sorry I overreacted. Tired of assholes like this guy."

"This is really strange. You do remember Big Jack did almost the same thing to some drunk on his dock at the bait shop. Did he teach you that move?"

"After that happened I asked Big Jack to show me what he did—it's really pretty simple and amazingly effective. Now, the jumping part isn't something Big Jack could do."

"My story is going to be he looked like he was going for a gun and you had to react quickly. None of these people in here will say anything at all to a deputy, not even to contradict our story. I'm just surprised you could move like that—I'm going to have to be nicer to you."

"Indian likes the sound of that."

They called an ambulance anyway, and also called the sheriff's department. While they waited for the deputies and ambulance they looked in Tito's backroom and office, but didn't find anyone. All the customers had left once it was clear nothing else was going to happen and that the deputies would be there soon.

The deputies had no problem believing that the bartender initiated the confrontation. The bartender regained consciousness and yelled that he'd been attacked by the fucking Apache and almost killed. It was pretty universally agreed that it might have been better if the Apache had killed the bastard. The deputies searched the bar and found a .38 special pistol, a sawed-off shotgun, and an impressive assortment of drugs. The bartender was going to be charged with a long list of crimes.

"How about we go find a nice quiet bar in a nice restaurant and have a beer or two and dinner?" Ray was ready for some less intense time.

"Firewater and steaks, nothing better for Indian—especially if old white man is buying."

Ray smiled. Tyee was ready for some quiet time too.

12

Beverly and The Kids

"Beverly, my goodness, it's been so long." Sue wasn't real sure she'd have recognized Beverly if she hadn't known that was who was at her door. She couldn't remember the last time she'd seen her, but she was fairly sure that she'd been just a teenager and probably weighed a hundred pounds less than she did now. Sue gritted her teeth and gave her a hug.

"Oh, Sue you look so great. My god, you are still beautiful! And you are so slim. My goodness, I must weigh twice what you do—don't you eat anything? Hey, meet my kids. This is Kay, she's eight, and the little one is Tom, he's six. Say hello to Sue, kids."

More or less hidden behind mom's girth were two actually quite beautiful children. The kids seemed polite, and they smiled and said hello to Sue. Sue was having a little trouble matching the kids' looks and manners to Beverly. *Must be the father's influence*, she thought.

Sue helped Beverly bring in the luggage and placed the children in one spare bedroom and Beverly in the other.

"Wow, this is a wonderful place. I had no idea when you said a cabin that it would be this large and so fancy. So where's your new husband? Did he hear I was coming and leave town?"

Bingo.

"Yes, he's away, but it had nothing to do with you being here. He was sorry to miss you. He's working on a case and he's in Ruidoso tonight."

"Well, maybe I'll be able to see him on our way back." Sue didn't like the sound of that, but let it pass.

"Beverly, since I wasn't sure when you'd be here I thought it'd be easiest and probably good with the kids if we just had hamburgers—is that okay?"

"The kids will love that—throw in few beers for me and I'll love it too. Do you need me to do anything?"

"Nope, everything will be ready in a few minutes. Come out to the kitchen and you can pick your beer. So tell me, what does your husband do for work?"

Beverly had found the refrigerator and the beer supply. She grabbed two bottles and sat at the kitchen table—the offer to help appeared to be something of a hollow gesture.

"Well Sue. I didn't mention this to you over the phone, but Chuck and I have called it quits. For about six months now he's been living with a girl who I'm sure isn't even legal in most states—shit, I think she's eighteen but I'm not sure. The man has lost his mind and his damned soul. He told me I didn't make him happy sexually anymore—what the fuck? Does he want me to be eighteen and slim after two kids and piles and piles of dirty clothes?"

"Beverly, I'm so sorry. How are the kids handling everything?"

"Jeez, I think they like the new girlfriend better than me. That's all they talk about when they come back from a visit, how neat it is to be with Molly. What fun Molly is. What a great time they had with Molly. Fuck, what kind of name is Molly for a grown woman anyway?"

Sue decided she needed a beer, too.

In an odd contradiction, the children seemed more mature than their mother. Beverly, who was nursing her sixth beer, had done nothing to help with dinner. The children, on the other hand, had pitched in immediately. They set the table and helped Sue bring in the burgers. They were quiet, polite, and very attractive. Sue began to wonder if Beverly had stolen these kids from someone else.

"Sue, I guess it's the long drive but I'm completely exhausted. If you don't mind I'm going to lie down a bit and rest up for tomorrow. Don't worry about the kids. They're pretty self-reliant."

Kay and Tom didn't pay much attention to Beverly as she staggered off to bed. They helped Sue clean up, showing unusual skill for kids that age. Apparently they were practiced at cleaning up after their mother.

Sue talked to them about school and whether they were excited about going to Disneyland. Both kids talked about school, about how they enjoyed their classes and school friends. With regard to Disneyland they seemed evasive, avoiding looking directly at her. Sue liked the children much more than she did Beverly. She made sure they were comfortable in their room and told them good night.

Sue had an uneasy feeling that Beverly wasn't being honest about what was going on and that somehow this was going to impact Sue personally. She just hoped that Beverly was gone before Ray got back tomorrow—she was pretty sure Ray wouldn't be impressed with her.

When Sue woke the next morning, she was sure she smelled brewing coffee—if that was Beverly she'd have to re-think her opinion of the woman. She put on her nicest bath robe—not the ratty one that was her favorite—and headed to the kitchen. It was Kay making coffee, while Tom worked on toast. Beverly was nowhere to be seen.

"Well Kay, how sweet of you to make coffee. How did you find everything?"

"Oh it wasn't hard. Most people keep their coffee stuff all in one place—once I found your place, it was all there."

Smart kid. "Guess you make coffee quite often for your mother?"

"She's a late sleeper. But I don't mind. I like the smell of coffee—even though I hate the taste."

About that time Beverly came into the kitchen wear-ing a robe that made Sue's ratty one look like a high fashion statement. Her overall appearance suggested that she'd slept in a cardboard box. Beverly said nothing, concentrating on the coffee machine. She poured a cup and added a massive amount of sugar, then sat at the kitchen table without a word of thanks to anyone.

"Sorry Sue. I'm just a bitch in the mornings until I have had at least two cups of coffee."

Sue had many things she wanted to add to that assess-ment, but decided to keep her mouth shut.

"Well I guess you'll be wanting to get an early start. Where do you think you'll stop for the night?"

"Sue, I was wondering if we could stay another night with you. I do want to meet your husband, and I'm feeling a little washed out for some reason. I'm sure I'll be feeling much better in the morning. Do you think that would be okay?"

Well, crap. Sue knew she should tell her to get in her damn car and go to Disneyland or else, but she also knew that she couldn't. Something was wrong, and screaming at this annoying woman wasn't going to help.

"What's really going on Beverly?"

"Well like I said, I'm just a bit tired today and tomorrow would be much better to start our drive again. And I really wanted to be able to meet your new husband."

"Beverly, either cut out the bullshit and tell me what's really going on or get in your car and go to California. Or go home. I really don't care."

Beverly started to cry. This is reflex for many women—when you're caught at something, cry, and see if the one who caught you can be bought off with tears. Works on men like a charm, not so much on other women. Sue waited without saying a word, her arms crossed, while Beverly shed some dramatic, but not very effective, tears.

"Shit, Chuck stopped paying the rent on the apartment—I was evicted. I called him and yelled at him and told him he'd never see his kids ever again. His lawyer called me later and told me they were filing divorce papers and in the interim asking a judge to award custody of the kids to Chuck's mother because I was an unfit mother and didn't have a place for them to stay. I was unfit—can you believe that shit? It's that asshole who's sleeping with a teenager, not me! Well, I lost it and threatened the lawyer—maybe even said I'd kill him, not real sure what all I said. He must have filed charges. I heard from a girlfriend that the cops were at my old apartment looking for me to arrest me for something. Well, I had to leave. You understand don't you? You were the only person I could think of. Shit, I'm sorry Sue, but I didn't know what to do. I'm such a loser. A big fat loser."

The tears that started this time were real. Sue looked at the kids, who had heard all of this, and realized that they'd known from the beginning what was going on. These were tough kids. Sue wanted to scream at Beverly, but realized that it'd do no good, so she went over and held her while she cried. The children came up to Sue and gave her a hug, and soon they were all crying. Sue was thankful Ray wasn't there—he might have shot the lot of them.

Sue spent much of the day trying to understand exactly what had happened with Beverly and her husband. While it did seem that Beverly had lost her cool with Chuck's attorney, there was no way to make this out to be Beverly's fault without addressing Chuck's infidelity. Plus, to make everything even more loathsome, it was the kid's babysitter he was having the affair with. Beverly had heard from the parents of the babysitter and they were looking at the possibility of filing criminal charges against Chuck. Beverly said the girl was eighteen, but just barely, and that there was some law in Colorado that made it a criminal offense for a man to have sex with a woman who was more than twenty years younger than he was. And to add dark humor to the whole mess, Chuck worked as an administrator at a huge church in Denver, and when word got out about his new relationship, he was fired. Lust had once again claimed many victims.

"Hey Ray, where are you?"

"Still in Ruidoso. Now don't yell. I'd thought we'd be leaving any minute, but things just kept happening. Rather than drive home in the dark, we're going to stay one more night and be home tomorrow. Got lots of stuff to tell you about the case up here. It's becoming more confusing by the minute, but there are some very interesting developments. How are things there?"

"Well it's probably just as well that you're staying. Beverly has some issues she hadn't told me about and is in a serious crisis."

"What the hell does that mean?"

Sue told Ray a brief version of the story. Ray was silent.

"I know you are not going to like this, but she has no one to help her. That rental I had in town is still vacant and I think I can get it now for even less than I was paying before. I won't let her and her kids stay here and mess up our routine, but I can't put her out in the street either."

"Sue, I understand. You do whatever you think is right. I love you."

"I love you too. And I really miss you."

Sue wasn't sure about her next decision, but she decided to ask Big Jack to dinner to meet Beverly. She knew Big Jack had been a lawyer, and by all accounts a very good one, and Beverly needed some legal advice. She probably should have run it past Ray first, but she went with her gut instinct and plowed forward.

"Big Jack, what kind of name is that? What, you're inviting someone over to meet Big Beverly named Big Jack?"

"Beverly, you need to control your mouth. I'm trying to help you, and you're making it very difficult. Now please shut up."

Beverly actually looked hurt. Sue could see that poor Chuck may have had reasons to wander off the farm.

"Big Jack's name has a long story behind it—yes he's big, but that's beside the point. I invited him to dinner because he's a friend, number one, but also because he used to be a hot shot attorney in L.A. and I thought he might be able to give you some advice."

"Oh."

"This isn't about romance, it's about your current mess of a life. You have two wonderful children, and you need to start thinking about what's best for them and stop just thinking about yourself. I think Jack can give you some options and explain the law a little so you can start fixing what's happened to you and your kids. Got it?"

"Yep. I'm sorry. You're being so nice, and I'm such an ass. Please, anytime it's appropriate you just tell me to shut up. I already owe you so much, and I know you really don't know me from anybody and here I just show up and lay my problems in your lap. Sue, I'm so sorry—I'll try to behave better."

Sue knew she was being conned, but at least it was better than the head-up-my-ass attitude she'd been getting up until now.

"I'll try to help you the best I can, but you've got to help yourself."

Sue was tired of making speeches, so she headed off to the outbuildings to get some steaks from the freezer. The outbuildings on the cabin property had once been used by drug smugglers as a storage and staging area. They'd made some improvements in the process, and then after Ray bought the cabin and decided to open the PI business the buildings had gone through a major renovation. The buildings now housed a state-of-art communication and computer center. They also boasted accommodations for Tyee, plus a couple of rooms for guests. Sue didn't want to put Beverly or the kids in those rooms, though, in case it'd be a distraction to the business activities. The outbuildings also had storage freezers that were used by everyone, including Big Jack, since the grocery store was some miles away in T or C.

Kay and Tom opted for hamburgers again, so Sue pulled out two steaks. She decided that she and Beverly could share one—it was clear Beverly was more than capable of eating the whole steak, but Sue was going to try to help change her ways if she could.

"Hello Big Jack, I really appreciate you taking some time to talk to my cousin." Sue had stepped out on the front porch so she could have a quick visit with Jack before she introduced him to Beverly. "She's something of a mess and can be a little annoying, but she has herself in a legal situation where you might be able to give her some advice about what she should do. I know you can't be her attorney, but she needs some direction or I think she may end up making things worse. I know I shouldn't have bothered you."

"Sue, it's no bother. Dealing with *your* crazy relatives will be a piece of cake compared to my nutso kin. Plus free steak dinner—that's top dollar legal fees for me right now. Don't worry about it—if I can help, I want to, and if I can't, at least you tried, right?"

"Thanks, Jack." Sue gave him a little hug.

"Jack, I'd like you to meet my cousin Beverly. Beverly, this is my friend Jack. And Jack, these are Beverly's wonderful children, Kay and Tom."

"Well hello everybody. It's nice to meet you. Hey Beverly, how about a beer." Sue had no idea if this was just Jack wanting a beer or if it was some kind of secret signal between beer drinkers, but whatever it was, it was the right thing to have said to get Beverly smiling.

Jack and Beverly grabbed two beers each and went out onto the front porch. Sue and the kids continued to fix dinner. Once again, Sue was amazed at how handy these kids were—they seemed much older than their ages and were so well mannered. Could this be a whole new movement in child rearing? Just be completely useless and self-indulgent as a parent, and your kids will turn out great?

Dinner was uneventful. The burgers got the thumbs-up from the kids, and the adults seemed to enjoy their steaks and salads. Beverly was even agreeable to having only half her normal serving. She seemed attentive to Jack, and Jack was very attentive to both Beverly and her children during dinner. Sue still wasn't sure she was doing the right thing, but so far nobody was yelling at anyone.

After dinner, Jack and Beverly grabbed more beer and went back to the porch. The kids helped clean up, but it was obvious that they were growing tired. Sue suggested that they finish the clean-up in the morning—for now, instead, she'd read them a story. Sue had some old books she had lugged along in her travels that had had special meaning to her as a child. She put the children to bed and started reading her favorite. She was so intently enjoying reading her old childhood book that she didn't notice the kids were drifting off to sleep— by the time she did, she suspected that they'd been asleep for some time. She made sure they were tucked in and turned out the light. Sue had never been much of a kid person, but she sure liked these two.

Sue made some unnecessary noise as an early warning signal for Jack and Beverly before opening the door onto the porch. She told her guests that the kids had gone to bed and that she was headed that way herself, asking Beverly to be sure the front door was locked before she turned in. Then she said her good-nights.

13

Ruidoso Again

Ray and Tyee met at a small breakfast place next door to the hotel called Bud's Breakfast. The atmosphere, and the age and appearance of the employees, suggested it was an old hippie establishment—which in Ray's experience meant exceptional food. He wasn't wrong. Maybe it was the mountain air, but the food was possibly the best Ray had ever had. It was just eggs and bacon with hash browns and toast, but it was close to perfect. The coffee was excellent, too. Tyee was obviously enjoying the sausage he'd ordered, and its aroma was amazing.

"We're going to have to remember this place—the food is just wonderful."

About that time, a man who appeared to be both the owner and the cook came over to their table.

"How was your breakfast?"

"Fantastic. I have never had better."

"Glad you enjoyed it. Aren't you the guy who was running the sheriff's department for a while?"

"Yeah, Ray Pacheco is my name, and this is Tyee Chino."

"Bud Jackson." Everyone shook hands.

"Bud, you're one hell of a cook."

"Well thanks, I appreciate your kind words. I was meaning to look you up. There was something I needed to tell someone about the murder of that creep Marino."

"Oh really. What's that, Bud?"

"The night he got shot I was in here cleaning up some. The place was closed and I didn't have the lights on, so not sure anyone could have seen me from the outside. It was pretty late. There are lots of nights I have trouble sleeping and this time I decided to do something useful, so I came down here to work on getting the grill spic-and-span. I'd made some coffee and was standing over there, just looking out at the street, when these two cars pulled up over there in front of the art gallery. I know he was shot further down the street, but this was maybe an hour or so before that happened. One of the cars was a sheriff's patrol car and the other was some kind of fancy foreign car. Big, maybe a Mercedes or something like that. Well the guy in the foreign car gets out and walks over to the driver's window of the patrol car, and before you know it they're arguing—he was really pissed, yelling at the guy in the patrol car. He reached in the window once and must have had the guy by the neck. The guy inside the car pushed the door open and knocked the other guy down. Then the patrol guy got out and I could see it was Deputy Marino. He came around and was kicking the other guy who had fallen—kicking him hard. I thought I should get out there before it got worse, but I was reluctant to jump into the middle of anything involving that asshole Marino."

"Did you know the other guy in the foreign car?"

"Yeah, I did. He's a regular customer. It was Dick Franklin, the guy who manages Ruidoso Downs."

Ray and Tyee exchanged glances.

"What happen next?"

"Well, like I said Marino is kicking Dick really hard, so I started towards the door. I wasn't happy about going, but wasn't going to let the little bastard kill someone right in front of me either. But then Dick got hold of Marino's ankle and tripped him up. Marino fell really hard and hit his head on his patrol car. Dick stood up and shoved Marino off of the hood of the patrol car onto the sidewalk. He looked around, like he was seeing if anyone had seen what had happened. He looked my way but I don't believe he saw me. Now I'm thinking maybe he's going to do something to Marino—but he doesn't. He goes around and gets in his car and takes off."

"So did you go out and help Marino?"

"Well, I was going too but just about then he gets up and gets in the car and tears out of here. I think to myself *I wonder what that was all about*. But I figured it didn't have anything to do with me, so I went home. Of course the next day there was all of the excitement about Marino being shot. I knew I should tell someone what I saw, but to tell you the truth I was a little reluctant until things became clearer as to what was going to happen around here."

"Well yeah, Bud you should've given us your information before—but I understand it's been hard to tell the good guys from the bad guys for a while. I appreciate you telling me now. The current Sheriff, James—he's a good guy and you can trust him."

"Yeah, people are starting to say that. Guess I should call him and tell him what I saw."

"That'd be best."

Ray and Tyee left and went back to the hotel.

"Guess we should check out and go see Dick Franklin."

"Sounds like the logical plan."

Driving up to the racetrack was an odd experience. Even though Ruidoso Downs was located in a small resort community with only a few thousand full time residents, it was state-of-the-art, with a huge grandstand. It was supported by tourists and gamblers, and had always been considered one of the premier horse racing operations in the region.

"Do you think Franklin makes a lot of money as the manager of the track?" Ray was genuinely curious.

"My understanding had always been this was one of the best jobs, money-wise, in this area. I know Dick was considered a top tier student and business prospect when we were at school. I'm sure he was heavily recruited—don't know what happened to him or how he ended up here."

"Were you good friends at school?"

"No way. He was very friendly the other day and said all of that bullshit about me being his hero. The guy is just full of shit. He was the star. I figured he thought I had some influence over the investigation and was sucking up. I was a good student and knew my stuff, but my god—I was an Apache from the reservation. This guy Franklin was a blue blood from some wealthy family on the west coast. The story that was whispered about him was that he was involved in something illegal and his rich family sent him to New Mexico to go to school as punishment. I was shocked to see him still in New Mexico—a big bucks job in this state is peanuts on the coast."

"The illegal stuff he'd been involved in, did you know what it was?"

"No, not really. Everybody said it was drugs, but that's what everybody said about everything. Especially California illegal—either some kind of weird sex thing or drugs. I actually found him to be an okay guy. He worked hard to make good grades, so while he supposedly came from money he didn't act like it all the time."

"Seems odd that he didn't go back to California. I mean, you and I like New Mexico, but it isn't California."

"There was a woman he was involved with who was from this part of New Mexico. Seems like she was from Tularosa. Most beautiful woman I've ever seen—Hispanic and drop-dead gorgeous. Besides that, she was smart and had an over-powering presence about her. Her heritage supposedly traced back to Spanish royalty, and it showed. Her family wasn't fantastically wealthy, but for that part of New Mexico they were loaded. Dick fell for her big time. I'd bet you the only reason he's still here has something to do with her."

"It's such a cliché, but most things center on sex and money. Lust and greed pretty well define the underside of our society. Do you think Franklin would be capable of killing Marino?"

"I'd have thought he was more a diplomat than a fighter. My guess back when we were in school was that he'd go on to law school and end up being some kind of lobbyist. But who the hell knows what somebody might do if given sufficient reason. He's already told us how much he hated Marino and this latest bit of news about some kind of physical confrontation sure supports the picture of him shooting the bastard. The part that doesn't make sense is that it looks like Marino put his window down to talk to whoever shot him. He had just had a fight with Franklin—why would he just sit there and wait for him to come up to the window?"

"Yeah, that doesn't fit the picture."

"My Apache grandfather once said, 'when evil dies, bury it quick, and never dig it up.' Do you think that maybe everybody would be better off if we just forgot about Marino's murder?"

"I have a feeling your grandfather was a very wise man. I also think that there are lots of people who'd be fine with the whole mess just going away. But in all my years in law enforcement I never thought it was my job to decide who was guilty or innocent—it was my job to follow the facts and arrest whoever the facts pointed to. It was the job of a judge and a jury to decide who was guilty. Maybe Marino deserved to be shot, but that doesn't change my job, which is to find out who shot him and arrest them—and that's what I'm going to do, if I can."

"Old man still thinks he's sheriff with a white hat."

"Yeah, it's hard to break old habits."

They headed toward the administrative offices. The racing season wasn't scheduled to start for another few months, and the place was quiet. When they entered the offices, no one appeared to greet them.

"Hello, anyone here?" Ray shouted toward the back rooms. The area seemed vacant, but if the front door was unlocked there must be someone close by. They went back out onto the main grounds. Off in the distance they could see a couple of people having an animated conversation and they began walking in that direction. As they got closer they could see that one was Dick Franklin, looking rather disheveled. Franklin finished his less-than-friendly conversation and started walking toward them.

"Well hello. Thought you guys had finished up your work in Ruidoso some time ago."

Ray and Tyee shook hands with Franklin. Up close it was obvious that today he wasn't the dapper man they'd seen last time. He wore old work clothes, and he hadn't shaved in several days. His eyes were bloodshot and in general he didn't look well.

"Just following up on some things so we can complete our report to the AG. Wanted to ask you about the last time you saw Marino."

If possible, Franklin now seemed to look worse.

"Somebody saw me didn't they?"

"Saw you when?"

"Listen I didn't kill the bastard—I wanted to, but I didn't. Sometime before he was killed, we got into a fight. I met him in front of that new art gallery downtown. We argued about money—I told him I wasn't going to pay his extortion any longer. I kind of lost it and grabbed him through his window. He knocked me down with the door and then started kicking me. I was sure he was going to kill me. I grabbed his foot and he went down, hit his head on the hood of his car. But he was alive. I got out of there because I was sure he'd start shooting when he came to. I went home and didn't go out again that night. I didn't kill him."

"Was there anyone with you?"

"Yes, Isabella."

"Isabella?"

"My wife, Isabella Ortega Franklin."

"Anyone else?"

"No."

"As a rule, wives are not real good alibis."

"Well Isabella hates my guts so I don't think she'd lie for me. She left me after that night. She said I was a coward for not dealing with a little shit like Marino and she wanted to be married to a real man. I said some things to her I shouldn't have. She went to her room and locked the door, and left the next morning. I'm sure she's gone to her parents place in Tularosa. No doubt she'd be pleased to tell you that I'm too much of a coward to have shot Marino."

The obvious gaping hole in his alibi—the fact that his wife had been locked in her room until morning—was something to keep in mind. Ray wasn't sure about this guy, but didn't want to close the conversation yet by being too aggressive with him.

"It seems that besides running an extortion operation, Marino may have been involved in illegal drugs. Did you know that he was distributing drugs?"

"Sheriff, I've had a suspicion that there was drug smuggling going on through the racetrack for more than a year. I didn't know who was doing it, but Marino and the old sheriff were my best guesses. I noticed that there were a lot of times that trailers would arrive with only one horse, when the trailer could easily have transported two, or sometimes even four, horses. It was sometimes the same guys bringing in two horses, using two trailers, when all they needed was one. That piece of shit I was just talking to when you showed up is somehow connected. He used to be the stable manager, but I just fired him. I've been going over the books since we're in the off season, and what I found is a pattern that should have been obvious to anyone. Something was wrong. I just confronted him, and he basically told me to go to hell—it was just about then that I saw you guys."

"Tyee, maybe you should head over to the barn and see if you can find that guy—what's his name?"

"Lewis Esparza."

Tyee was headed in that direction when an old pickup came fishtailing out of the barn. Lewis Esparza was driving and he was headed right for Tyee. Ray pulled out his old service revolver and was ready to stop Esparza when a shot rang out. The truck carried on under its own momentum, but Ray could see that Esparza had been shot in the side of the head and was dead. The pick-up swerved towards the paddock area and slammed into a concrete barrier. Ray, Tyee, and Dick all headed over to the barrier and got down behind it for protection.

"That shot had to have come from the grandstands. Sounded like a high powered rifle. If someone was up there, how'd they get down?" Ray directed the question at Franklin.

"There are five exits that go out the back and three that come out the front. The exits have stairs, but you can get down them pretty damn quick."

They stayed behind the barrier and listened to the old pickup releasing steam from a broken radiator.

"Where's the closest phone?"

"Back in the barn. There's an office right inside the door and a phone on the wall."

Tyee said he was going to the barn to call the Sheriff's department. Ray wasn't real comfortable with it, but considering the time that had passed, it was likely that whoever had taken the shot was probably long gone. Ray pulled out his service revolver and told Tyee that if there was another shot to hit the ground and Ray would cover him. Tyee gave Ray a look that said *you've got to be kidding*. Then he headed out. There was no further shooting.

Ray and Sheriff James had a heated conversation about Ray and Tyee being in Ruidoso investigating without having let the Sheriff know. Ray apologized, but it was halfhearted. They filled the sheriff in on what they'd learned and then discussed the shooting. The deputies had searched the grandstand area and found a spent cartridge from a .30-30 rifle, but no other evidence.

Ray and Tyee were eventually able to leave and head toward T or C. They debated about stopping in Tularosa to see Isabella Franklin. On the one hand it felt like it might be pointless. If she was in her room and didn't come out until morning, she couldn't say where her husband had been that night. But, of course, they only knew that from her husband. It felt like something they should cover, just in case.

On the other hand, the murder of the stable manager had introduced a whole new level of confusion, taking them back to the idea of someone trying to tie up loose ends. If the stable manager was the main contact for the drugs, he must have known who was behind the operation. Obviously Dick Franklin didn't shoot him, so there had to be someone else.

Ray wasn't entirely comfortable not following up to verify Franklin's alibi, but he was also anxious to get home. He knew the investigation was a long way from being over and he was unsure what their role was going to be, if they had one at all. It was Ray's nature to take an investigation through to its completion, but running a PI business wasn't the same as being a sheriff. He had less authority, for one thing, and he had to keep an eye on the cash flow to make sure the bills were being paid.

"Tyee, my instincts are to push hard until something breaks, but in this case it might be best if we just headed home until we're sure what our position is going to be in this—any objections?"

"None from me, partner."

They headed for home without much conversation. It was going to be a long drive.

14

College Days

Albuquerque, New Mexico

Dick Franklin had lived a charmed life in many ways. His parents had money, and Dick more or less assumed that he'd have money, too—his parents' money. Then his parents went nuts and kicked him out with next to nothing. Well, "next to nothing" included tuition at the University of New Mexico in Albuquerque, plus room and board. Still it *felt* like nothing. They'd done it because he'd been caught selling drugs to some of his classmates in high school. Sure, it was a bad thing to have done, but it didn't justify him being disowned—it was only pot.

But Dick adjusted. From an early age he'd had a chameleon-like way of adapting to whatever circumstances he encountered. He would use his personality and his brains to make the best of his exile to New Mexico—in a second tier school, he should be a star. As it turned out, it took all of his attention during the first year just to meet the minimum grades required to remain in school. His parents threatened to stop paying if his grades didn't improve. He had no idea what he'd do if he couldn't go to school, so in his second year he actually learned to be a student.

As he began to study and attend classes more diligently, he discovered that he was actually pretty good at it. He was a born salesman, and he turned his substantial charms on the professors and administrators, sucking up to anyone who could help him succeed. And he did succeed.

Part of his commitment to success at school involved abandoning almost all his social activities. He studied and then he studied some more. He knew a few people, like Tyee Chino, but mostly he remained a private, somewhat isolated person. Even his connection to Tyee was academic—Tyee had helped him with a couple of classes they shared. He had thought the guy was intimidating because he was such a huge Apache Indian, but he'd turned out to be exceptionally smart, and he'd been a big help to Dick as he took on more challenging courses.

Everything changed when he walked into the student lounge one afternoon and took a seat in a community booth with his coffee and newspaper. As he sat down, he looked into the eyes of the most beautiful woman he had ever seen. She was like a picture, a glamorous portrait—something unreal. He'd never seen anyone who literally took his breath away until that moment. She looked up at him and smiled—he thought he might faint.

"Hello, sorry to bother you, my name is Dick Franklin." He was a little surprised that he could actually talk.

"Hello, I'm Isabella Ortega."

Her voice was wonderful. Dick realized he was staring, but he couldn't seem to stop. He took his seat, but forgot about his paper as he began talking to her. The conversation was mostly just meaningless chatter, giving Dick an excuse to keep his eye on the beautiful Isabella. She told him that her family was from Spain, but that they now lived in Tularosa in the central part of New Mexico. Dick gave a very brief synopsis of his background, hinting that his family consisted of rich Californians, which was true, but leaving out his current status as an exile. Dick asked Isabella on a date. She said no, she didn't date. Eventually Dick did find out where she was living on campus—one of the high dollar sororities. Beautiful and maybe with family money—Dick Franklin was very interested.

Over the next few months, Dick spent considerable energy trying to impress Isabella. While maybe the most beautiful woman Dick had ever seen, he discovered that she was also one of the most aloof. She seemed most comfortable when people kept a distance. At first Dick had tried some very direct tactics, but that seemed to be the wrong approach. He'd sent her cards, and once even mounted a sign outside her sorority house asking for a date. She sent him a note saying that he should stop or she'd notify campus security.

Dick didn't give up, but he made his approach more subtle. He had discovered that she was a philosophy major. Dick had taken a lot of philosophy courses, and he began sending Isabella letters discussing his thoughts on various philosophers. Eventually she began to write back. While they lived on the same small campus, they established their relationship entirely through these letters, never meeting face to face during this stage.

Not only was Isabella drop dead gorgeous, and her family had money, but she was smart. Their letters became the focal point of Dick's life. He'd been attracted to her because of her beauty, but now he fell in love with her mind. Her words were very formal, but revealed great insight.

Isabella was a much stronger person than she appeared. Her manner was subdued, but she was courageous and outspoken in her beliefs. She was totally committed to her family and their welfare. Her parents were central to her life, and her devotion to them was awe-inspiring, especially for someone like Dick, with his troubled family background.

They exchanged letters, often four or five times a week, for months before they met again. Dick had trouble concentrating on his school work as a result of his preoccupation with Isabella. He asked her to have coffee with him at the student union and set a time in the late afternoon. He wasn't sure if it would be considered a date or not, but he'd framed his request in such a way that she could at least rationalize that it was only a casual meeting at school—in case she still didn't date.

Dick was in the student union almost an hour before the time for their meeting, still unsure as to whether or not she'd show. They'd gotten to know one another over the months of letter-writing, but he was still unsure who she really was. Intellectually he understood her beliefs and ideas, but emotionally she was still a mystery.

He spotted her as soon as she entered the student union. He'd forgotten how striking she was—many eyes turned her way as she walked toward his booth.

"Isabella, I'm so glad you could make it."

"Is Dick short for Richard?"

"Well, yes it is, although I have always gone by Dick." He wasn't real sure he understood the point of the oddball question.

"May I call you Richard?"

"Sure."

"Richard, I have fallen in love with your letters. I still don't know if they really represent you or not. I'd like for you to visit me in Tularosa this weekend if you can."

This was said with no visible emotion at all—it sounded more like he was being asked to a job interview. Dick was uncertain whether things were going the way he wanted or not. Jeez, he was only looking to date this woman—but as a result he'd spent months pining over her and now she wanted him to meet her parents. And they had yet to have a single date! Was this some kind of seventeenth century courting?

"Sure, I can be there."

"Good. I have written out the directions and the best time to arrive. I'll see you then." She turned and left.

What the hell? This whole experience was strange, as if they might be married within a few days but had yet to hold hands. Dick—or Richard—was going to have to give this some serious thought. Beautiful or not, weird was still weird.

Throughout time, beauty's allure has conquered the warning flag of weird, and this time would be no exception. Dick pulled into the long drive of the Ortega's house. As he followed it, a magnificent hacienda came into view. He'd seen houses like this in southern California, but none larger or more magnificent. Even without the many acres of land that made up the estate, the house alone must have been worth millions—even in Tularosa, New Mexico.

When he pulled up in front of the house, a man came out and opened his car door. He told Dick, in broken English, that he could leave the car there with the keys in—Dick was to go inside.

The entrance to the house took him through a large, walled courtyard. There was a fountain, and there were all kinds of exotic plants. At the end of the courtyard was a massive wooden door—obviously the main entrance. As he approached, the large door opened and there was Isabella. She looked like a character in a film.

"I'm glad you could make it Richard, please come in."

He was still uncomfortable being called Richard, but it appeared that he'd endure almost anything to be near this woman.

"This is the most beautiful house I've ever seen. How long have your parents lived here?"

"A long time. My father's family owned a great deal of the land that now makes up southern New Mexico for hundreds of years. Most of the land was unsettled, but the ownership was clear according to Spanish law. But the Mexican government wanted to sell the land to the United States. A dispute over what land belonged to our family and what they'd be paid in the deal with the US resulted in the Mexican government illegally confiscating the land."

"Wow, international intrigue. When did this happen?"

"That was in the 1850s. Eventually my family received ownership rights for a substantial amount of land outside of the Mesilla Valley, where most of the original disputed land had been, and also received a substantial sum as consideration for all of the other land. As of today, the land this house is located on is all that remains."

"It feels like I'm in another country. Have you always lived here?"

"Yes, I was born here. My parents didn't have children until late in life and the birth was very difficult for my mother. I was born in, and have always lived in, this house. The only exception has been my time at the university. My parents will join us a little later—as I said, they are older than normal parents would be for someone my age, more like my grandparents, and they enjoy their afternoon siesta. We will see them later for dinner. Let me show you the hacienda."

As they made their way into the interior of the house, it became much cooler. The walls were adobe and stucco, with a variety of tile floors. All of the ceilings were exquisitely detailed, with many features that were new to Dick. The overall effect was inviting and sophisticated. Most rooms contained what he guessed was very valuable original artwork—all of it seemed to be museum quality. Dick wasn't very knowledgeable, but he could tell this had to be some very expensive stuff.

"The artwork is very impressive. Who's the art collector in your family?"

"That would definitely be my mother. She was a world-famous artist before she married my father. Much of the artwork is hers, and she has very carefully selected the other art. It's her great passion."

Isabella showed him into an enclosed garden room full of bright red bougainvillea. The colors were almost overwhelming. Dick found himself smiling—the room seemed to radiate joy.

"I just can't tell you how lovely your house is—it just seems full of happiness."

"Thank you Richard. It has always been a special place for me—and this room was where I'd go anytime I was a little down. Just being in the room with the flowers would always cheer me up."

She directed Dick toward a bench positioned at the side of the room. He was seeing her in a different way—she seemed more settled and mature here than she did at school.

"Richard, I'm twenty-one years old and according to my family traditions I should marry soon. My mother concentrated on her career as an artist and didn't marry until she was much older and she feels it was the biggest mistake she made in life. She has told me I must return to our heritage and I should be married."

Dick had nothing to say. He hoped his mouth wasn't hanging open. Was she proposing to him?

"My mother wants me to return to Spain to find a husband—I have told her that I'm in love with you. She's not overly happy about that, but will let me decide who I marry. Richard, would you like to marry me?"

Now his mouth *was* open. Jeez, what does he say? *What I'd like to do is sleep with you—not real sure about marriage.* His mind was racing—beautiful woman, very wealthy family—he could sure do a lot worse. He was in the process of a cost-benefit analysis when he realized she was waiting for an answer. He looked into those beautiful eyes.

"Of course I'll marry you."

That evening Richard met her parents. They were friendly, but somewhat distant. He had the feeling that he should never cross Isabella's father. While he was every bit a gentleman, there was something very hard about the man that gave Dick the shudders.

Within days, wedding plans were being developed for a very large ceremony to be held at the family hacienda in two months' time. Dick talked to his parents, who were overjoyed and made plans to be there for the ceremony. He hadn't seen Isabella since he returned to Albuquerque. He'd continued to write her letters, but she didn't write to him, and he began to suspect that she hadn't returned to school after they'd gotten engaged. He called her several times. Isabella's mother had returned one call to Richard, saying that Isabella was out of town shopping for the wedding and honeymoon. She'd call him soon.

The whole effect was to make everything seem mysterious. Why had she not called him? Why did she ask him to marry her? Couldn't she marry just about anybody? Why are her parents so weird? Why is she so weird? Dick was growing less sure about his decision each day. It was just not right—and he needed to find out why.

He headed out to Tularosa. Right or wrong he was going to confront Isabella, maybe even tell her that he'd changed his mind, that he couldn't be treated like he had no say in the matter. He didn't even know if she was there. When he pulled into the long driveway, he started having second thoughts about being there. What exactly was he being forced to do? If he didn't want to marry Isabella, he could say no. It suddenly felt like he was whining about being ignored. Was he really that weak?

He parked the car, and immediately someone came out to meet him. While he was getting out of the car, he saw Isabella standing at the door. She was so incredibly beautiful. He felt foolish.

Without saying a word, Isabella came down and took his hand and guided him through the house toward a casita beside a beautiful pool. He started to ask her a question, but she placed her fingertip on his mouth and guided him into the luxurious casita. They made love. It was a passion Dick had never experienced.

Hours later, he realized that he'd do whatever Isabella asked him to do.

15

Back Home

Truth or Consequences, New Mexico

Ray and Tyee made it to T or C just before sunset. While Ray loved his old beat-up Jeep, it wasn't the most comfortable ride for long trips, and they both stretched and moaned a little as they climbed out of the vehicle. Happy came running, jumping around and madly wagging his tail as if he hadn't seen them in years—dogs really know how to greet people. Ray gave Happy a good rub—he was glad to see the dog and glad to be home.

As Ray entered the cabin, he was greeted by Sue with a very aggressive kiss and hug. Not exactly on the dog level of jumping and tail wagging, but for a human it was a great start. Ray began to respond, when out of the corner of his eye he noticed a rather large woman staring at him. He pulled away.

"Hello, I don't believe we've met." Ray extended his hand toward Beverly.

"Oh, Ray. It's so great to meet you. Sue has told me all about you—you being Sheriff, and your new business, and the fishing—just everything, and it's so exciting. I just couldn't wait to meet you. Your cabin is so wonderful and the business buildings—what a clever idea to have the business offices and computer centers right here by your cabin. It's just so amazing."

"Thanks."

"Beverly, Ray's just had a very long drive, so why don't we give him a little time to unwind. Ray maybe you'd like to lie down for a little while. Beverly and I'll get dinner started."

Ray could tell Sue wanted him to leave so she could kill Beverly for being such a motor mouth. Ray said thank you and headed to his room. Sue came into the bedroom and shut the door.

"I'm so sorry about Beverly. She's just so hyper all the time and will not shut up. I gave her a beer—that usually calms her down for a while. Her kids are the exact opposite. They're so calm and polite and they help with fixing meals and cleaning up. Beverly doesn't do jack shit. I've got to get her out of here before I go nuts. I'm starting to sound like her aren't I?" Ray gave Sue a hug.

"Don't worry about her. If she's going to stay around for some time, just put her in that rental in town or put her in the extra bedrooms in the outbuildings. Don't worry about disruption to the business—we'll adapt. Just don't let her upset you."

Sue held on to Ray for some time. She knew everything would be better now that he and Tyee were home.

"Where are Beverly's kids?"

"If you can believe this, they're with Big Jack. It's just amazing. Big Jack and Beverly seem to have a developing thing, and her kids just love him. I'm not sure if he's given them beer and cigars, but I can't imagine he's the best influence on children. For reasons that probably defy logic, the kids like him and he likes the kids."

Ray had a genuine laugh at that. Big Jack and Beverley would be a sight to behold—throw in some kids and it started to sound like entertainment.

"Can I help with dinner?"

"No, it's stew and it's almost ready. I'm going to warm some bread and we can eat. I'm going to see if Tyee wants to join us and of course, Big Jack and the kids. Definitely going to need plenty of beer."

Ray chuckled at Sue and told her to call him when it was ready. Sue smiled and went back to the kitchen.

Dinner was actually very comfortable. Sue noticed that Big Jack seemed to have a calming influence on Beverly—or maybe it was the five beers. Everyone was on their best behavior and the food was delicious. Beverly's children impressed Ray with their manners and willingness to jump in and help with any chore that needed to be done—plus they were very quiet. A good time was had by all.

The next morning Ray gathered Sue, Tyee, and Big Jack in the conference area in one of the outbuildings for an update on where they stood regarding the Ruidoso matter.

"First, we still don't know who shot Marino. The possibilities are extensive, including people we don't even know about. That's something I'm becoming more and more concerned about. This could have been someone from Marino's past that we're completely unaware of, who shot him for reasons that have nothing to do with Ruidoso."

"How would we investigate that?"

"Tyee, I think that's the point—we couldn't. It might be a crime that we can't solve."

"Well shit, that's not very satisfying."

"No it's not. But it may be the reality. He obviously had a criminal past and had accumulated a lot of enemies. Based on what we've learned, this guy deserved to be shot, and we have lots of candidates who might have done it. While I think we have to consider that it wasn't someone local, I'm still inclined to believe that's the most likely possibility."

"Sheriff Rodriquez's killing seems like a professional hit. It could be what it looks like, or it could be someone trying to make it look that way. He was shot with a .22 as well, but that's the only similarity to Marino. Now we have the shooting of the stable manager, Lewis Esparza. He was shot long distance with a .30-30 rifle, with no known motive. And there's no question in my mind that all of these killings are connected."

"No doubt the connection is the drug trafficking." Tyee had said this from the beginning.

"Yes, it's the only thing that might bring these killings together. We know that the Sheriff and Marino were doing something more than Marino's strong-arm protection racket. There was some reason that the sheriff hired Marino, and the protection demands didn't start until the Sheriff was hospitalized. So the sheriff hired Marino for some other reason. Best guess would be that he was somehow connected to the drug trafficking."

"Someone we need to talk to is Tito. We had a little scene in his bar and his bartender was accidentally hurt by Tyee, so he may not be open to talking to us."

Big Jack jumped in. "Accidently hurt by Tyee—what the hell does that mean."

"He said very prejudicial things about Indians and I decided to correct his misunderstanding of Indian ways. In the process his shoulder became accidently dislocated."

"Ray, what is this—you and Tyee fighting? My goodness, tell me you don't do that sort of thing."

"Sue, it was Tyee not me."

"Tyee, what the hell? My husband is too old to be getting into brawls."

No one was happy with the way that came out, including Sue once she realized how it sounded.

"Sorry, you know what I mean."

"Well, yeah, unfortunately I do know what you mean." Ray smiled as he said this which made it okay.

"So here we are, we have three killings and no idea who might have done them. We have a list of prospects but no real evidence. Plus—and this is a big thing—we don't have a client. Our first involvement, through the AG's office, has been terminated. We have no one covering our fees or our costs. While I don't like it, I think we should drop the matter. We can't go off spending time and money just to uncover who shot this creep Marino. What do you all think?"

"Ray, the biggest issue I have with that, is that if we don't keep looking into this nobody else will. It'll be dropped. Three murders, and no one will be held responsible."

"Yeah, you're right Tyee. I don't like it either—that's why we went to Ruidoso. But from a practical point of view, I don't see how we justify any more time on this without a client."

"Well I agree," Big Jack said. "We're running a business. I think it's for shit that people have been killed and we don't have the authority to go at this full-bore and find out who did it, but keep in mind who was killed. I'm not saying anybody should get away with murder, but really, Marino—the list of people who wanted him dead looks like a phone book. The second victim is the probably crooked Sheriff, who it would appear was killed by his drug running business partners—how the stable manager fits in I don't know. I'm just saying that these are more than likely not innocent people who need justice. It's probable that all of this happened because of their criminal activities and selling illegal drugs, so there may not be too many people in Ruidoso who give a shit if we find the killer or killers. I vote we drop this and find some paying clients." Everyone nodded in agreement—Tyee a little less than the others, but he still agreed.

"I think we should spend more time on getting Big Jack elected mayor and then contact the FBI and push them to give us some work."

"Okay, we all agree that we'll drop the Ruidoso matter."

Everyone stood and headed for coffee or out the door. While they didn't have an active case at the moment there were other things that needed tending.

The day after their meeting, though, Ray got a call from the governor's chief of staff. Once off the phone, he called everyone and requested that they meet again in the conference room that afternoon

"Looks like maybe we are not done with Ruidoso after all. The governor's chief of staff called this morning and said that the governor would like to meet tomorrow in Santa Fe to discuss how to proceed on the matter. He said the governor wants our firm to continue to investigate the murders—we're rehired."

"I guess that changes everything."

They made plans for Ray and Tyee to go to Santa Fe the next afternoon so they could meet with the Governor. There was a discussion about whether Ray should contact Tony, but the decision was made to leave that until after meeting with the governor. It might turn out to be that Tony was the reason the governor had contacted them directly.

Sue and Ray attended a rally that evening for Big Jack. The turnout was very impressive, probably because of free beer, and the crowd was enthusiastic. Big Jack gave a spirited speech, promising to be an honest mayor and to represent all of the people, not just his cronies, the way the current mayor did. Ray thought Big Jack had real promise as a politician—all those years as a lawyer had been great training.

Beverly attended, along with her children. She was very attentive to Big Jack. She was smiling more, these days, and even seemed to be walking in a different manner. There was something developing—but Sue and Ray silently agreed that they didn't want to talk about it. As the evening progressed and more beer was served, Sue and Ray decided it was time to leave and offered to take the children home with them.

The next morning the kids were up fixing themselves breakfast, but Beverly had apparently not made it back to the cabin. Sue said she thought she must have stayed at Big Jack's to help clean up, prompting skeptical looks from both kids that seemed to say that she must really be pretty dim if she really believed what she was saying. Sue let it go.

Ray and Tyee were ready to head out about noon. Ray could see that Sue wasn't pleased with the way things were happening with Beverly and the kids. Otherwise she probably would have gone to Santa Fe. Happy, on the other hand, was pleased to be staying at home with his new best friends—the kids. Both children had adopted him as the one sure thing that existed in their lives. You could always depend on dogs. Ray took Sue aside.

"Look Sue, you've got to fix this Beverly thing. She's somebody you haven't seen in over twenty years, and she isn't your responsibility. I know you want to help, but you can't let her mess with our lives this way. Her kids seem great—I'd think that has something to do with their dad. You're allowing her to hide from their father, and maybe that's wrong. Look, I don't know exactly what's right, but what's happening right now doesn't seem like it. If you want, I could get involved and help."

"No Ray, I don't need you to get involved. It's my problem." Sue wasn't pleased.

"Sue, I'm sorry. I don't want you mad at me. I told you I'd support you in whatever you decide, and I will. I'm just not sure that she can be a mother to these kids if she ignores them. Maybe your cousin is a part of the problem in her marriage. You can't fix this problem—only she can. Help her but don't let her become dependent on you. If she's going to stay here she has to get a job and pay her own way—and someone needs to tell the father where his children are and that they're safe."

"You're right. I'm not mad at you as much as I'm mad at myself. She's manipulated me from the beginning and I need it to stop. I'll do something today. Thanks Ray. I guess I needed a nudge to get me doing what's right."

16

Governor Johnson

Santa Fe, New Mexico

Ray and Tyee were in the colorful central eating area of La Fonda after spending the night at the hotel. Since the investigation was now being funded by the governor, having breakfast in an extravagant environment before their appointment with him seemed appropriate. The La Fonda Hotel was located on the famous Santa Fe Plaza, and had been serving some of the best Mexican breakfasts—without customers having to wait for a table—for many years. They enjoyed their breakfasts and both agreed that they might have to settle for salads for lunch.

"I've never met a governor. Should I bow?"

"Well I guess that'd be up to you, Tyee. Keep in mind Governor Johnson is an old fart whose family probably were Indian fighters back in the day. So I don't think you want to piss him off with your wiseass antics."

"Wiseass antics?"

"Oh, I'm sorry. I meant to say your college-educated wiseass antics."

"Much better."

"The Governor can be a little difficult at times. There's no question that he'd prefer to be living in the nineteenth century verses the twentieth. But he has a keen sense for what's right and wrong—and it doesn't matter who you are. If you've been wronged, the governor is on your side. He and I butted heads a couple of times when I was sheriff—he wanted me to do what he said and didn't want to discuss my point of view. Anyway we learned to work together and I think we might actually have become friends. But if you cross this governor, you better be ready for a fight."

"Sue has given me specific instructions not to fight with anyone without her permission, so I guess I'll be on my best behavior."

"Excellent choice."

Several blocks south of the Plaza on Old Santa Fe Trail was the state capitol. The governor's office was located on the fourth floor. While the distance was probably walkable, they drove to be sure that they were on time for their appointment.

The capitol building, known as the Roundhouse, was surrounded by acres of gardens. The effect was to place the building away from the active community, in a more serene environment. Ray always liked coming to visit the building, mostly due to the peaceful nature of the surrounding gardens.

They entered and went to the fourth floor, which was only two flights up since they'd come in on the second level. They located the governor's office.

"Mr. Pacheco and Mr. Chino, the governor will see you now."

"Well son of a bitch. Sheriff Pacheco, how the hell are you? Hey, this must be your Indian sidekick. Oops, hope I didn't offend anyone. Every fuckin' thing I say seems to offend someone."

The governor was known for his bombastic manner. Some people found it endearing, some found him to be a loudmouth fool. He was term-limited and had two years left in office and had said, on more than one occasion, that he didn't give a big fuck what anyone thought.

"Good to see you, Governor. This is my partner and friend, Tyee Chino."

"Tyee Chino, it's great to meet you. I heard about you pounding on that bastard bartender in Ruidoso. Maybe I should give you some kind of damn award. My god, you really are a big fuckin' Indian."

Everyone shook hands. Tyee seemed stunned by the governor's manner—the governor had that effect on a lot of people.

"Well come over here and sit down and I'll tell you why I asked you to come see me."

They took seats around a conference table in the corner of the large office. The governor seemed thoughtful before he spoke.

"Tony Garcia handed in his resignation a couple of days ago. I think he's been one of the best attorneys general this state has ever had—he's also become my friend. I'm greatly saddened by his decision to quit. Ray, I know that you and Tony have been close over the years—do you have any idea why he'd be quitting?"

"Governor, he's been troubled by something ever since we started discussing the events in Ruidoso. I've sensed that he was holding information back from me since the beginning. He told me that he hadn't reacted as quickly as he should have and that he blamed himself for the mess down there. I don't know what it's about, but something or somebody is causing Tony real anguish."

"Yes, I know what you mean. He hasn't been candid with me either—it's like he's become someone else. Even though I didn't want to, I've accepted his resignation. He made it effective immediately. I asked him not to do that, but he said no. Now I'm worried that there's something criminal involved. I don't know what's going on, but his behavior the last few days screams to me that he's running away from something pretty bad. I want to know immediately what this is about. I don't want Tony to leave the state and then find out he was involved in something illegal while he was the fucking AG in my administration."

"I'll need to meet with him at once. Governor, this is only a guess but I think it has to do with his wife or her sister."

"Well yes, meet with him. You've my full authority behind you to do whatever's necessary, including arresting him if he won't cooperate. I have to know what the hell this is about."

Ray and Tyee shook the governor's hand and said they'd let him know as soon as they knew something.

Once outside, Ray steered Tyee over to a bench in the gardens.

"Tyee, I was wondering if you could contact your guy at the FBI and see if they'd run a background check on Tony, his wife, and her sister."

"I can ask. If we're working on something for them they're always cooperative, but this may be different."

"Yeah. I know. If they say no, so be it. But ask. I'm just having a hard time finding the connection to Tony in all of this."

"I can go back to the hotel and make calls. Do you want me to walk and leave the Jeep for you?"

"No. You take the Jeep. I'm going back to Tony's office. If he's there, I'll try and see him. No matter what, I'll leave him messages that will make it clear he better contact me or I'll have the state patrol pick him up. Whatever happens, I'll walk back to the hotel. I need some time to think about what's happened."

Tyee headed out, while Ray went back inside the capitol building and directly to the AG's office. He wasn't surprised that Tony wasn't there, and asked his secretary to locate him.

"Sorry, Mr. Pacheco. I don't know where Mr. Garcia is at the moment. I've placed calls to his house and to other places I thought he might be this morning, but I haven't been able to locate him."

"Could I use Tony's office to place a call to his house?"

The secretary said that was fine and gave him Tony's home number.

"Tony, this is Ray. Not sure why you're not answering your phone, but we need to talk. The governor is very concerned about what's going on and has asked me to get involved. You need to call me at La Fonda by two this afternoon—if I haven't heard from you by then, I'll involve the state police and have you arrested. In the meantime, I'll notify the state police to alert all airlines that you should not be allowed to leave the state, and tell them to take any other appropriate action to prevent you from leaving. You know better than anyone that this may not be completely legal, but the Governor is getting pissed at the fact you're not telling him what's going on—and when the Governor gets pissed he doesn't care about legal niceties. Give me a call at La Fonda and let's prevent this from becoming even worse."

Ray left, thanking the secretary, and began walking back to the hotel. The weather was pleasant and there were interesting shops and restaurants along his path. Ray made a mental note that he and Sue should come back real soon and spend some time in Santa Fe, enjoying the ambiance and the great restaurants.

The walk back took about thirty minutes, and Ray felt refreshed when he arrived. He was going to his room when he saw Tyee in the dining room.

"It is lunch time isn't it? How did your phone call go?"

"They seem responsive. I gave the FBI the names and some location information as best I knew it. He said that he'd get back to me ASAP. Of course ASAP could mean a week from now."

"Tony wasn't in his office. I called his house and left a somewhat threatening message—gave him until two this afternoon before I bring in the state police and have him arrested. I'd think that would prompt either a mad dash to the border or a call."

They both studied their menus. Santa Fe is the highest US state capital, at 7,000 feet. That's forty percent higher than the mile-high city of Denver. The height can create problems for people who haven't adjusted, causing altitude sickness among other things. One side effect—a drawback or maybe a benefit, depending on your point of view—is that it seems to contribute to an enhanced appetite. Of course this doesn't make the hundreds of restaurants in Santa Fe unhappy.

Both Ray and Tyee settled on Mexican food, Ray going with a burrito and Tyee selecting enchiladas. They both ordered beer and settled back to relax while waiting. To hell with the salads. A few moments later a man approached them.

"Mr. Pacheco, I have the Attorney General holding on the phone for you. If you like, you can take the call in my office." Ray guessed that the man was the manager of the hotel, although he hadn't introduced himself. Ray got up and followed him to a small office down a hall.

"Well Ray, now you're threatening to arrest me. And by the way, you're right, that's completely illegal unless you've got a charge to bring against me. I expected this of Governor Blowhard, but from you I expected better."

"Tony, you left me and the governor no choice. All I want to do is talk to you. When can we meet?"

There was a pause and Ray could feel the tension through the phone. Tony was about ready to explode.

"Okay. I'll meet you in La Cantina at Coyote Café. That's the rooftop bar above the Coyote restaurant. It's just a couple of blocks from the La Fonda."

"When?"

"At two this afternoon." He hung up.

Ray went back and finished his lunch, filling Tyee in on what had happened.

The Coyote Café on Water Street had just recently been opened by Mark Miller. An instant hit, it was almost impossible to get a reservation. Not a big concern to Ray, since he understood that it was a little pricey and probably didn't serve his favorite green chili cheeseburger. He climbed the stairs to the rooftop bar and looked around for Tony—who wasn't there. It was a couple of minutes before two, so Ray asked to be seated and hoped like hell Tony would show up. If not, bad shit was going to happen.

Ray became increasingly nervous as time passed. Somewhere around two thirty Ray was about ready to leave and contact the state police when he saw Tony come in. He looked like he'd aged years just in the few months since Ray had last seen him.

Tony came over, but said nothing to Ray. He took a seat and ordered a beer. Ray joined him.

"Tony, I'm sorry you're having problems. Whatever it is, I'm sure we can find some kind of solution."

"Ray, I know you mean well, but there is no solution other than to resign and leave. I know the governor's worried that I've committed some major crime that will bite him in the ass after I've gone, and I guess I can't blame him for being concerned. I think I've been negligent in my job, but there has been no crime committed by me or my wife that will embarrass the governor."

"Why don't you tell me what this is about?"

"Ray, I told you before that Marino was my wife's half-sister's ex-husband. When I found out who was causing the problem, I delayed acting because of that connection. As a result, people got hurt. That's it. I didn't do my job because of my wife. As a result I've decided to resign—end of story."

"Bullshit. Tony, that doesn't make any sense. You didn't act as quickly as you should—so fuckin' what? That's not even a firing offense, that's a get-your-ass-chewed-out-by-the-governor offense, and you know it. Tell me what's going on."

Ray's voice had gone up a little, causing a few people to turn their way.

"Ray, if you're going to yell at me, I'm leaving."

"Sorry."

For a while they sat and drank their beers. Ray wasn't sure how to proceed, so he just waited.

"What's the Governor going to do?"

"If you don't give me a believable story, he's going to arrest you. Until he can find the truth—legal complications be damned. And you know he'll do it."

"Yes, he would. Ray, this is difficult but I'm going to tell you what I know. You need to convince the governor not to pursue this with me or it'll blow up in his face."

"Tony, tell me the truth and the governor will stop. Threatening him will only make him dig in, not let go."

"Yeah. You've been a good friend Ray. I'm sorry I got you involved in this."

"I still don't know what *this* is."

"Right. As you know, I met my wife in Houston. I was a prosecutor there and we met when she was arrested. It started because her fiancé had overdosed and she found the body. She panicked and ran. There are lots of details here that I'll tell you if you want, but for now I'll give you the short version. She was arrested mostly for being overdressed in a shitty neighborhood—that was when I met her. The desk sergeant called and said they had a high-class woman in custody and he thought someone from the district attorney's office should come down and talk to her. That was me. Eventually she told me about her fiancé and we sent someone to his apartment—but there was no body. In fact, a body was never found. I helped her, and I fell in love. I probably cut some corners to protect her. While there wasn't a body, her fiancé was a major player in politics and very wealthy. He was also gay—their engagement was just a facade to appease their families. His disappearance became a big deal—lots of pressure from a lot of politicians, including the mayor, to find him or recover his body. Nothing happened. Without a body or other evidence of foul play, no charges were ever brought. She was the prime suspect, but never charged. Because of my less than professional way of handling the matter, I was fired. We married and ended up in Las Cruces."

"Love makes us do strange things."

"It does. Well, that was in our past until a few months ago. When things started happening in Ruidoso, I made a call to talk to Rodriguez, but I was told Marino was in charge so I talked to him. Once I introduced myself, he started laughing. Turns out Marino had a connection with Houston. He was a thug there, just like he'd been his entire life. He claimed that he was the one who disposed of the body of Kate's—my wife's—fiancé's body. Said he was his drug supplier and that he'd been directed by his bosses to get rid of the body so that it wouldn't point back to their drug operation. While he's cleaning up the mess, according to him, he finds Kate's bags. Coming from the airport directly to her fiancé's apartment, she had her carry-on with her. When she panicked and ran, she left the bag. Marino claims he had the bag and evidence that she was at the apartment when the fiancé died. Of course I got angry and told the bastard that I'd have him arrested that day for all of the shit he was doing in Ruidoso and also for trying to blackmail me and my wife. Once again, he just laughed. That's when he told me that Desk Sergeant Nelson would be more than willing to testify that I'd covered up my wife's involvement in her fiancé's murder."

"My god, are you talking about the Police Chief?"

"Afraid so. And Nelson was there, and would definitely be able to make quite a case against me and my wife. It'd all be lies, but it'd destroy my career and hurt my wife more than you can imagine."

"So what happened then?"

"Nothing. He said I'd be hearing from him, but in the meantime I should do nothing about Ruidoso. So that's what I did—nothing. I waited to hear what he and Nelson wanted. Somewhere in there I called you and asked you to look into Ruidoso. I thought that might be a way to stop him without him knowing that I was the one who did it. And then, of course, he was killed. I never heard from Nelson, so I don't know if Marino just made that part up or not. But there's no question it's the same Nelson as the Houston sergeant, and without question he and Marino knew one another in Houston."

"Is that it?"

"Yes."

"Don't see why you're quitting."

"I may not have broken the law, but there's no question I violated my ethics. I let that hood blackmail me into keeping quiet while he strong-armed a bunch of people. Even if I could rationalize what I did in some way, it doesn't change the fact that I've lied about a lot regarding my wife and what had happened in Houston. I've lied to the people, I've lied to the governor. The only way out of the problem is to resign. I haven't committed a crime, but I've violated my oath of office and I have to leave. Nothing will come along later to embarrass the governor."

"What happens now for you?"

"I've made a few calls and it looks like we're headed to Boston. That's where my wife is from and she has lots of connections there. I've even had a call from a Boston law firm about an interview once we get there and get settled in. I'm sorry this has been such a mess—I'm sure I could have handled it better."

"I just hope it all works out for you, Tony. I'll talk to the governor and encourage him to let it go. It can't be in his interest to start something with you when he's not sure what actually happened. I'm sure I can get him to calm down for now. Let me know if I can help in some other way. It's been a pleasure knowing you."

"Thanks, Ray. You're a good man."

They shook hands and left the bar. Tony waved as he headed down the street. Ray wanted to believe him, but something still smelled wrong.

Ray contacted the governor and went over what Tony had told him. The governor said he'd accept what Tony had said for now, but wanted Ray to continue to investigate what had gone on in Ruidoso and find out who killed "that asshole Marino and the dumb fuck sheriff." Ray knew the governor wasn't considered politically correct by anyone's standards, but he liked the way the old fart talked.

17

Chief Nelson

Ray and Tyee got an early start out of Santa Fe and expected to be in T or C around noon. They had gone over most everything the day before, so the drive so far had been quiet and thoughtful.

"Guess the next move might be to talk to the Police Chief."

"Yeah. Kind of hard to believe all of the connections back to Houston. I've known Nelson for some time, but he never mentioned his background. Kind of figured he was from some place around here—never would have guessed he was part of the Houston police department."

"Starting to sound like he was the connection to Marino that maybe got Marino a job in the sheriff's department in the first place."

"Well, if they were both in Houston at the same time— which is what we're hearing—a policeman knowing a crook isn't that strange. Cops hang out with crooks, in a way. It just seems so different from what I was imagining. Now we need to rethink everything. Did Nelson help Marino get his job? Was Nelson involved in the drug trafficking? When we first went to Ruidoso and I went to see Nelson, he said Marino was evil and should be dead. So I guess the biggest question is--did Nelson kill Marino? Or—if Nelson was involved in the drug trade—did he just say that to throw us off his trail, so he would sound like everyone else who hated Marino?"

"And the other part is whether Nelson knew Marino was threatening Tony and implicating Nelson in some kind of blackmail scheme." Tyee made a good point.

"Tyee, if we're going to spend this much time on the road, I may have to upgrade our vehicle. I love my old Jeep, but it may be time for something a little bit more comfortable."

"Amen!"

They discussed logistics and decided that it'd be foolish to delay seeing Nelson. So they'd stop in T or C for the night and head out first thing in the morning for Ruidoso. Ray knew Sue would be pissed, but it couldn't be helped. He just hoped things were calmer at home.

"Ray, are you deliberately staying away because of this crap with Beverly?"

"Sue, of course not. Look, I don't want to drive to Ruidoso to avoid Beverly or anyone else—matter of fact I'm sick and tired of driving to Ruidoso. What I'd like to do is stay home and be with you."

Sometimes Ray was just lucky and he'd say the right thing—this was one of those times. He and Sue held each other for a long time, realizing how much they'd missed their time together—alone.

The next day was gloomy. It was cloudy, with a fine drizzle falling. Not your typical New Mexico desert weather. Ray had been outside playing with Happy and was a little damp. Happy liked the cool weather and was the only member of the household who seemed to be in a good mood.

Ray sat at the kitchen table and had another cup of coffee. He wasn't eager to get back in the Jeep. Kay and Tom were preoccupied with some sort of board game and had given Ray wide berth—probably based on instructions from Sue. Ray thought the kids were okay, but he didn't appreciate them being left there while their mother was off doing who knew what. He hadn't seen Beverly since he'd got home the previous evening. He and Sue had avoided the subject of Beverly, both sensing it wasn't a good subject—due mostly to the fact that neither one had any idea of what was going to happen. Sue came into the kitchen and poured herself a cup of coffee.

"Guess we're headed out. Take care, and if you need anything give me a call. We'll be staying at the same place downtown."

"Be careful Ray." Sue seemed weepy and Ray felt bad. He wasn't looking forward to the work ahead of him in Ruidoso, but he'd take that over Sue's problems with Beverly any day. He gave her a hug and left.

"Don't say giddyup."

"I wasn't going to say giddyup."

"Sure you were, until I told you not to."

"Nope. I never say giddyup this early in the morning."

"What does the morning have to do with giddyup?"

"Ray, you'd make one piss poor Apache scout."

Ray was pretty sure that was a meaningless response, using the Indian angle to deflect him, and decided it was time to ignore Tyee Chino for at least fifty road miles.

By midmorning the clouds had broken up and it turned into a sunny day. The drive to Ruidoso was becoming very familiar—and not very interesting. As they entered town, they both felt a sense of dread—as if things were going to happen and they'd need to be alert.

"I think we should go see Sheriff James before we check in to the hotel. We need to make sure he's up to speed on what's going on and what we're planning on doing."

"Yeah, we may need some back-up on this trip."

The Sheriff was in his office and seemed genuinely pleased to see Ray and Tyee.

"The police chief?" Ray had just told Sheriff James about what they'd learned from Tony.

"I know. It's not what I was expecting either. And of course at this point we still don't know what's true."

"What's your plan, Ray?"

"Well we sure don't have any evidence that the police chief was involved in anything, so there are no grounds to arrest him. The statement by Marino involving Nelson could have been complete bullshit—again, there's no actual evidence that what Marino said was true. So I think the best approach is a low-key, non-confrontational interview to see how Nelson reacts. My plan is to go to his office after we leave here. Tyee will stay outside while I go in and talk to the chief. Not sure how I'll start that conversation, but I'll have to let him know that he's now a suspect in the murder of Marino—then see what happens."

"What do you want me to do?"

"I guess just be available if this blows up in my face."

Ray and Tyee headed back towards the center of town, parking in front of the police station. Ray gave Tyee a glance and a nod of the head and went into the office. The Chief was definitely in, all three-hundred-plus pounds of him, asleep in his chair.

"Chief. Chief. It's Ray Pacheco." The chief stirred.

"Oh, fuck. Guess I fell asleep Ray. Come on in. What are you doing back in my town?"

"Just trying to close some things out Chief. The Governor wants to make sure we do all we can to find out who killed Marino and the sheriff. He's asked me to continue the investigation. Something kind of strange came up in a conversation I had with Tony Garcia—he said he knew you when you worked at the police department in Houston."

"Really. Well yeah, I worked in Houston. Tony was an assistant DA there at the same time."

"Little surprised you had never mentioned you were a policeman in Houston."

"Why's that Ray? We're not exactly asshole buddies—are we?"

"Yeah, guess that's true. The other thing Tony said was that Marino was also from Houston. Did you know Marino in Houston?"

"Fuck. I knew that would eventually bite me in the ass. Yeah, I knew the little shit. Look Ray, you know the world is a big place, but in lots of ways it's also small. Who'd ever guess that I'd bump into Marino in Ruidoso?"

"Yeah. That's a strange coincidence. So you just saw him in town one day?"

"Yeah. Just like that. I was doing a walking patrol and there he was standing in front of me. Like I said, I knew him in Houston because he was always in some kind of trouble with the law—he was a thug. You know how police work is— you spend most of your time around criminals. So anyway, he was always around being charged on one thing or another. I'd have figured the little shit would have been dead by now, but there he was standing in front of me. He said he had moved in with his cousin or something and was lookin' for a job. Told me all of this bullshit about going straight and how he wanted to get into law enforcement. Well shit, I don't know I guess I believed him. Anyway, before I knew it I had told him that I'd ask the sheriff if he needed any help. The guy was always a good salesman—he went over to the sheriff's department and before I even had time to think about it, he had a job. I was shocked that Rodriguez would hire him without checking him out. But hell, it wasn't my problem."

"So you steered this known thug to the sheriff, who hired him as a deputy without running a background check."

"Yeah. Unbelievable isn't it?"

"Tony mentioned something about his wife being in trouble in Houston. Do you know about that?"

"Hell yes, I know. I was the one who called Tony and told him about that woman. My god, she was one good lookin' woman. I can sure see why Tony did what he did."

"What did Tony do?"

"Didn't he tell you?"

"He said he may have stepped over the line to help her."

"Well that's putting it pretty fucking mildly."

"So what did he do?"

"Look Ray, if he didn't tell you I'm not going to tell you. What the hell are you doing here anyway?"

"Do you have an alibi for the night Marino was shot?"

"Fuck. I get it. The governor needs a scapegoat. Tony Garcia needs a scapegoat. So why not the useless old police chief. Let's hang him by the balls. Is that it Ray?"

"You didn't answer my question?"

"Fuck you. If you're not going to arrest me, then get the fuck out of here, now!" Ray left.

Ray and Tyee got into the Jeep and headed towards the hotel.

"How did it go?"

"Well, he's been alerted and he acted like a trapped animal. He attacked me—but just verbally. But he took the offensive—didn't seem surprised that it was happening. Now I guess we just wait and see what he does next."

They checked in and agreed to meet in about thirty minutes for a drink before dinner.

"Had a return message from my FBI contact. He ran all the names and what information they found more or less matches up with what we know. Tony is from Oklahoma, graduated from OU and landed a job in Houston. Reports seem to indicate he might have been fired, but their information wasn't specific. He married Kate and they moved to Las Cruces. His wife, Kate, is from Boston and was raised by her father, who is a multimillionaire involved in international currency trading. No known criminal charges on either one. The sister, Lisa, was also raised by her father after her mother—also Kate's mother, obviously—was killed in an auto accident—police suspected that drugs were involved in the crash. Lisa's father has had connections with organized crime, but the FBI thinks it's been incidental and mostly the associations he had were with people from his old neighborhood in Miami. The FBI isn't sure about the dad, but said he was a very tough businessman and had on occasion been suspected of heavy-handed dealings with customers, suppliers, and employees. They said any dealings with him should be done with caution."

"Well Kate's rich father sure explains Tony's lack of concern about leaving his job here. Good to have millions somewhere to fall back on."

"Yeah, should make the transition to Boston painless."

"Not sure what I was looking for in their backgrounds, but that wasn't it. Lisa's father's Miami association with organized crime types could explain how Marino got into their lives, but it still seems odd that the daughter marries such a loser and that the father allowed it."

"I sometimes get the odd feeling that we're the only ones who don't know what's really going on."

At that very moment, Deputy Samson came into the restaurant and looked around the room. Once he spotted Ray and Tyee, he headed their way.

"Sorry to interrupt Sheriff, but Sheriff James thinks you should get over to the hospital as quickly as you can."

"Why? What's happened?"

"Someone tried to kill Tito Annoya. Shot him with what we think was a .30-30 rifle while he was leaving his cabin. Hit him in his shoulder. The doc says he should survive, but he lost a lot of blood by the time someone notified nine-one-one and an ambulance could get back to that cabin. He's going in and out of consciousness. The sheriff thought you might want to be there if he's alert enough to question."

"Absolutely, deputy. We'll be on our way right now."

The hospital in Ruidoso was located in a small building on the edge of town. They entered and immediately saw Sheriff James.

"Ray, he's not awake right now. He keeps going in and out. When he was awake the last time he was rambling on about the bastards that were going to kill him, but never named anyone. Is this just another coincidence or is this the result of challenging the chief?"

"Not real sure what anything's about. I always thought Tito was involved with some kind of drug operation, but how this fits together is beyond me right now."

"I'll tell you one thing, within the last month or so the drugs in Ruidoso have dried up. We actually had a known drug user come into the office and complain that there were no drugs on the street—first time I ever had that happen."

"Sort of looks like our little drug dealers are closing up shop and getting rid of evidence and accomplices."

"Sheriff, your prisoner is awake and demanding to be released—I'd say he's better."

They followed the doctor down the hall to the room where Tito was. Amazing—one minute he's almost dead, the next he's raising hell because he wants to be released.

"Tito, I'm going to read you your rights. The doctor here is going to note that you are awake and aware of what is happening." Sheriff James started reading from a laminated card.

"Wait a goddamn minute—are you arresting me?"

Sheriff James started reading from the card again, and this time finished without interruption.

"Do you understand these rights Tito?"

"Yeah. Get on with it."

"Do you know who shot you?"

"No."

"Tito, a couple of hours ago one of your bartenders was arrested for illegal possession of a controlled substance. The amount he had on him will place him in the dealer category, and he's facing maybe twenty years in prison. He's decided that you should go down with him. He's given us a statement that implicates you in the distribution of drugs through your clubs. At this time I'm placing you under arrest for drug trafficking."

"Damn bartenders. I always hated every wiseass, useless bartender who ever worked for me. Look Sheriff, maybe I was moving a little pot every now and then—but hell, that's not a major crime."

"Not the story we're getting. It seems you've been distributing significant quantities of heroin and cocaine, both in Ruidoso and Albuquerque. We believe that, as we start to dig further, the bartender here is going to be just the first who'll be willing to point the finger at you."

"Look, shit, man. I need a deal. What kind of deal can I get?"

Ray had been waiting for this kind of opening.

"Tito, my name's Ray Pacheco and this is my partner Tyee Chino."

"Ah, yes, the fucking Indian who broke my bartender's arm."

"Actually, I believe it was only a dislocated shoulder." Tyee couldn't help himself, he smiled.

"Tito, we work for the Governor. He wants things cleaned up here in Ruidoso and we want to know who killed Marino, Rodriguez, and the racetrack stable man, Esparza. If you can help us the Governor will be grateful, and can help you a lot."

"That's just a bunch of fuckin' talk. Tell me exactly what will happen if I give you the information—and I want it in writing."

Asshole had suddenly turned into a lawyer. "Tito, I think you're misunderstanding what's happening here. If you decide not to give us information then what will happen is you'll be charged with every crime we can think of, and with the help of your not-so-loyal employees you'll be looking at forty plus years—and guess what, wiseass, at your age that's very much like a life sentence. You've got about five minutes to make up your mind or there's no deal."

Ray turned and started to leave the room.

"Okay, hold on. I just need someone to give me their word that I won't get more than five years. Hey, I'm going to give you the big guys—you've got to give me a break."

"Tito, I'll give you my word that I will—and the Governor will—work to get the best deal possible for you. We'll go to bat for you as a cooperating witness. I can't guarantee anything beyond that—the other option is we put you back on the street, where it looks like you're at some risk of being shot again."

"Fuck."

"Is that some kind of answer, Tito?"

"Yeah. Okay I'll tell you what I know. But look, I may not know what you think I know."

"Do you know who killed Marino?"

"No. There were plenty of people who wanted him dead, and a bunch of them are here in Ruidoso. But I never heard anyone claim to have killed him, or even to know who did it. What I heard was thank god he was dead, but no bragging or anything. Most everyone thought it must have been someone from his past who found him here, shot him, and left."

"Do you know who killed Rodriguez?"

"Jeez. Man I don't know who killed anyone. Okay, I'm a small time drug dealer—I don't know anything about killing."

"Let me ask you again, do you know who shot you?"

"No. I was leaving my cabin and *bam*—I was shot. I didn't see anything. Then I was on the ground and figured whoever did it would be there any minute to put a bullet in my head. Next thing I know my nosy neighbor, Mrs. Pratt, was screaming up a storm and running around yelling for help. I guess that scared off whoever shot me. Mrs. Pratt finally calmed down enough to call for help."

"Okay, you don't know who shot you. Who were you getting your drugs from?"

"Sheriff Rodriguez."

"Sheriff Rodriguez was supplying you with drugs?"

"Well it was actually usually one of his deputies, but they worked for Rodriquez."

"Did you ever have any personal contact with Rodriguez?"

"Sure. A lot of the time he'd be the one who collected the money. Plus, he'd come into the bar a lot. He was always acting like a big shot—most everyone in there hated his guts, but he thought he was something special."

"Where was Rodriguez getting the drugs?"

"Never really knew, but almost had to be Mexico. Also had something to do with the racetrack."

"What do you mean it had something to do with the racetrack?"

"A couple of times Rodriguez got drunk and said he had to go to Ruidoso Downs and pick up his shipment."

"Did he mention anyone at the racetrack by name?"

"No, but I always thought it was the stable manager, Esparza, the one who got shot."

"Was the police chief involved in any of this?"

"The police chief? You mean Nelson?"

"Yeah."

"Nelson is a fucking joke—what would he be involved in?"

Sheriff James stepped in and started getting the names of the deputies involved and trying to pin down dates and how the quantities of drugs that were involved.

Ray and Tyee stepped out into the hallway.

"That didn't go where I thought it would." Ray was disappointed they hadn't gotten more.

"No. Why is someone trying to kill Tito if that's all he knows?"

"Yeah, good question. I'd say Tito is holding something back, maybe he's trying to negotiate, or maybe he's just plain stupid, but there's no way we're done with Tito."

18

Dick Franklin

The next morning Ray and Tyee headed to the breakfast place next door, Bud's—possibly the best reason to visit Ruidoso. The food was just amazing and they really appreciated the low-key atmosphere. When they walked in, Bud saw them and waved. They found an empty booth and seated themselves. The waitress brought menus and coffee and a beautiful smile. Ray decided she must be Mrs. Bud. They placed their orders.

"I guess one approach might be just to wait until everyone gets killed and there is only one person left standing—must be the killer." Tyee always took the direct and simple path to a solution.

"The, we-have-no-idea-what-to-do-next approach."

"Exactly."

"First thing is our schedule. I have no idea what might happen today, but I think we need to leave tomorrow morning. Obviously we would both rather be at home, but also I'd like for you to spend more time on the Internet getting as many details as you can on all of our players."

"Sounds good to me."

Their food was served and their attention shifted to the delicious-smelling offering. This was one great place to eat breakfast.

After their meal they headed down to the sheriff's office to check in with Sheriff James. Ray thought that after visiting with the Sheriff they should go to the racetrack and see if Dick Franklin was available for some additional questions. Sometimes the only thing you can do in an investigation, when there's no clear path ahead, is to keep poking the various parties until something pops.

Sheriff James seemed glad to see them, but was obviously much more focused on the day-to-day operation of the department. He didn't show a great deal of interest in the Marino matter, but he was concerned about the shooting at the racetrack and the Tito ambush.

"We found casings at the Tito cabin, just like at the racetrack. Somebody is being very sloppy to leave those behind. We've sent them to the lab, but our initial examination seems to indicate that they came from the same gun. Of course that doesn't mean the same shooter, but that sure would be my guess right now. As soon as we know for sure it was the same rifle, we'll let you know."

"How's Tito doing?"

"They released him from the hospital, so we have him in jail right now. The prosecutor is working on the charges to be filed—and, yes, he heard from the governor's office about going easy if Tito will give us something we can use. So far there hasn't been a lot, although it does look like we'll be able to charge a couple more of the old deputies based in his testimony."

Ray and Tyee chatted with the sheriff about how things were going in general in Lincoln County. The sheriff was very upbeat about the overall reduction of criminal activity in the community and the type of support he was receiving from the citizens. He said that crime was way down, and he was very pleased to be a part of the team that had turned things around. He thought getting Tito behind bars was the last big step toward returning Ruidoso and the county to being a well-run, law-abiding community. Ray made a note to inform the governor once again about what a great job Sheriff James was doing.

Next stop was Ruidoso Downs and a visit with Dick Franklin. "Since Franklin admitted he was concerned about drugs being moved through the racetrack, do you think that eliminates him as part of the drug trafficking?" Tyee was driving while Ray rested his eyes.

"Don't know Tyee. Franklin sure seems to be at the center of something. But if he was the drug dealer, why'd he bring that up to us—unless he thought it was coming out anyway and maybe it was a way to deflect the spotlight from him. Could the stable manager actually have run the racetrack operation without Franklin knowing?"

"I keep going back to when I knew him in school. It was obvious he could be less than honest, maybe even sneaky, but I just don't think there was anyone who'd say the guy was a drug dealer type—and no way a killer. He just wasn't that person."

"Well people change."

"Yep, they do."

They parked in the track lot and went around back to the administrative offices. The doors were locked and there didn't seem to be anyone around. They walked toward the stable area, looking for someone. In the back there were a couple of workers cleaning the barn area.

"We're looking for Mr. Franklin. Have you seen him?"

Both men shrugged their shoulders and went back to work—apparently English wasn't their first language. Ray attempted his embarrassing imitation of someone who could speak Spanish and just got smiles from the workers—he had no idea what he'd just said. He finished with "buenos dias," and they left. He always regretted not making the effort to learn Spanish.

As they went behind the barn, they found another man working on a tractor that was apparently used to level the track area.

"Good morning."

The man greeted Ray with a nod. "We're looking for Mr. Franklin. Have you seen him today?"

"Not today. And that SOB better show up pretty soon, because we're supposed to be paid. Plus we've got a ton of work to complete if we're going to be ready to open the track next week, and Dick hasn't been around the last two days. This time of year he'd normally have hired ten or more extra hands to help us get ready. I have no idea what the hell is going on. Do you know where he is?"

"Have you tried his house?" For this obvious question Tyee received a hard look from the worker.

"Hell yes. I've tried everywhere—even in Tularosa. They say he's not there and then just hang up. If he doesn't show up in the next hour, we're going to walk and this track isn't going to open on time."

They left the unhappy worker and went back to the Jeep. Taking their own advice, they decided to swing by Franklin's house. As soon as they pulled up, they could see that more than likely nobody was home, and probably hadn't been in days. There were newspapers on the driveway and the mailbox appeared to be full. Just in case, they parked and went to the front door and rang the bell. No answer.

"Looks like Franklin has flown the coop."

"Or maybe the guy with the .30-30 got him."

"Guess we better look around the house." They did, but found nothing.

They drove down the hill to a service station, and while Tyee filled up the tank Ray called Sheriff James. He filled him in on what they'd found that morning and said that it appeared that Franklin had left, although it was also possible that he was another shooting victim. The sheriff said he'd send a patrol car to the house to search the outside again—he was reluctant to push too fast, what with Franklin being a leading citizen, but he said he'd ask a judge to give them permission to enter the house later today if nothing changed, for a welfare check. Ray thought he should just bust the door in and see if anyone was there—but Ray wasn't the sheriff of Lincoln County.

"What now, oh noble leader?"

"I think we should go to Tularosa and see if we can visit with Dick or Isabella Franklin."

"Sounds like a plan."

They were on the right side of town for it, so they were quickly out of Ruidoso and headed toward Tularosa, about forty minutes down the mountain. They had passed through this area on each of their trips without paying too much attention to it. The highway went through some commercial areas, but didn't approach the neighborhood where the Ortega hacienda was located. They had gotten directions from the sheriff when they'd considered stopping there on their previous trip.

They turned off of the main highway and headed into the foothills. After about two miles, they found the entrance to the estate. The driveway was very long and climbed high into the foothills. The entire property became more lush and manicured as they went. Climbing over a small rise, they could see the house—it was almost unbelievable. Located in this remote area was a huge Spanish hacienda with amazing plants and flowers, looking for all the world like something from a Hollywood movie.

"Wow. That has to be worth millions even here in the back waters of New Mexico. I've never seen anything like it."

"You never knew this was here when you lived in Mescalero?"

"Never. I didn't live far from here but the res was like another world—we didn't socialize outside of our designated place."

They pulled up in front of the house. The place looked abandoned, but within a short time armed guards appeared carrying semiautomatic weapons. One of the guards came over to the Jeep and opened the door.

"Maybe you didn't see the private property signs."

"We are here to see Dick or Isabella Franklin—we're officials with the governor's office."

The guard gave a snort. "Who gives a fuck—I said turn around and get out of here," he said in a very unpleasant voice.

"I think you should tell someone that we're here before you threaten us."

"Listen you dumb shit..."

"Stop. I'll handle this." This came from an elderly man who had the bearing of a king—or maybe a god. But he also had an odd cast to him that gave the impression that he wasn't fully aware of where he was.

All the guards backed away as the old man walked down the stairs toward the Jeep. Ray and Tyee remained sitting in the vehicle.

"Who are you?"

"My name is Ray Pacheco and this is Tyee Chino. We work for the governor and would like to speak to Dick or Isabella Franklin."

"I have met your governor—he's a buffoon. What does the governor want with Dick Franklin or my daughter?"

"Some people have been killed in Ruidoso and there's some reason to believe it's related to drug operations that are using the Ruidoso Downs racetrack as their delivery point. We'd like to discuss this with Dick Franklin. We wanted to talk to your daughter to confirm some earlier statements Franklin made regarding his whereabouts when one of these killings took place."

"My daughter is divorcing Dick Franklin because he's weak. Franklin isn't here. You should leave before you offend me and I have these men kill you." He turned, as if dismissing a pair of stray dogs, and returned to his magnificent abode.

Ray eyed the guards and realized there was no doubt that with nothing more than the flick of the old guy's wrist these men would kill them. He started the Jeep and gradually left.

It seemed to take a long time to finally reach the highway and get headed back to Ruidoso.

"You know, I had the feeling that for no reason at all that old man might have had us killed."

"Yeah. I had the same feeling. Not very comfortable to be around someone who'd do that on the slightest impulse. That's one very frightening guy."

"Do you think Dick or Isabella were there?"

"Tyee, I have a bad feeling about Dick Franklin. After meeting Isabella's father, I think this isn't a family that would have a friendly divorce. I have no idea about Isabella. All I've heard about her is how beautiful she is, but if she inherited anything from her father she could be trouble. What did you think of her in school?"

"I didn't know her at all. I saw her a few times with Dick, and there is no question she was a knockout. Most people described her as cold and a little scary, but I don't remember ever talking to her."

They headed back to Ruidoso and went to the sheriff's office.

"Do you want to file charges against them Ray?" Sheriff James had listened to their story and was amazed there could be such an armed camp in his county.

"No, I don't think that would move things forward. But if you ever have to go in there, you better be prepared. These are very bad people with lots of weapons."

"I think it's time we head to the Franklin house and get inside."

Ray and Tyee followed the three patrol cars back to Franklin's house. They stayed in the Jeep as the deputies busted in, then almost immediately came back out and got on the radio. Ray and Tyee stepped out of the Jeep and waited.

"Well, we've got another body. Dick Franklin is dead inside—probably since some time yesterday. It's either a suicide or someone made it look like a suicide. There's a note. You and Tyee can go in if you want and take a quick look. We can meet at the office and go over the note."

Ray and Tyee agreed. They entered the house. Franklin was sitting at a large desk in a home office. He'd been shot in the right temple and had a large part of his skull missing. It was obvious he'd been dead for hours. The gun, a .38 special, was on the ground by the desk. They examined the area around the desk and the rest of the room, but didn't see anything significant. They left for the sheriff's office as the deputies went about their crime scene responsibilities.

The sheriff handed Ray a typed note inside a clear plastic bag:

I have done things that are wrong. Because of what I have done, people have died. I'm sorry. This is all because of drugs and greed. I wanted to make money so I could be independent of my wife's family and be able to leave this state. I'm sorry for what I have done and the people I have hurt—most especially my wife, whom I love very much.

I started the drug dealing business with Sheriff Rodriguez. We got our drugs from a connection in Mexico who shipped the drugs in the horse trailers. My stable manager first told me he could do this if I was interested—I should have fired him and told the Sheriff, but I wanted the money. I talked Rodriguez into to helping me, and he brought in Tito.

My wife was never involved and didn't know.

Please forgive me for the harm I have caused. I have no choice but to take my life. I love you Isabella.

Dick Franklin

"Not much of a confession, did Franklin have Marino and Rodriguez killed? We know he didn't kill the stable manager—at least not on his own—because he was there with us when it happened. Nothing is solved by this note."

"Yep."

"Let's say this is a real suicide note and confession. If he had killed Marino, Esparza the stable manager, Rodriguez, or taken that shot at Tito, wouldn't he admit it? So if it isn't a real suicide note, and the real killer shot Franklin, why wouldn't he include in the fake suicide note that Franklin killed all of those people?"

"Beats the fuck out of me Ray, but I'm telling you I don't believe Dick Franklin committed suicide." Tyee seemed angry.

"Looks like the only thing this note does is clear Isabella—maybe that was the whole idea."

19

Home Alone

Neither Ray nor Tyee was in a good mood. They even skipped breakfast at Bud's, heading home first thing in the morning. Skipping the joy of breakfast at Bud's was a strong indication that the trip was going to be long and quiet. Ray wasn't happy with the situation, but Tyee was truly pissed about the whole mess. And Ray was sick and tired of driving to Ruidoso and needed a break from everyone involved.

They were headed out of Las Cruces before they attempted a conversation.

"Once we get in I'll call the Governor and give him an update. I think our focus should be on getting more information about Isabella's father. He seemed like he might be a little unhinged. Maybe you could do some research on the computer and see what you can find. My plan is to remain in T or C for a while and let things settle down. I'm going to talk to Sheriff James about putting some kind of alert out on Isabella, but other than that it looks like we're in the waiting game again."

"I can do the research as soon as we get back. I agree that we need to stay out of this Jeep for a few days—I think you're starting to get on my nerves." Tyee smiled. They both knew a little space would be welcome.

As they pulled into the driveway and parked, they were greeted by the best greeter in the world—a dog. Happy jumped and wagged with great doggie joy, both Ray and Tyee gave him a good rub. Tyee said he'd see Ray later, then headed toward the outbuildings where he lived and worked. Ray went into the cabin with Happy following.

"Hello, anyone home?" No sound. They were probably a few hours earlier than Sue was expecting. The early departure and the very few stops along the way had gotten them back in record time. Ray went into the kitchen and decided to fix a pot of coffee and just relax. The phone rang.

"Hello."

"Hello, this is Chuck, Beverly's husband. I'm waiting at the Lone Post Café, but no one's here. Is there something wrong?"

"This is Ray Pacheco and I just got back into town, so I don't know exactly what's going on. Were you expecting to meet Beverly at the Café?

"Yes. She and her cousin and somebody named Big Jack were supposed to meet me. I am expecting that I'll be able to take the kids back to Denver."

"There's no one at my place, so I'd guess they may be on their way into town to meet with you."

"Okay. Thanks." He hung up.

Interesting development. Ray debated about calling, or even driving into T or C to see what was happening, but decided he could use the peace and quiet.

He sat down with his newly brewed coffee and glanced through the mail. Sue handled all of the household expenses, so he skimmed through the pile and put it aside without much interest. His life had always been about working. Getting up on a schedule, going to work on a schedule, eating on a schedule—the few months when he'd tried to break those habits by retiring and doing nothing hadn't been enjoyable. He craved the structure of his routines. But since his marriage to Sue, he'd wanted to spend more time just being with her, so now the schedules and the demands of his new career were starting to annoy him. Had he made a bad decision starting this business? He wasn't sure.

Of course some of this attitude could come from being tired after all of the driving they'd been doing, as well as being upset that they hadn't been able to nail things down better. Everything still felt unsettled, and Ray didn't like that. He got up and went outside with Happy. Maybe a walk with the dog would help him unwind.

There was no walking with Happy—he liked to run. Watching the dog get such joy out of simply running started to make Ray feel better. He'd done that when he was a kid—just taken off running for no purpose other than the joy of doing it. What happens to people that they lose the joy of being alive? He started jogging a little. Before he knew it he was running—not as fast as a kid or a dog, but running, and smiling. He thought, *you old fool, you're going to fall and break your neck.* But that didn't stop him, and soon he was laughing.

On the way back to the cabin, both Happy and Ray walked slowly—they were tired. In sight of the cabin, Ray sat on an old log and started tossing a stick for Happy to fetch.

This went on for some time—he hadn't felt this relaxed in a long while.

"Looks like some of the tension is gone."

"Yeah. I even ran some with the dog. This is a great place to be."

"Old man running with dog sounds like trip to hospital."

"Don't tell Sue, okay?"

"Sure. Didn't take long to find out lots of stuff about Mr. Ortega. Andres Ortega was by all accounts once a member of organized crime in Mexico—some call it the Mexican mafia, later known as the cartels. Ortega was a leader of a huge crime family that had operations in Mexico and the U.S. from the 1950s through the 1970s. The FBI says that he was suspected of running the vast empire from his hidden hacienda in New Mexico. Sometime in the '70s he was overthrown by younger toughs, who expanded the drug business and increased the level of violence. But Ortega was still honored because of his age and history. The FBI and DEA files indicate that they don't suspect him to have been involved in anything illegal since the '70s, and that they haven't monitored his activities closely since that time."

"A big time international crime boss living in isolation in the hills of New Mexico—who would have thought? Any mention of his wife or Isabella in the records?"

"More or less just footnotes. His wife died about five years ago. The files mentioned that his daughter is involved in his care. My contact at the FBI said he was once considered to be the top dog in all sorts of illegal activities, but today they don't believe he's involved at all."

"Guess even drug lords get old and retire."

They both absorbed this, imagining what it might mean—if anything.

"Tyee, I think I need to apologize for being on edge lately. I like what we're doing and I want to keep doing it, I just need to set better priorities around being at home with Sue. This running all over the state is making me nuts."

"White man must fish more—chase evil men less."

"Let's go fishing tomorrow, how about it?"

"Perfecto."

Sue was anxious about going to the meeting between Beverly and Chuck Evans. She'd learned a lot over the last few days of having Beverly and her kids living with her. She knew that Beverly was an unaware mother who was totally absorbed in her own life and took her great kids for granted. Ray had told Sue there had to be a better parent involved for those kids to have turned out so well-behaved and mature, and of course Ray was right. As soon as she talked to Chuck on the phone, Sue knew that he was the source of the kids' composure.

Chuck's concern was one hundred percent about the kids. He said that if the kids were better off with Beverly, that's what he'd want—but he hadn't seen that in many years. He told Sue that Beverly was going through a mid-life crisis and didn't need the responsibility of children at this point. He was candid with Sue about his "mistake" in having an affair with the young woman who used to be the kids babysitter—but as he explained it, there were a lot more extenuating circumstances than Beverly had told her.

Chuck and Beverly had been separated for over a year when he started his relationship with the other woman. He said Beverly had had at least two live-in boyfriends during that time. During the majority of the separation, Chuck had complete custody of the children. He was even concerned about Beverly. He told Sue he was sure that she was having all sorts of identity issues, and that this was compounded by the fact she had gained so much weight. He thought that Beverly should concentrate on getting herself together and not worry about the children until she was better prepared to deal with them.

After Sue's conversation with Chuck, she immediately confronted Beverly, who broke down and cried and asked for sympathy—but never once took responsibility for anything. Sue told her she should grow up and that she should get the kids back with their dad where they belonged. They didn't talk for the rest of that day.

That evening, with the aid of Big Jack, Sue was able to talk to Beverly and convince her that it was in everybody's best interest to work out a deal between Beverly and Chuck for a divorce—and that the kids should be with him until Beverly was better able to handle them. Big Jack was sympathetic to Beverly, but also firm. He discussed the legal realities and told her she could win custody, but probably couldn't move out of Colorado without the court's permission. After about an hour of discussion on the various points, Beverly's position changed and she decided that it was Chuck's responsibility to take the children.

Once they'd reached that conclusion, Sue had called Chuck and asked him to meet them in T or C. He had immediately agreed and said he'd be there by the afternoon of the next day. They agreed to meet at the Lone Post Café.

Now they were driving to the meeting. Thanks to Beverly they were about thirty minutes late, but Sue was sure that Chuck—who had driven ten hours—would be there waiting.

"Kids, I bet you didn't know that I used to work at this restaurant we are going to."

"Really, were you the cook?"

"No. I waited on tables."

"Wow."

That was the great thing about kids—they were so easily impressed.

"Once we get inside I'm going to get you two a special booth and have the cook fix you one of the best green chili hamburgers you'll ever taste—how about that?"

"Great. Great."

They parked in front and everyone got out. Big Jack was supposed to meet them there, but Sue didn't see him. They went inside. Sue was greeted with hugs by what seemed like everyone on the staff. She got the kids situated and saw Beverly talking to a tall, thin man in the back. She headed that way.

"You must be Chuck?"

"Yes. And you must be Sue, nice to meet you." They shook hands.

Chuck said that he wanted to go say hi to the kids and left. Beverly stood there, frowning. About then, Big Jack walked in and Beverly's mood changed completely for the better. Big Jack was busy glad-handing everyone in the room and slowly making his way back to where Sue and Beverly were seated. Big Jack came to Chuck and gave him his standard please-vote-for-me greeting. Once they realized who they each were, they stepped aside and had a few words, then they joined the ladies at the booth. Big Jack slid in beside Beverly—something of a challenge—and Chuck sat next to Sue.

"Chuck, I'm pleased to meet you and I want you to know that while I'm an attorney, I'm not here in that capacity—I'm here as Beverly's friend. She and I have talked extensively, and I believe candidly, about what would be best for everyone for at least the next few months. So, if I may, I'd like to address the issues and make sure everyone is agreeable."

"Please, go ahead Jack." Chuck seemed to be as well-mannered as his children, possibly not a coincidence.

"Beverly, I'm going to say some things that you may have said to me in private, so if it upsets you then please ask me to stop, okay?"

"Yes." Beverly didn't want to be at this meeting.

"First, the children. I have never met more polite, well-adjusted kids in my life. Beverly may not have ever said this to you, but she gives you all of the credit for that. She's told me that you're a much better mother than she ever was." Beverly frowned, Chuck grimaced.

"With that in mind, it's critical that the children return to your care at once. I know that's why you're here, to pick them up, but I think it's important to say some of these things out loud. You are to be congratulated on an excellent job raising your children." Once again no one said anything, although Chuck did nod.

"Second, you two need to be divorced. The separation may have had a purpose at the beginning, but now it's just getting in the way of you both moving on with your lives. I think this can be a simple process with no confrontation. We can put together a list of things we would like to happen related to financial matters, and we will try to keep it reasonable. Regarding the children, Beverly agrees that you should have primary care, but that she should have visitation rights. Unless there are hidden assets that I haven't been told about, there's no reason this can't be an agreement of only a few pages and you can get it signed and done in a matter of weeks. On a very personal note, and I have already said this to Beverly, you two should decide to be friends as best you can so that you don't impact your children. I think in this case that would be mostly about not being nasty with one another. Many marriages end in divorce, believe me I can attest to that, but that's no reason for there to be petty bickering after the fact. You both care about your children so act like it."

Big Jack had said his piece. Everyone was quiet.

"I agree with what you've said Jack. Beverly, I'll do my best with the children and I'll try and be a good ex-husband."

Sue was so impressed with this guy—she thought that given the opportunity she might just slug Beverly.

"I have a lot to learn, Chuck. I know I need to grow up. I do love our children, I'm just a lousy mother. You're a good man Chuck." Beverly lowered her head and cried. Maybe they were genuine tears.

Everyone stood, ready to move on. Big Jack and Chuck exchanged contact information and discussed logistics related to the divorce papers. Beverly, to her credit, went over and hugged her kids. She told them she'd see them soon—they said they'd like that. The kids came over and gave Sue a big, loving hug. Sue was touched, and teared up a bit. Everyone said goodbye.

Outside, Beverly left with Big Jack. Chuck left with the kids. Sue was ecstatic to be going home alone.

Sue and Ray spent the evening and some of the night getting reacquainted. Just what they needed.

20

Dinner Party

Sue decided to have a dinner party, inviting Big Jack and Beverly along with Tyee. When she asked Beverly if they could come, she was surprised that Beverly insisted on cooking the meal.

"Look Sue, at this point I owe you more than I'll ever be able to repay. Please let me cook the meal. We can do this at your place, but let me get all of the ingredients and cook a meal for you and your guests."

"Sure, if you really want to."

Sue set the date for Saturday night, one week away. She wasn't completely sure about letting Beverly fix the meal, but she was reluctant to turn down any offer from Beverly. She told Ray, but he wasn't too interested—he hadn't invested the time in Beverly that Sue had. Ray did ask an interesting question, though—was Tyee bringing a date? Suddenly Sue had a new project.

Sue and Ray attended another beer bash on behalf of Big Jack's mayoral campaign. Ray questioned the logic of holding it since it looked like the same people showed up as at the last one. But there was no question that Big Jack and Beverly loved this environment. One thing that had changed since the last event was that Beverly had set up a taco tent, and the smells coming from that direction were wonderful. Even more impressive were the lines of people waiting to get their tacos. They were free, so you'd expect demand, but the crowd was more enthusiastic than might be expected—Beverly actually got a standing ovation from her customers.

Sue prodded Ray toward the tent—she had to try a sample of Beverly's wares. As they got closer, they could read the menu, which included tacos filled with smoked chicken with chipotle sauce, Korean barbeque, mushrooms, grilled steak with bourbon sauce, and honey mustard chicken. So far so good. They finally made it up to the counter, where Chester was taking the orders with a big smile.

"Hello Chester."

"Well hello, Mr. and Mrs. Pacheco. Nice to see you."

"What best on the menu, Chester?"

"We've probably sold—well, I mean given away—more of the steak than anything else, but my favorite is the smoked chicken."

They ordered one steak and one smoked chicken, and both smelled wonderful. When Sue caught a glimpse of Beverly, it seemed like she was having the time of her life. They found a spot to sit and sampled the food.

"Wow. This is some good stuff."

"Wow is right. This is delicious. Wonder why she never mentioned her food skills before."

"Maybe she didn't want to become the house cook." An annoying but logical answer.

As Big Jack started his speech, some of the guests headed to the beer tent to stock up—Jack usually shut off the free beer after his speech. Ray and Sue headed back to the taco tent for seconds.

"These are amazing Beverly, I had no idea you were such a great cook. I'm starting to really look forward to next week's dinner."

Beverly gave her a genuine smile. "Thank you Sue, for being so great."

Maybe Beverly was an okay person after all. After Big Jack's speech, Ray and Sue headed home.

"I want to invite Nancy to the dinner next Saturday as a date for Tyee—what do you think?"

"I think I'd let Tyee find his own date."

"But he won't, so I need to invite someone. Ray, he's still depressed after all of these years about his wife and his failed marriage. He needs help to get some love back in his life. Just like you did." Oops. That got Ray's attention.

"Just like I did?"

"Yeah. Just like you did. If I'd just waited on you, we'd both have been dead before anything would have happened. Ray come on, I need to help Tyee rejoin the human race. My god, even Big Jack has a girlfriend—can you imagine if you were Tyee, how that would make you feel—Big Jack has a girl-friend and you don't?"

"Who is this Nancy person?"

"She's the new girl at the café. She's from Albuquerque, but her parents moved up here about three months ago to re-tire. She moved in with them for a little while to help them get everything set up. She's really cute. She quit her job as a paralegal to help her parents, and she works part-time at the café. Did I mention she's real cute?"

"Listen, this is your doing. If it blows up in your face, don't drag me into it, okay? And by the way, do you think she'd want to be Tyee's date?"

"Good question. She may not know who he is—which could be helpful. Most of the people who've been around here for a while know him as 'that scary Indian'—but they don't know him the way we do. I think she'd come because it's at our house and we'll be here."

Ray walked off to the kitchen shaking his head. In the ultimate head-in-the-sand position, Ray thought romance just blossomed, kind of naturally, but Sue knew better. He'd be sure to warn Tyee about Sue's plans.

The next day Sue went to the café and had coffee. During Nancy's break she was able to talk to her and invite her to the dinner. Nancy didn't initially show a lot of enthusiasm. Sue mentioned that the party would be a small gathering with Big Jack, the guy running for mayor, and his girlfriend Beverly, who was going to do the cooking, and of course her and Ray—and Tyee Chino. The list of attendees made the nature of the invitation obvious. Nancy didn't give Sue an answer, so she hung around for a bit to see if they could talk on Nancy's next break.

"Sue, I appreciate you trying to fix me up with someone, but the timing is probably not right. I told everyone that I moved here to help my parents get settled in with their retirement, and that's true, but I also moved because my relationships with men have been a disaster. I just wanted to get away for a while and not think about men. So it's not you or your Mr. Chino, I'm just too gun-shy right now."

"Oh bullshit, Nancy. What are going to do, become a nun? I'm just asking you to dinner. Yes, there will be an equal number of women and men, but Tyee is no masher—he's a gentleman. You can have polite conversation with him or ignore him—he won't attack you. Plus, you'll get to meet some people in a social situation and it'll make you to start feel more at home here. So, can you make it or not?"

Maybe Nancy figured that she probably had nothing to fear from Sue, but decided not to risk refusing anyway—she said yes.

Being a natural worrier, when Sue hadn't heard from Beverly by Saturday afternoon, she began to feel concerned. Had Beverly changed her mind, had she forgotten, was the whole thing some kind of cruel joke? But just as panic was starting to set in, Beverly and Chester showed up with a truckload of goodies. They started bringing in the food, most of it already cooked, and the aromas were fantastic.

In all the days that Beverly had been a guest in Sue's house, she hadn't done a thing, but tonight she handled everything. They made two trips with the food, and then Beverly left to get dressed. She was back in a surprisingly short time and began the final preparations. She also helped Sue set the table and seemed in a great mood. She looked very attractive in an outfit Sue had never seen before, along with skillfully applied make-up.

Big Jack showed up a few minutes early and quickly found a beer. He also was dressed in a way that Sue hadn't seen before, with a well-tailored, expensive suit. This dinner party had already brought out surprises.

Next to make an appearance was Nancy. She was lovely. She had brought a bottle of wine and seemed more relaxed than Sue had expected after Sue had pressured her into coming. The dress she wore was beautiful, and it was enhanced by her very attractive, trim figure. Sue thought she was actually better looking than she'd remembered.

Ray was busy helping everyone get something to drink and seemed to be having a nice time. He chatted with Nancy, and Sue could tell he liked her. She had the kind of little girl charm that many men couldn't resist.

Tyee finally arrived. Sue hoped that arriving late wasn't some kind of macho bullshit—then saw him and realized that he'd known Nancy would be there and had dressed for the occasion. At six-foot-four, with long, braided, black hair and an obviously muscular body, he wasn't someone anyone would miss, but dressing in an absolutely gorgeous suit and tie gave him a movie star quality. He was an extremely handsome man, and quite a hunk. Sue glanced at Nancy and realized she was staring at Tyee. Sue stepped over, grabbed Nancy's hand, and guided her over to Tyee so she could introduce them—and she gave the other woman's hand a squeeze along the way to snap her out of her glazed gawking.

Once Nancy and Tyee started talking, they hit it off without any help from Sue. They discovered that they had many connections from Albuquerque, where they'd both lived for many years. Nancy had also gone to the university there, although she hadn't graduated. They seemed to be doing fine, and Sue relaxed. Ray gave her a smile.

The dinner was a smashing success. Beverly served honey-chipotle roast chicken with a green chili sauce, acorn squash with honey butter, and asparagus with a honey-lime based sauce. She had made amazing rolls with more honey and butter, and for desert she prepared sopapillas with a special spiced honey. "Nobody ever complained about too much butter or honey," she said. Everyone raved and ate, then raved some more and ate some more. Beverly was a star.

21

Confession

Ray hadn't realized how tired he was until he'd had the previous few days to rest. He'd been so busy, he had worn himself out and hadn't even been aware how bad he felt until he started to feel better. He had to promise Sue, an easy thing to do, that he'd be more aware of his health and his limitations and not push himself so hard in the future.

The time they had together during these slower days was special. Ray made every effort to enjoy what a wonderful person Sue was and how much he appreciated her humor and wisdom—and the sex wasn't bad either.

Ray let Happy out for his morning romp, then decided to join him and take a walk along the path down toward the lake. The weather was turning and the morning air was crisp. He was about to start running, then remembered his promise to be careful and not kill himself—Sue's exact words. On his return from his walk he stopped in at the office to see what was going on.

"Morning Tyee, how are you on this fine morning?"

"Well, you're in a good mood."

"Yes, I am. Although, since everybody notices with such shock when I'm in a good mood, it must mean most of the time I'm an asshole. That right?"

"Indian not understand English."

"Very funny."

"I was just going to head up to the cabin to give you a message. Some officer from the Albuquerque Police Department said that a woman walked in this morning and announced that she wanted to confess, but only if you were there—he wants you to call."

"Some woman? Did he say what her name was?"

"No. He just wanted you to call him as soon as possible."

Ray went over to one of the desks and called the number.

"Albuquerque Police Department."

"Officer Clarke, please."

"Just a moment, please."

"Officer Clarke."

"This is Ray Pacheco, you wanted me to call you."

"Mr. Pacheco thanks for calling. Kind of a strange deal. A woman walks in this morning and say she wants to confess, but she'll only talk if you're here. We don't have any idea what this is about, but this woman is absolutely gorgeous and very upper-class, so we decided we'd call you and see if you knew what it's about."

"Did she give you a name?"

"Just her first name—Isabella."

"I'll be there in a few hours—don't let her go."

Ray went back to the cabin looking for Sue, but apparently while he'd been out she had gone shopping. He went back to the office and asked Tyee if he'd look after Happy. He told Tyee what was happening and that he was going to Albuquerque immediately. They discussed Tyee and Happy going with him, but it just created logistical issues so Ray decided to go by himself.

He got in his Jeep and headed out. He had a full tank of gas, so he wouldn't have to stop until he got there. What was this about? Isabella wants to confess to what? Where had she been the last few days? He had no answers, so he just concentrated on driving.

"Ray Pacheco to see Officer Clarke."

"Sure, come on through—he's in the last office on your right."

"Officer Clarke? Ray Pacheco."

"Come in Mr. Pacheco, have a seat. I've been told that you're some kind of special officer for the governor and I should do what you say—is that right?"

Ray chuckled. "Well, I do work for the governor. Doing what I say will be up to you. Where's Isabella Ortega?"

"We're holding her in an interrogation room. She's just been sitting there for hours, like she's meditating or something. We've offered her food and something to drink, but she's only taken water. Damn, she's the most beautiful woman I think I've ever seen. What is it she's wanting to confess to?"

"I'm not sure officer. She's been involved in some things in Ruidoso over the last few months, including the apparent suicide of her husband. I guess the best way to find out what she wants to say is to go ask her."

Officer Clarke took the hint and showed Ray to the interrogation room. Ray entered and stood at the door. He felt as if he knew Isabella Ortega after discussing her so much as part of the events in Ruidoso, but he'd never seen her and for a moment he was stunned. People had said she was beautiful, but the words didn't do her justice. But when she turned her eyes up and looked at him, he saw a real person, someone feeling great pain.

"Isabella Ortega, my name is Ray Pacheco."

"I have to tell you what has happened."

Ray shut the door. There was a tape recorder on the desk—he adjusted it and made sure it was working.

"Isabella, I need to record what you're saying so there are no mistakes. Do you agree to that?"

"I do."

Ray turned on the recorder and stated the date, her name, and his name.

"Tell me what happened."

"My father was powerful—he controlled whole armies of men. He was rich and famous. But my mother died about five years ago, and he died with her—not completely, just his mind. He lost his power and his money. As soon as the scum knew he was weak, they took over his businesses, cut off his money. I was the only thing he had left. I had to help him, so I did."

She told her story. Andres Ortega had been the top gangster in all of Mexico for years. He ran all kinds of illegal activities, but he was generous to the people, who loved him. His family had owned property in what was now New Mexico for hundreds of years, long before the area became part of the United States. He had established a secret getaway in

Tularosa. She told how he had married Clara and had been so much in love with both the woman and the artist. They'd had a child, and he had softened. As he became more and more of a father and a husband, he lost much of his power. He decided he didn't want to go back to Mexico, so they just stayed where they were.

Even though he wasn't the head of a criminal organization anymore, he still received money—lots of money—from its activities, because he knew the names of the people involved and the locations of their dealings. He knew where they kept money, drugs, prisoners, guns—all of it—and if they didn't pay him they'd feel his wrath. He was a legend and they all feared him. Much of the fear was a result of the fact that, although they hadn't seen him in years, if someone bad-mouthed him or threatened him, they died. It was as if he could hear them and always found a way to punish them if they did him wrong.

Once the stupid police chief, Nelson, came to see him and asked if he would supply Nelson with drugs that he could sell. Nelson said he knew about his Mexico connections because he had once been in the Houston police department. Her father laughed at the idiot and kicked him out. He told Isabella about it, saying how ignorant Americans were.

Her parents wanted her to marry a Spaniard, but that wasn't something she wanted. Instead she chose Dick Franklin, deliberately picking someone she could control—plus it made her parents mad, which in that moment she wanted. After they were married, though, she fell in love with Dick. She stayed away from her parents and began to enjoy an almost normal life. But then her mother died. Her father went crazy, accusing people of hiding his wife. He even attacked some of the employees—everyone started leaving.

Word got out about her father and his madness. The cartel stopped sending money. Her father slipped deeper into madness and started hiring all kinds of thugs to guard the hacienda. He refused to see Isabella and accused her of killing her mother. What money still remained was disappearing fast.

"At that point, I could have abandoned my father—who wasn't in his right mind anyway—or I could try to help. I can't tell you how much my parents meant to me. I adored them both, and for many years they were my entire life. I couldn't turn my back on my father. Of course I didn't have money, but I did have connections. I contacted the police chief and asked him if he was still interested in buying drugs. The pig of a man said he was."

"Dick was running the Ruidoso Racetrack, and it seemed natural to me to use those facilities as a distribution point. I convinced Dick to hire Lewis Esparza as a stable manager because he was one of my connections and would do what I told him. He helped set up the system of transporting the drugs with the horses from El Paso to Ruidoso. Nelson recruited Sheriff Rodriguez, another law enforcement moron, to move the drugs from the racetrack into town or to Albuquerque."

"Nelson told me about running into that thug Marino in town—he remembered him from Houston. He said he didn't trust Rodriguez and wanted someone on the inside who was tougher to make sure nobody was stealing from us. I didn't care as long as I was getting my slice. They started using Tito somewhere along the way to move drugs through his clubs, and he was the main pipeline to Albuquerque. And at no time did my husband know anything about any of this."

"I was getting what I wanted—money—which I gave to my father. He was wasting it on his paranoid delusions, hiring guards and increasing security. I knew it couldn't go on, but I didn't know how to stop. Dick and I became distant. I could tell he was suspicious of my activities—going to my father's all of the time. He accused me of having an affair. He was very upset. And then this moron Marino starts strong-arming people for money. We had a nice deal going with the drugs, and it wasn't bothering the good people in the community, but now this nut is threatening my husband along with all of the other businessmen. I couldn't believe it. I told Nelson I was going to shut everything down unless something was done about Marino."

"And then poor Dick goes to meet Marino to tell him he wasn't going to pay him any more money. Marino laughs at him and tells him it's his wife who's running everything. I have no idea how he knew that, but Dick went crazy and tried to strangle him—they got into a fight and then Dick left and came home. He confronted me and I eventually told him what I've been doing. He tells me to leave. He said he wants a divorce—that my whole family has always been crazy and he's going back to California."

"I left and went to Tularosa. My father confronted me and I told him that I'd screwed up everything, including my marriage. I told him Dick was going to divorce me and said it was his fault. I screamed and told him that I hated him. He hit me, then he hit me again and again. I got away and ran to my room and locked the door. He pounded on the door for a while, but then left. As soon as I thought it might be safe, I escaped and drove to Albuquerque to the hospital."

"Mr. Pacheco, I believe my father had Dick killed. In some strange, twisted way he must have thought he was helping me. One of the investigators here told me about the contents of the suicide note, that it said I wasn't involved in the drug dealing. Dick didn't commit suicide and he didn't write that note. Only my father would try to clear me with a fake suicide note—no one else would care. I think my father is completely out of his mind—he doesn't know what he's doing or why. He has to be stopped." She put her head on the table and cried.

Ray waited for her to stop crying.

"Do you know who killed Marino?"

"No. My guess would be Nelson. I guess you might be able to make a case that I ordered it, but that's not what I meant when I said something had to be done to stop him. I just wanted him gone, but I think that Nelson took it as an order to kill Marino."

"Do you know who killed Sheriff Rodriguez?"

"No. My guess is that it has something to do with my father. Where he was killed and the way he was killed is exactly how it would be done by the cartel."

"Someone took a shot at Tito, do you know anything about that?"

"No, nothing."

"Isabella, you're going be charged with drug trafficking. Also, if Nelson killed Marino you'll be charged with murder, or at the very least accessory to murder. The more you cooperate with the investigators and prosecutors, the better it'll go for you. Do you know where you father is now?"

"He could still be at Tularosa. He's not thinking straight at all, so he could do almost anything—plus those thugs he has working for him will do whatever he says. If he's left, the only place he could go would be Mexico."

"When did you last talk to you father?"

"When I left after he hit me. I've been hiding, trying to figure what to do. I haven't talked to anyone."

"Do you know where Nelson is?"

"More than likely still in Ruidoso. I doubt he even knows that I've disappeared, so he's probably still waiting before he runs."

Ray stood and turned off the recorder. He looked at her. How could someone who had everything lose it all so fast? He knew he shouldn't, but he felt sorry for her.

"I work for the governor—maybe he can help you. I'll tell him your story. Good luck Isabella."

22

Home Sweet Home

Ray got into his Jeep and started home feeling terribly sad. There was something so upsetting about Isabella's story—it made him want to be in Sue's arms.

Officer Clarke had made a copy of the tape and he gave one to Ray before he left, saying that he'd call the DA's office and let them know that trafficking charges should be filed. While most of the dealing had been done in Lincoln County, the confession included references to crimes in Bernalillo County, so the Albuquerque prosecutors could file charges to make sure she continued to be held in custody. Ray had told the officer that he was worried about her safety if she was released, and that she should be placed on suicide watch.

Ray also asked the officer to contact the sheriff's office in Lincoln County and ask them to arrest and hold Police Chief Nelson on charges of drug trafficking and on suspicion of murder.

The drive home went by quickly, and by dusk he was pulling into the cabin driveway. He parked and walked to the door. There was no greeting, from human or dog, but then Ray realized he hadn't called anyone to let them know he was headed back. He went inside and turned on the light.

There was a note.

Tyee told me you had to go to Albuquerque. I'm sorry. I hope you get to come home tonight. Happy's with Tyee. I went out to have a cup of coffee with Nancy. I may have started something—she seems real taken with Tyee. Anyway, I should be home by seven. Love, Sue.

Ray walked down to Tyee's and went into the office. Happy was in the corner, sound asleep. He quickly responded when he saw Ray and gave his usual joyful greeting. Good ol' dogs.

"Hey, what happened?" Ray hadn't seen Tyee sitting behind his computer. Ray gave him a shortened version of the story.

"What a tragedy."

"I know—it's very depressing. But it's beginning to all point to Nelson. Funny, I remember telling you that he was too lazy to be involved, and now it looks like he may be the key to everything." He shook his head. "Think me and my pooch will call it a night. See ya tomorrow."

Ray and Happy went up to the cabin. Ray felt nervous and unhappy and decided to have a scotch and water—unusual for him. He'd just fixed his drink and was sitting at the kitchen table when Sue walked in. He was happy—even a little relieved—to see her, and they hugged while Ray told her Isabella's story. Sue cried, and it surprised him. He fixed her a drink and they sat and thought about all the complexities life throws at us.

"I'm not sure, but there's some chance that Nancy's in love with Tyee."

"What does Tyee say?"

"Nothing to me or Nancy. That's why she called me—she wants more help. I know you told me not to get involved, but I just wanted Tyee to have a date—I had no idea that she'd fall in love."

"Well, the election for mayor is next week so let's do a watch party. You can invite whoever you want. We can do it in the large space in the outbuilding. It'll be less formal and they can get a chance to meet again."

"Well my, my—aren't you romantic."

"Actually, I am." He took her hand and they left Happy to sleep alone—which was fine with him.

Ray decided to go down and see how Big Jack was doing, just two days away from Election Day. It had been a while since he'd been in the store, but ever since Chester had arrived the whole experience had changed. One of the unique things about Big Jack's store had been the smell—some people thought it was offensive, but Big Jack said it was authentic. Somehow Chester had eliminated it. He'd been interrogated about the source of the smell, but so far had refused to say what it had come from. Many people thought it was best simply not to know.

The store was an eclectic collection of the old and the modern. The old was Big Jack, while Chester had brought in modern shelving and displays. The result seemed like a study in indecision—who was in charge here? Ray wasn't sure. Big Jack owned the store, but in many ways it was now more Chester's store—although Big Jack had declared the dock areas off limits to Chester's modern ways. Ray found Big Jack in his usual spot, drinking a beer and smoking a grotesque-smelling cigar.

"I'm surprised Chester lets you smoke that thing so close to the store."

"Fuck Chester. You know he's a skinny little shit—anytime I want I could pound him into the ground."

"Well, we have a short fuse today."

"Fuck, Fuck. I have no fuse at all. I don't know Ray. It's like I'm all wound up and ready to pop. I have the election. I have Chester, who wants to do some kind of business school analysis of the bait shop. What the fuck is that? It's a fuckin' bait shop. And then there's Beverly—which is your goddamn fault."

Ray was rethinking his decision to drop in for a friendly visit.

"Jack, I'm not sure anything about Beverly is my fault. If it is, I guess I'm willing to apologize, but to tell you the truth I'm not real sure what you're talking about."

"Well, okay, not your fault. It's your wife's fault—same difference."

"What's the problem with Beverly?"

"She wants to open a restaurant in the fucking bait shop. Can you believe that? A fucking restaurant."

"Okay, Jack. I'm trying to understand. What's the problem with her opening a restaurant in the bait shop?" Ray could think of several potential problems, but wanted to hear what specifically was bothering Jack.

"It would just change everything. Guys come in here to talk fishing, and sports, and to talk about women. How the hell can that go on with a woman in the store fixing tea and shit?"

"She wants to open a tea shop?"

"Fuck no. She wants to sell tacos. And don't get me wrong, those are some of the best damn tacos I've ever eaten, but it's just not right."

Ray figured he understood. Big Jack was protecting his turf. First it had been Chester, with all of his improvements, and now Beverly wants to invade his space. The bait shop had never been about making money, it was about a certain attitude. Big Jack had the attitude, most of his regular fishing customers had the attitude—Chester didn't, and obviously a woman wouldn't. Big Jack was probably still pissed that Chester had managed to get rid of the offensive smell—now they'd have to meet health department standards. It was more than the man could take.

"Beverly's a lot of fun and I'm enjoying being with her. But opening a restaurant? I don't know—it just seems too permanent."

"Have you talked to Beverly about this?"

"Not yet. That's why I'm so tense. Fuck. I guess I'll have to talk to her, but I really don't want to. Maybe Sue could talk to her?"

"I'd imagine Sue would say you need to handle your own problems with Beverly. Maybe you should rethink this problem with the restaurant. I sure understand it would change the atmosphere you've nurtured for the store, but things are changing. You're going to be mayor—that means you won't be here as much. You have responsibilities with the PI business. Maybe having Beverly around the store to help Chester when you're not here isn't a bad idea. And you say it's permanent—it probably isn't, but if it is, is that so bad? This isn't a marriage, Jack, it's a business deal. You write up a lease where you share a percentage of the restaurant's sales, and if Beverly makes a go of it maybe you'll make some money."

Big Jack's frown indicated deep thought. Ray wasn't sure about a restaurant in the store, mostly because of the location. The bait shop had customers but most of that business was early-morning fishermen, who weren't likely to be taco customers even if you were open early. There were a lot of people living around the lake, but it was still a good trip for most of them to get to the bait shop. Ray had the feeling this would be a very temporary project that Beverly would soon tire of.

"Well hell, Ray, guess I won't fight it. Just keep the costs down and see what happens—no reason to start a fuckin' war if it's not going to work out anyway."

"I think that's a wise decision. Now how about some coffee?"

Ray sat on the dock with Big Jack and went over the status of the Ruidoso matter. Jack felt bad for Isabella, as Ray and Sue had, and was surprised that the do-nothing police chief might turn out to have been the trigger for all of this grief. The conversation quickly turned to the election and what Big Jack thought would happen.

"Hard to tell about the election. You know, when we helped the sheriff get elected it was county-wide, and he carried most of the districts outside of the city limits—but this election is just the T or C district. I know I have the support of all the lake people, but they can't vote. My guess right now is that it'll be very close. Mayor Martinez still has his followers, as well as people who owe him something, or who are just afraid of what I might do—so he'll get votes. Some people will vote for me because they hate Martinez, but there are people who'll vote for him because they think I'm an outsider who could screw up their town. So I see it being very even, with only a few votes deciding the outcome."

"Yeah, I agree, it'll be close. People at the café have told Sue that the Mayor is telling all the city employees that if you're elected you'll fire them all and give their jobs to people you'll bring in from LA."

"Not a bad idea."

"What *will* you do if you're elected?"

"You know I've thought about that. Almost every city employee is some kind of Martinez crony. I wouldn't fire them, but I'd gradually put standards in place for each job and some kind of testing procedure to ensure that the most qualified person gets the position, whether they had a connection with someone or not. So the first move would be better hiring practices. Second, I'd look at annexing more land around the lake. Martinez did some of that, but he did it for the wrong reasons—this lake people verses city people thing needs to stop. Third, I would look at increasing tourism. I know every politician in the world says something like that, but it's still a good idea. I was wondering if maybe there was some way the city could invest some money in the Hot Springs Inn. I know there'd be legal issues, but the city needs a focus—maybe revitalizing a landmark would be just the thing. Anyway, I'd try and be active and positive for all of the people of the town."

Ray stood up and began clapping. "Three cheers for the mayor!"

Big Jack stood and took a bow.

23

Confession Two

Ray hung up the phone, walked over to Tyee's desk, and took a seat.

"That was Sheriff James. They tried to execute the warrant for Police Chief Nelson, but he'd already skipped town. Said it looked like he left in a hurry and wasn't coming back. The sheriff has put out alerts to all the sheriff departments in New Mexico and some in Texas, and he's notified the police departments in Albuquerque and El Paso. They searched the police office and found a .30-30 rifle. They'll be sending it to the lab to compare it with the casings that were found. They're filing murder charges against Nelson."

"Think Nelson killed Marino?"

"I do. The first day I talked to him it was obvious he hated Marino. He should have been the number one suspect from the beginning, but it just seemed out of character for him to shoot Marino with a little .22 pistol. Anyway, they'll find him soon—can't see Nelson blending into the background. Sheriff also said that they went to Tularosa with a small army to arrest Ortega, but he'd also left. There was a gardener still there working—said even though everyone had left he felt responsible for the plants. He said they were all fired a couple of days ago. Looked like everything valuable had been removed from the house. The sheriff said he was sure Ortega must have headed to Mexico, so he's notified the border patrol and El Paso officials that Ortega's wanted for questioning in a murder."

"Bet he's never heard from again. He's not Nelson—he'll disappear into Mexico."

"Yeah, I think you're right."

"What's on our horizon? Any other cases pending?"

"Well, it just so happens that I had a call from the governor's office. His chief of staff wants us to do a research project into the San Juan County Sheriff's Office. They're concerned about purchasing patterns involving old military equipment. The governor thinks the sheriff has started his own white supremacist militia and wants to know if we can analyze the data and prove that they've transferred weapons and other hardware out of the department. They've given me access codes to various state databases."

"Does that mean a visit to Farmington in our future?"

"I hope not."

"We could visit my Navajo brother warriors. The Navajo and Apache wars are part of our common history fighting the evil white man."

"You're starting to make me nervous."

"Good."

Tyee concentrated on the San Juan computer project, while Ray worked on enjoying changes in his current daily schedule. Ray had thought about having a conversation with Tyee about Nancy, but decided that he'd already butted in as much as he was comfortable with and would let Sue go ahead as the sole matchmaker in the family.

"Ray, got a phone call for you from the El Paso Police Department."

"Ray Pacheco."

"Mr. Pacheco, this is Sergeant Vargus with the El Paso PD. Sheriff James from Ruidoso asked me to contact you. Larry Nelson, the police chief from Ruidoso, was captured this morning. There was a standoff at a motel in downtown El Paso. He was trying to get out the back and fell from a first story window. He hit his head on the concrete and also broke a leg. The biggest thing, though, is that he had a heart attack. He's in the University Medical Center, in intensive care. If you want to see him, you better get here quick."

So much for the slower pace he expected. Ray got details regarding the location of the hospital and how to contact Vargus.

"How about a trip to El Paso?"

Ray and Tyee headed out immediately, and the trip took about two hours. All the way, Ray was hoping that Nelson wouldn't die before they got there. It seemed like a harsh thing to wish for, but he wanted to wrap up the open questions about the events in Ruidoso. He didn't hate Larry Nelson, but it was nonetheless his actions that had led to five people dying— maybe he didn't do it personally, but the things he'd set in motion had made it happen, so the responsibility was his.

The hospital complex was a large, sprawling group of buildings. They left the Jeep in the parking garage and went inside. Ray asked for directions to the IC unit, and they were directed into a maze of hallways that eventually led to the IC area. Finding their way back to where they'd started without help would be impossible.

Ray introduced himself to the guard on duty, who said that he'd been cleared by Sergeant Vargus. They entered the IC unit, where a nurse stopped them and asked them their business. Ray told her he was there on behalf of the state of New Mexico, where the patient had committed several crimes, and he wanted to ask him some questions. The nurse wasn't pleased and left in a huff to find someone with more authority who could kick them out.

Larry Nelson looked bad—he appeared to be dying before their very eyes. Ray's approach softened.

"Larry, can you hear me?"

Nelson didn't move and Ray wondered if maybe they were too late.

"Well, if it's not the asshole Pacheco and his Indian fighter."

Larry Nelson—still alive, still annoying.

"Larry, you know you're in IC and in bad shape. You broke some things when you fell and you also had a heart attack."

"Yeah. Old fuckers like me shouldn't be on the run—we aren't very good at it."

He seemed to be responding to the stimulus of having someone to talk to.

"Can you tell me what happened in Ruidoso? Did you kill Marino?"

"Ray, you don't have to shout, my hearing is okay. Yeah, I'll help you clean up the mess I made. You know Ray, I'm no fuckin' saint, but I didn't mean for anything to become deadly.

I just wanted to make some money so I could retire. It was going to be so simple. I knew about Ortega and his drug connections from my time in Houston. When I found out he was living down in Tularosa, I thought it'd be simple to just ask him to sell me drugs—well, that was a stupid idea. I thought the old fart was going to have me killed that very day. So I just forgot about it—I had no idea how I could get drugs from Mexico unless Ortega arranged it, so the deal was over. Then one day that beautiful daughter of his, Isabella, came to see me. She said she could supply the drugs."

"Then you recruited Sheriff Rodriguez, Tito, and Marino?"

"Well, sort of. I definitely got Rodriguez involved. He and I used to drink together. He was involved even back when I went to see the old man. Rodriguez was the one who brought in Tito. Marino was just a coincidence. I saw him on the street in Ruidoso. I knew him from Houston—a thug of the worst kind, mean and violent—but when I saw him, I thought he might be useful in controlling Rodriguez and anyone else who got in the way. I thought I'd be able to keep a tight rein on Marino—man, was I ever wrong. The guy just went nuts with power. Then, when Rodriguez bailed out, Marino completely lost it. I was going to kill him—had to, there was no choice. But I wasn't the one who did it—somebody shot the bastard before I could."

"You didn't kill Marino?"

"That's right. I wanted to kill him, maybe the only person I really wanted to kill—he was so fucking evil. But I didn't. Someone else got to him first."

"Do you know who?"

"Nope. The list of suspects has to be long, but I have no idea who actually did it."

"Did you kill Lewis Esparza?"

"Yes. I knew things were coming to the end. Esparza told me he was done with the drugs and he was going to tell Franklin what was going on. He said he wasn't afraid of Ortega any more. My guess is that Isabella got Esparza involved, but she implied it was her father who was in charge. I couldn't let Esparza implicate me. I'd gone to the racetrack to kill him when I saw him arguing with Franklin. At that point I'd decided I was going to kill both of them. I climbed up the grandstands with the rifle, but at that moment you showed up and Esparza went into the stable. I was debating what do to when he drove out of the barn and headed toward your Indian buddy. On impulse I shot him—then I took off. I knew it was all over and I just wanted to clean up what I could, get out of town and hide somewhere."

"What about Tito. Did you try to kill him?"

"Yes. The bastard called me and said he was going to make a deal with you. He said he wouldn't implicate me, yet, if I'd pay him some ridiculous amount of money. He said he could survive a few years in jail for selling drugs, but that I'd die in jail. I either pay him big bucks or he names me as the leader. I figured he was hiding at his old cabin so I went up there and waited. Shot him, but I could tell he was still alive—and then this old woman shows up screaming her fool head off. I got out of there."

"Do you know anything about the Rodriguez murder or Franklin's suicide?"

"I had nothing to do with any of that. My guess is that Ortega had Rodriguez killed. Rodriguez told me he was going to El Paso and was going to use Ortega's name to find a new source that he'd use to sell drugs in Denver. Rodriguez was so stupid, he thought he could just go shopping for a drug dealer. I told him that was the dumbest thing he had ever thought of and that it'd get him killed. Regarding Franklin, I can't imagine why he would kill himself. He had nothing to do with the drugs going through the racetrack—that was all his wife, and she had said to me that he didn't know about it. My guess is it was Ortega again. I'm not sure why he'd do it, but Ortega has a history of killing people when they get in the way."

"Marino talked to Tony Garcia, the AG, and told him that he had proof that Tony's wife was involved in the murder of her fiancé in Houston. He also said that you'd back him up. Did you know about any of that?"

"Jeez, Marino was some kind of crazy. I knew nothing about any of that—he was just flat out lying. Of course you already know that I knew about Tony and how he screwed up his career in Houston because he fell in love, but I never talked to Marino about any of that."

"Do you think Marino would have any way of knowing about the murder that happened in Houston?"

"Who the hell knows? He was a complete lowlife, so whenever anything bad happened it was always possible he was involved. Where that guy was supposedly killed—or died or whatever—was the area of town where Marino hung out, but I don't know anything about Marino that ties him to that crime. If I had, I'd have had him picked up—the mayor and everybody downtown was driving us nuts trying to find someone to pin that on. I'd have tossed them Marino in a New York second."

"Sheriff James found the .30-30 rifle and they'll match the bullets and casing. You've been charged with the murder of Esparza, the stable manager, and the attempted murder of Tito. If you live Larry, you'll be extradited back to New Mexico to stand trial."

"Ray, I think I'll die in El Paso and save fuckin' New Mexico the trouble. I'm tired now, so why don't you and your Indian pal get the fuck out of my room." Nelson looked even worse than when they'd arrived, if that was possible. The conversation had taken a toll and he was obviously in pain.

About that time the nurse came in with a doctor in tow. The doctor directed Ray and Tyee to leave immediately and they complied. After asking for assistance—twice—they managed to make it back to the parking garage.

Without hesitation, they headed home. The only stop, besides for gas, was in Las Cruces, where Ray insisted that they stop at a Whataburger for a green chili cheeseburger and fries. Tyee didn't object—he had soft serve ice cream, his favorite.

The next day Ray put together a report to the governor outlining what they'd learned from Nelson and Isabella Ortega. He faxed it to the governor's private fax line, then called Sheriff James and filled him in on what had happened.

"Ray, we were notified this morning that Nelson died during the night."

Ray decided it was time for a walk with his dog. Seemed like he was spending a lot of time thinking about life and death lately. Maybe it was an age thing. After his first wife died, Ray didn't worry about death—in a way, he'd felt ready for it. There hadn't been much to look forward to except for getting older. But since his marriage to Sue life had become more valuable than ever—and it was slipping away.

That night Ray held Sue and told her he loved her. She started to cry. Ray wasn't sure why, but he didn't mind.

24

Tacos

Beverly's Taco Stand had become the talk of the community. At lunch time there were lines circling the building, with people driving in from T or C in groups. One man ordered fifty tacos, saying that he'd established a delivery service.

Big Jack wasn't sure if he was happy with the success or irritated by it, but Beverly was ecstatic, blossoming before their eyes. Despite working with delicious food every day, she was losing weight. She smiled more and laughed a lot. She was experiencing something she'd never had before, success—and in a small town sort of way, fame.

After high school Beverly had gone to culinary school in Boulder, Colorado. She was an excellent student, but had never pursued a career because of her depression. Instead, she married Chuck and had children, but she'd been miserable as a mother and housewife. She ate compulsively and gained a lot of weight. She knew she was driving Chuck away, but she didn't care—she was too absorbed in self-pity. Now she felt alive. She wanted to sing and dance and tell everyone how happy she was—it was getting a little annoying.

Chuck and Beverly had signed the final divorce papers, and while there was some lingering sadness it seemed that they both felt good about their break-up. Chuck reported that the children were doing well, and made sure that Beverly knew she could visit whenever she wished. He was definitely too good for the old Beverly.

"Hey cheer up Big Jack. Remember, you're getting a share of the sales as rent."

Big Jack didn't look cheered up. He grabbed a beer and headed out to the dock. Even self-absorbed Beverly knew that something was wrong. She followed him.

"What's the matter Jack? Did I do something wrong?"

"It's not you, it's me. Tomorrow's the election—I actually may become mayor. But I'm not sure I *want* to be mayor. Your success is wonderful, but it's changing everything. Chester changes shit like that's his fuckin' goal—just to change shit. Everything is changing. I don't know that I want it to change."

"Jack, in a very short period of time you've given me the confidence to try to make myself better, to try to please you if I can. If you don't want change, then I don't want change. We'll put everything back the way it was, okay? Well maybe not that infamous *smell* I've heard about."

Big Jack laughed. Not one of his infamous falling-over-on-your-back sort of laughs, but a genuine, good laugh.

"I think I'm scared."

"Yep, me too. You and I can be something, or we can just be friends—I just want to be with you. You don't have to make any commitment to me. And whenever you want me gone, just say so and I'll leave. I know I dropped in out of nowhere and have taken up a lot of space in your world, and you've been generous and kind. I owe you a lot."

Nancy had started working for Beverly in the taco stand. It was only open during lunch, and her parents' cabin was just a short distance away, so it was much more convenient than working at the café. And of course, it gave Nancy more opportunity to see Tyee, although as best she could tell he wasn't very interested. Sue had said he was still upset about his failed marriage.

Nancy had always been described as cute, and she hated it. When people said *cute* she always heard *plain*. She'd tried to make herself more attractive, but it was a lot of effort and usually just attracted the wrong kind of men. She was a serious person who took everything too seriously. Her parents had been telling her to lighten up since she was about ten. They were ex-hippies who seemed never to have taken anything seriously, except maybe their child. At times, as she was growing up, she'd felt like she was the only grown-up in the house.

The move to the cabin on the lake was perfect for her parents. This was the lifestyle they'd always wanted. But it wasn't so perfect for Nancy. She didn't mind the location, but the isolation sometimes made her feel like she was being punished for something. She wasn't very outgoing, but she enjoyed being around people, and the more the merrier. Going for days at a time seeing just her mom and dad was wearing thin very quickly. At the same time, she was nervous about trying to make friends since she'd screwed things up so badly in the past. Sue was wonderful, and she immediately trusted her, so she'd made the attempt with Tyee, and wouldn't you know it she was genuinely attracted to him, but he seemed uninterested. More of life's mysterious ways.

The election watch party was the following day at Sue's, and Nancy was going to make an impression on Tyee one way or another.

"How many tacos did you say?"

"One hundred."

Nancy stared at the guy. Then she recovered and began looking around for Beverly—she was going to need some help.

Sue and Ray had spent the morning together. She was getting worried about him—he was starting to act like a puppy, always right there following her around. She knew he was feeling the pressures of all of his responsibilities, and he was becoming increasing conscious of his age as well. She thought it was nonsense to worry about it, but couldn't say that to him. Maybe they needed a vacation.

"Ray, how about we do a little traveling?"

"Traveling where?"

"How about Paris?"

"France?"

"Yeah."

"I don't want to go to France."

"How about San Francisco?"

"Maybe."

Sue made up her mind—they'd take a vacation to San Francisco the following month. She needed to get Ray out of his funk. No Happy, no Tyee, no Big Jack—just the two of them for a week. Done, plans made. She'd tell Ray later, after she'd bought the tickets.

✺

"Tyee, did you know that Nancy works at Beverly's Taco Stand now?"

"No."

"What the hell's wrong with you, Tyee? You know she likes you, but you act like it's some damn big burden to be nice to an attractive girl. So tell me what the hell's wrong with you?" Sue had lost her patience with the big, dumb Indian act.

"Sue, I know you mean well. But I'm not interested in a relationship right now."

"Well then when? Five fucking years from now? Maybe ten? Are you just through with life? You just going to hang out with your computers? What's wrong with you?" Oops. Sue had a history of losing her cool, and now she had done it with her good friend Tyee—who definitely didn't deserve it.

"Sue, sit down. I don't know what's wrong with me. You being angry at me isn't helping."

Sue couldn't have felt worse. In a bid for the Illogic Hall of Fame, Sue began to cry.

"Okay. Please stop. I'll go see her, okay?"

"I'm sorry Tyee. I care a lot and just want you to be happy."

"Okay, mom. I said I'd go see her." They both laughed.

25

Election Day

Today the good people of T or C, New Mexico would decide who should be their mayor. The results would be close. Most people had made up their minds weeks before, and the town seemed evenly split.

The current mayor, Martinez, had been in office for a long time. He had lots of friends due to his practice of only hiring people to work for the city who promised to be his friend, and he had lots of enemies—mostly because he was an arrogant, overbearing, crooked politician.

Big Jack was running as the anti-Martinez candidate. He and Martinez had developed an intense dislike for one another, so the campaign had often been nasty. Big Jack was okay with winning or losing—mostly he was more than ready for the campaign to be over. The bickering and accusations had become absurd and childish.

Big Jack closed the bait shop at four o'clock and headed to the *Pacheco & Chino* office, in the outbuildings on Ray and Sue's property next to their cabin, for the watch party. They were expecting maybe a hundred people to pass through at various times during the evening. He'd heard that one of the El Paso TV stations and one from Albuquerque were sending crews to monitor the results and report them live from city hall. This was unusual for T or C, and most people suspected it was because of the nastiness of the race. Whatever the reason, it meant that they should know the results by around ten that night.

Beverly had gone to the watch party early to prepare the food and stock the bar. She would serve various finger foods—mostly using the same ingredients as her tacos—and Chester and Tyee were helping out, bringing in wine, beer, and ice. Serving a hundred people took more food and drink than most people realized, and the biggest problem was keeping the various items either hot or cold over an extended period of time. Beverly was nervous about Big Jack. She wanted him to win, but she wasn't sure what that might do to their schedule. She enjoyed being around him and didn't want him sitting in the mayor's office in town. On the other hand, hoping he would lose was just not right.

Sue and Ray were busy, too. Their biggest challenge was finding room for the guests to park their vehicles. They had cordoned off a nearby street that was very rarely used and planned to have people park their cars there. They also had some fairly flat land about half a mile away where people could leave their cars, and they would run a shuttle service from there to the party using Ray's old Jeep. They were busy putting up signs in various locations, directing people to these options.

"Hey Ray. There is a call for you in the office."

Ray waved to Tyee to let him know that he heard. He went up to the office and picked up the phone.

"Ray Pacheco."

"Hello Ray, this is Tony Garcia."

"Well my goodness, Tony. Good to hear from you. Are you in the neighborhood or something?"

"No, I'm in Boston. Look, I have some things we need to talk about and I have something I need to give you, can you come to Boston?"

"Talk about? Give me something? What's this about Tony?"

"I'd really prefer to talk to you in person."

"Can't you come here, or I could meet you in Albuquerque."

"Maybe I'm being paranoid, but I don't want to be in New Mexico."

"What's this about?" Ray's tone took on an edge.

"It's about the things that went on in Ruidoso. I know what happened with Nelson and Franklin. But there's something you need to know and I won't discuss it on the phone or leave Boston. So if you want to know, you'll need to come here."

Ray paused. His gut was telling him that he needed to find out what Tony knew—and he needed to do it now. He made a decision.

"Give me your number. I'll call and book a flight. Once I have the details, I'll call you. I'll try to be there tomorrow. I hope you know what you're doing, Tony." Ray got his number and hung up.

Ray went and found Sue. "We need to talk a minute." He told her what had happened. Sue knew how to book a flight—he didn't. He asked her if she wanted to go with him.

"Ray, you go find out what this is about and come back home. I'll call right now and try to get you out early in the morning and—depending on schedules—back tomorrow evening. If I can't, then I'll book you a hotel and get you back the next morning." She left to take care of the arrangements. Ray felt nervous.

As Ray went back into the main room, he noticed that there a small band was busy setting up in one corner. He hoped they wouldn't be playing loud rock and roll, but based on the ages and appearances of the band members it probably was. He headed to the opposite corner and took a seat. He was sitting there when Sue came back.

"Connections aren't good. I got you out early in the morning from Albuquerque on TWA, but there'll be a stop in Dallas and you'll get in Boston late afternoon—so most of the day will be flying or waiting, sorry. So, no question you'll be spending one night. I booked a room downtown at the Hilton—not cheap. Coming back isn't any better. You'll leave a little after noon and get back to Albuquerque around nine. It'll be eleven or later by the time you drive home—one long day. You sure you want to do this?"

"No, I don't want to. And I'm not sure I can bill the Governor for this, either. Asshole Johnson probably won't pay until he knows what Tony wants first. Sue, I'm on edge and need a break."

"I agree. Screw it Ray, I'm coming with you—and damn right we're billing the fucking Governor—it's his case."

That got Ray's attention. "You sure you want to leave at some god-awful hour in the morning just to sit in an airport or on a plane all day? I appreciate the thought, Sue, and I love you very much, but no, you don't have to go and watch me. I'll be fine. If I'm too tired when I get back, I'll get a room in

Albuquerque and drive home the next morning. Still it's nice to have a mother hen." He gave her a hug.

By about four o'clock most everything was in place to accommodate the expected crowd. Within a matter of minutes the place was full—and it began to look like they'd underestimated the size of the crowd. Beverly was scrambling for more beer and food. The band, per a request from Sue, was playing at a softer tone than the way they'd begun, with much less screaming—even so, most people stayed on the other side of the room.

Nancy came in looking absolutely stunning. She saw Sue and waved.

"Nancy, you're gorgeous. That's such a wonderful dress. I'm so glad you came—come on over here and get some food and a beer. Or do you prefer wine?"

"A glass of white wine would be perfect." As if by magic, Tyee handed Nancy a glass of white wine.

"Hello. How did you know I'd want white?"

"Sue told me."

"I did not." Sue poked Tyee in the arm and went off in search of Ray.

"Actually I had a glass of red and a glass of white—and if you'd said beer, I had one parked on that table next to you."

"Think Big Jack is going to win tonight?"

"Not sure anyone knows that yet. I know Martinez is a creep, though, so I hope Big Jack wins—although Big Jack has one or two faults of his own."

"Do you have faults Tyee?"

"None."

"Well, it looks like false modestly isn't one of your faults."

"Nancy, don't think I'm being too forward, but you looked particularly attractive this evening."

"Well okay, that's a little bold, but I accept your compliment. Why don't we sit down?"

Sue walked by and smiled at them, then continued on to deliver more beer to Beverly.

"You know Sue is trying to fix us up."

"Yep. She seems to have a need to fix everyone. Ray and Sue are special people. It wasn't that long ago that I was a complete drunk. I was a part-time fishing guide living in a tent. Now I'm Ray's and Big Jack's partner and I only occasionally drink too much."

"Why were you so low?"

"I thought I'd failed at life. Apaches are taught to be tough and I felt weak. I just didn't want to face my failures."

"What happened to drive you to that point?"

"I bet Sue's told you that I was married once, right?"

"Yep."

"Well it failed. She was a wonderful person who fell in love with someone else. I hadn't had many relationships and she was the world to me—when she left, something happened inside me. I thought I wanted to be dead. I just didn't know how to deal with it. I couldn't go home, because the way people there saw it I'd abandoned my people to be with the white people. So I went into hiding as a drunken Indian fishing guide."

"I've had two relationships with men. They both ended because the men said I had a screw loose and didn't know how to enjoy life. I moved here with my parents to hide. I thought I was just one of those women who couldn't be with a man, until I saw you. I'm not any different from before, but I wanted to be with you." Nancy blushed. She had never talked like this, much less to someone she hardly knew.

"Nancy, if I asked the weird band to play a slow song, would you dance with me?"

"Yes."

The music wasn't very good, but Tyee and Nancy didn't care.

"Ray, look at Tyee. Does he have a different expression on his face?"

"I think he does. I have to admit that Nancy cleaned up pretty good." He got a slug to the shoulder for that.

"Ladies and Gentlemen, we have some numbers from city hall. They have counted 60% of the ballots and it stands Martinez fifty-two percent and Big Jack forty-eight percent." A spattering of boos greeted the news, then people went back to drinking and eating.

"You know, it's funny Sue. I haven't thought much about Big Jack losing. I guess I just assumed he'd win."

"Well, it's not over yet. Hold your horses—our guy is going to win." Ray stepped back a bit, thinking he might get another shoulder pop.

There had to be a hundred and fifty people at the party by this time, which meant there must be a real mess outside as far as the parking went. Ray decided that it wasn't his concern at that moment, so he didn't bother looking.

Big Jack got up in front of the crowd and quieted everyone down, including the band.

"Before we get anymore results, I want to say a few things. You all know that I arrived here under some strange circumstances and was mostly just running the shop for a few years. But recently, mostly because of Ray Pacheco, I've become a part of this community. I probably would have said that I didn't want to be a part of anything, much less a community, but I was wrong. The support you've given me over the last few months, despite my being an outsider, has been wonderful. I may have to rethink my whole attitude about people. But let me tell you, win or lose the election tonight, I've already won. So I want you to have a good time and no matter what happens, we have all won something. Thanks."

There was a standing ovation and some cheering. Ray wasn't sure what was happening to the people around him, but it seemed like they were becoming better, more complete humans. And he realized that he was doing the same, even at his age—he was growing. He'd read about old people losing control of their emotions, and now he fought back tears, but he felt a huge warmth for his new friends.

The band started again, playing whatever kind of music it was that they played, driving everyone to move back to the far side of the room.

Some guy went to the front of the room and called for quiet.

"Got more results. Ninety-four percent of the votes have been counted. Martinez fifty percent, Big Jack fifty percent." Everyone cheered.

A tie would be something else. Maybe Martinez and Big Jack could have a duel on Main Street at noon—that'd get TV coverage. Ray decided he needed a beer.

The evening began to drag on. If they'd counted ninety-four percent of the votes an hour before, why was it taking so long? Some people were leaving—most had work or school in the morning.

Finally, the guy came back in with his paper. He held up his hands for quiet.

"We have a winner. With fifty-one percent of the vote, our new mayor: Big Jack Parker!" Everyone began clapping and screaming. The band started making noise. Where was Big Jack? After a slightly frantic search, they found Big Jack asleep in one of the spare bedrooms and dragged him back.

"Well as you can see, I'm tired. Thank you all very much. I'll try to make you proud to have voted for me—but right now I need to go home and go to sleep. Good night."

Big Jack had won.

26

Father and Son Talk

Ray got up more or less in the middle of the night to get packed and have time to drive to the Albuquerque airport.

"Ray Pacheco, you be careful. If you get tired, you stop somewhere and rest. And call me when you can and tell me what Tony has to say." Sue was awake, but just barely. They had postponed most of the clean-up from the night before until today—and there was going to be a lot of it.

"Don't worry about me, Sue. As soon as I know what the hell this is all about I'll call you. You be careful too, and don't work too hard putting things back together." They kissed and hugged. Ray gave Happy a good ear rub, then headed out to the Jeep. Man it was dark.

There was a little fog on the way, so it took him a bit longer than expected to get to I-25. Once on the interstate, though, he made good time—there were almost no other cars. One of the unforeseen advantages of his old Jeep was it had such a rough ride no one could possibly fall asleep behind the wheel—unless they were dead.

The airport was on the south side of town, which helped. Ray decided to use the short term parking—he was sure that he'd be in no mood when he got back to look far and wide for his car. He checked in with TWA and waited. There were few people in the airport that early in the morning, and it had an abandoned feel. Ray had only brought a carry-on bag, so he was ready to go. The wait wasn't long, and soon he heard his boarding call. This early flight originated in Albuquerque, so he figured it probably wouldn't be full—that proved to be an understatement. The plane could probably hold over a hundred people at capacity, but it looked like only about twenty had boarded. Ray sat back and tried to relax. He wasn't an avid flyer, and although he didn't mind it, he still felt a certain tension as they prepared for takeoff. The miracle of flight, especially in something weighing so many tons, was still something of a mystery to him.

Once in the air, Ray relaxed. He leaned back, then surprised himself by dozing. The early hour had several advantages—one was that it was easy to go back to sleep. As the plane was descending, he woke and found to his surprise that he'd slept the whole way to Dallas. He deplaned with the other passengers and found the gate for his next flight—which wasn't for a couple of hours. He located some coffee and began his wait.

Ray had debated with himself about calling his son. Michael was an attorney in Boston, and their relationship since Ray's wife died hadn't been good. His son became angry when Ray told him he was remarrying, and they hadn't spoken since. On impulse, Ray decided to call.

"Hello, I'd like to speak to Michael Pacheco, please."

"Just a moment."

"Pacheco."

"Michael, it's your dad. How are you?"

"Something wrong Dad?"

"No. Nothing wrong. At the last minute I needed to come to Boston to meet someone. I'm going to be in Boston later today, towards evening. I was wondering if maybe we could get together for a drink or something."

"Well, I don't know. Where are you staying?"

"The Hilton downtown."

"That's actually very convenient to my office. Who are you meeting?"

"Well, you know this stuff is sort of like your legal stuff Michael, so best if we don't talk about it."

"Sure, that's fine. I was just wondering if your meeting place was around here that was all."

"Yeah, sure. The guy I'm meeting works for a law firm downtown, Taylor, Jefferson and Clinton—mean anything to you?"

"Dad, that's where I work."

"I didn't recognize the name. My goodness I'm getting terrible at remembering stuff."

"It's not you, Dad. I changed firms. I probably didn't mention it specifically, but when I gave you that new contact number for me it was because of the new job."

"Interesting coincidence. Well, I should be at the hotel around five. I still have to call my appointment and make sure when we can get together, but I imagine I'll see him tomorrow morning—so if you'd like we could plan on meeting for a drink at five thirty or so—how does that sound?"

"Sure. I'll see you then." His son hung up. For some reason Ray thought it was a little abrupt—but maybe that was his imagination. Then he called Tony.

"Tony, how about we meet for breakfast tomorrow at the Hilton?"

"Sure that'd be perfect."

"Tony, you do know that my son, Michael, works at the same firm as you—I just found this out from him. He said he'd told me he'd changed firms but it didn't stick with me and I didn't make the connection to you."

"Well sure, I knew Michael was your son. I had no idea that you didn't know he worked here. Does that make it a problem to meet with me?"

"Tony, my son and I are not real close. I'm going to have a drink with him tonight—but until I talked to him today, I didn't know he worked at the same place. I don't really see this as a problem and I won't mention your name if you're concerned on your end."

"Your son is a good guy, but yeah, it's probably best to keep our conversation confidential—although he knows that you know me. I mentioned it to him when I found out who he was. What the fuck—you can tell him you're meeting with me, that it has something to do with cleaning up some messes I left and the governor asked you to get involved. Ray, I need to go, so I'll see you tomorrow morning at the Hilton." Tony also abruptly hung up—maybe it was a Boston thing.

Ray heard the call for his flight, so he gathered his stuff and boarded. Unlike the first leg this flight was packed, and he ended up on the aisle. It was going to be a long flight. They quickly got everyone situated and began the taxi to the end of the runway. They were held briefly, but then they were quickly airborne. Ray tried to sleep, but it wasn't going to happen. He shut his eyes and pretended.

After an uncomfortable, bumpy trip they began their descent into Boston. The landing was smooth, and the passengers quickly deplaned. With only a carry-on, Ray headed directly to the hotel shuttle area. Once he was on the Hilton bus he sat back and tried to relax, tired but glad to be on the ground. He'd have time to check in and maybe refresh a bit before meeting Michael. He was a little apprehensive.

The check-in process went without a hitch. Soon he was in his room and washed up, feeling much better than he had. Entering the bar, he didn't immediately see his son, and he decided to take a seat at the bar so he could watch the entrance as he sipped a beer.

"Hey Dad, I was already here. I have a booth over in the corner."

Ray got up and shook Michael's hand. Then, after a brief pause, gave him a hug. Michael didn't respond—they went to the booth.

"Sorry, I didn't see you over in the corner."

"No, I should have spotted you. I think you must have come in while I was in the restroom."

"So, how are you son?"

"I'm fine, just fine. You must be tired after being on a plane almost all day."

"Yeah. Not the best connections out of Albuquerque, especially on a last minute deal."

"Dad, I can guess who you're here to see. I've met Tony Garcia and he said you two were friends from his time as the DA in Dona Ana County—then of course he became the AG of the state. He said you were doing some special work for the governor—sounds like a big deal."

"No, not really. I actually started doing some investigative work for Tony and then lately, have ended up working directly for the governor. And yeah, my meeting tomorrow is with Tony—he said it was fine for me to tell you. There was something of a mess at the end of Tony's time as AG's office and the governor wanted me to talk to Tony about some loose ends."

"Long trip for just a conversation."

"Yeah. A little bit more complicated than I'm making it sound—the governor and Tony are kind of at odds. Anyway, I'll meet with him tomorrow morning and then it's back to Albuquerque."

"How's your wife?" Michael asked it without obvious emotion one way or the other.

"She's good. I know you don't approve and that's fine—but this has been a good thing for me."

They were both quiet. Ray was remembering how close he'd been to his son while Michael had been growing up—and now here he sat, unable to think of anything to say.

They chatted some more about Boston and Michael's job, but didn't return to anything related to Ray's life—especially Sue.

"How about you Michael, any girlfriends in your life?"

"Actually, Dad, there is someone. We've been dating for a few months now and she's become very special to me. If you were staying longer, I'd have liked for you to meet her."

"That's great, son. I know your mother would be very pleased to know you're with someone. She worried about you a lot more than she let on."

"I know. She was a great mom."

"She was a great mom and a great wife. Just because I've remarried doesn't mean I don't still love your mother. She was the best thing that ever happened to me. And I know you won't believe it, but she'd be the first person to be happy about my relationship with Sue."

"Yeah, I know she would be. I just need more time to absorb everything. I'm glad you were able to visit. Listen Dad, in a couple of months I have some vacation time coming and I'd like to bring Terri, that's my girlfriend, out to New Mexico to visit you and Sue and show her where I used to live."

"That'd be just fantastic. You're very welcome to come and stay with us anytime. You're going to be surprised when you see the cabin—it's actually pretty impressive."

Maybe sensing that this was as good as it was going to get, they said their goodbyes and gave each other a hug. Ray knew they had crossed an important line that might let them finally connect again—he hoped so.

Once in his hotel room, the toll of the day hit Ray pretty hard. He called Sue and gave her an update on the meeting with Michael, and she was pleased that it had gone well. He said he'd call her the next day after his meeting with Tony, but now he needed to go to sleep. Which is just what he did.

27

Confession Three

Ray woke up starving. He realized that he hadn't eaten much of anything the day before and had completely skipped dinner. He got dressed and headed down to the dining room. He was going to be early for his meeting, but his primary goal at this point was some kind of breakfast.

Ray was just finishing his breakfast when he saw Tony, who came over and they shook hands and exchanged greetings. Tony just ordered coffee, and Ray was glad he hadn't waited on the guy to have his breakfast.

"Ray, I know the governor is still pissed at me and I guess I really don't trust him. He really is an odd duck, and I was worried that if I came back into New Mexico the old bastard just might have me arrested. I'm sorry to have made you come all of this way, but there's something that I need to share with you. I wanted to do it in person."

"It's fine Tony. I got to see Michael last night for a little while, and that's something that needed to happen to get us talking again—so I should thank you."

"Your son really is a sharp attorney, Ray. He's one of the stars at the firm. Not sure what went wrong with you and him, but it's good that you're trying to fix it. My story involves family, too. As you know, my wife and I have some unusual history back in Houston, and most of her family history isn't exactly normal. Some of what I'm going to tell you, you'll know, other parts you won't—but it's the truth as best I know it."

"I told you before that Marino was blackmailing me to stay out of the affairs in the sheriff's department because he claimed he had information to prove that my wife was involved in her fiancé's murder. And that the Police Chief Nelson, who'd been in the police department in Houston, would back him up. First, my wife had nothing to do with whatever happened to her fiancé. He was a childhood friend of hers and she agreed to the fake engagement so he could get his family off of his back about him getting married. He was gay and he lived in Houston in order to be away from his family in Boston, who didn't know. He was very active sexually and was a heavy drug user—she suspected both cocaine and heroin. He was worth millions, even independent of his parents' money, because of an inheritance from his grandfather. But he was also a good businessman and was making lots of money in Houston."

"Should have just told Marino to fuck off, but I didn't. I was worried about my job and the effect it would have on my wife, so I ignored the fiasco going on in Ruidoso. I even misled the governor, told him it was under control when obviously it wasn't."

"But then something strange happened. My wife's half-sister, Lisa Collins, called and said she was going to be in Santa Fe and wanted to meet Kate. They had talked a little over the years, but they'd never met. Kate lived with her father in Boston after her mother ran off. The mother ended up in Miami and remarried and had another child, but Kate never saw her after she left."

"Kate meets her sister at a restaurant on the Plaza. Her sister tells her she's looking for her ex-husband, who had taken some sentimental items that had been given to her by her grandmother, and she wants Kate to help. She says her ex is working as a sheriff's deputy in Ruidoso. Kate asks her the ex-husband's name, and she tells her it's Martin Marino. Well, you can imagine—Kate almost fainted. How was it possible? The person who is messing with *our* lives is the ex-husband of her half-sister from Miami, whom she'd never met before? Kate told me she felt like there was some big evil cloud that had followed her most of her life—she got upset right there in front of Lisa. Of course Lisa didn't know what was going on."

"So Kate tells Lisa the whole story—about the fiancé, about Marino blackmailing me—everything. Lisa was livid, just uncontrollably angry. They had to leave the restaurant because Lisa was so out of control. They found a bar down the street and continued the conversation. Lisa says she wants to go and see Marino—she says she can stop him from causing all of this harm. She's adamant that she's going to Ruidoso. At first Kate was against the idea and felt it would only lead to more trouble—but she couldn't talk Lisa out of the plan. Kate decided she would support her sister. Maybe she could talk some sense into the ex-husband. At that point, Kate called me and said she and her sister were going to Albuquerque to just look around and do some shopping. She said they might even spend the night. I remember thinking that it was really unlike her, but maybe she just needed some private time with her sister."

"Kate said that they headed out, then stopped in Albuquerque. They were planning on driving to Ruidoso that day, but they stopped so Lisa could call Marino. Kate didn't hear the conversation, but when Lisa got back in the car she told Kate that she'd talked to Marino and he'd agreed to meet with her. He said since it was going to be so late he'd meet her in front of a bar in downtown Ruidoso called Tito's, and they set a time."

"At that point they headed out for Ruidoso. Kate has told me that Lisa didn't say much as they drove—she seemed quiet and calm. Once they reached Ruidoso and drove down Main Street, it was easy to find Tito's Bar. There weren't a lot of people out. The bar seemed to be the only place open. Kate parked down the street some. They sat there for about fifteen minutes before a sheriff's patrol car pulled into the parking spot in front of the bar. Lisa got out and told Kate she'd be back in just a minute. Kate said she was worried that Lisa might get hurt."

"Lisa walked down the street to the patrol car. Kate could see that, as Lisa approached the car, the window rolled down. There was some kind of exchange between Lisa and the person in the car. It looked like Lisa was very angry. Just as Kate was thinking that maybe she should go down there and make sure everything was all right, there were gunshots—not real loud, but no question it was gunshots. Kate could see Lisa standing outside the patrol car holding a small pistol—she got out and ran toward Lisa, who seemed to be in shock. Kate looked into the car and saw that the person in the car had been shot several times, all in the head. She grabbed Lisa and took her back to their car. Lisa was in some kind of trance and hadn't said anything. Kate waited for a minute, expecting that at any moment someone would come out of the bar or something—but nothing happened. She decided to leave. She drove Lisa back to Albuquerque, checked into a motel, and put Lisa to bed."

"Jesus, Tony. You're telling me that Marino's ex-wife shot him and your wife was an accessory."

"Yes, Ray. It's a mess. When Lisa finally snapped out of her daze, she told Kate that when she asked Marino about getting her things he took he just laughed and said he'd thrown away all that junk a long time ago. For some reason having him throw her useless treasures away was more than she could stand, and she killed him in a fit of anger."

"Where did she get the gun? She couldn't have brought it on the plane from Miami, could she?" Ray, always the investigator, was already looking to fill in all the gaps in the story.

"No. When she got to Albuquerque, she went to a gun shop by the airport and bought the gun. There's a waiting period in New Mexico, but she offered the shop owner five hundred dollars and he gave her the gun right there and then. I know this sets it up as a premeditated murder. She can claim she shot him on impulse, but she must have planned on something or why buy the gun? She told Kate she bought the gun to scare Marino—she didn't plan on shooting him."

"Where's Lisa now?"

"She's in Miami. She knows I'm talking to you. She may fight extradition, I don't know. She and Kate have talked some, but her father is advising her. I think he's already hired some top dollar lawyers who'll fight tooth and nail to keep her in Florida."

"What about your wife?"

"She's scared, just like me. I think a case can be made that I committed a crime, too, by moving my wife out of state knowing that she was an accessory to murder. Now you can see why I wasn't coming back to New Mexico. I can assure you she didn't know her sister was going to kill Marino, but as soon as she drove her back to Albuquerque any claim of innocence was over. I don't believe Kate was thinking of anything other than getting her sister someplace safe, but I understand the legal consequences."

"This probably isn't relevant right now, but I can't help being curious. Does your wife know why her sister married Marino in the first place?"

"Lisa told her she was taking drugs and that Marino was her supplier. And she was rebelling against her very strict father, so one night while she was under the influence of drugs she married the creep. They'd gotten a license on some previous drug binge, so with the license in hand and the waiting period over, they found a justice of the peace and entered marital bliss with the blessing of the state of Florida. Lisa said she immediately regretted it, but once her father started screaming at her and saying it was the dumbest thing she had ever done she instinctively started to defend her decision. A very stupid mistake by a spoiled girl. When Marino left she was glad to be rid of him. She'd learned to hate the man in the few short months they were married."

"There's more Ray. Once Kate thought Lisa was emotionally stable enough, she bought her a ticket and sent her back to Miami. By then she knew she was involved in helping Lisa escape out of state, and that she could be charged as an accessory to Marino's murder. Kate called me from the airport and told me what had happened. I couldn't believe it—our world just turned upside down. I immediately put in place a plan to resign and leave for Boston. With her connections in Boston, and her family's money, that was our best chance of fighting extradition back to New Mexico. I told Kate to wait for me in Albuquerque. I packed a bag for her and drove to the airport. When I got there, I couldn't believe how upset Kate was. Everything had been going so great for us, and now it had all blown up—again."

"I had to really convince Kate to leave—she didn't want to go without me. She said she should just give herself up. I talked her out of that. Eventually she agreed that she should go to Boston. Then she gave me the gun. She'd found it in the car—apparently Lisa had accidently dropped it, or maybe meant to leave it there. Kate said she found a hand towel in the trunk of the car and had wrapped the gun in that. She handed me the towel. I opened it and it was amazing—it was tiny, like a little toy, but it had killed a man. I wrapped it back up and put it in my pocket and we bought tickets for Kate. The first flight out of Albuquerque was going to Denver, so we got a one-way ticket—once she was in Denver she'd buy another ticket to get to Boston. I waited with her until it was time for her to board. She was crying most of the time."

He paused to gather himself.

"After Kate left, I found the pay lockers in the terminal and put the gun in one of them and paid for the maximum amount of time. Before I left New Mexico, I found a place near the airport where I could rent lockers by the month. I put the gun there. Here's the key."

"Will Kate testify about what she saw that night?"

"I don't know. Kate's very upset right now and having trouble deciding what is right. I think her first instinct was to protect her sister, but after some thought I think she's begun to wonder why her sister put her in that position in the first place. I can't answer your question at this point."

"The gun will tie back to Lisa and prove to be the murder weapon, but that might not be enough to convict her without corroborating evidence, especially a witness."

"I understand. I'd like to be in a position to tell you what we will or won't do, but I don't know. I called you out of a sense of obligation to both my wife and the law. Believe me, this hasn't been an easy decision. I thought that if we continued to hide the truth it would get worse for everyone. I believe that Lisa can make a case that it wasn't premeditated, but an impulse, a fit of rage. The gun is a problem, but good lawyers can get around that. What do you think the governor will do?"

"Well, as you know he can be very volatile, so he could just go berserk, call out the National Guard, and threaten to start a war with Massachusetts—or he could avoid getting involved at all. He knows Marino was an evil man causing all kinds of mayhem for the good citizens of Ruidoso, so having him dead is probably not a bad thing in the eyes of the governor. He's going to be sympathetic to your wife protecting her sister. Probably the person he'll be most angry with is you. The governor values loyalty over everything else and I think he'll feel that you've been disloyal. But according to our legal system disloyalty isn't a criminal offense. My guess is that the governor is sorry you left, because he liked you and you were doing a good job, but now he's moved on to other matters—

seems to be some shenanigans going on in San Juan County that have him upset."

Tony chuckled, which was good to hear. Ray thought he looked very tired.

"I know it's bizarre but I'm going to miss the governor."

"Tony, as you know I'm going to turn over all the information I have to the appropriate authorities. At this point I'm not real sure who that is, but there's no question that the legal wheels are going to start turning. At any time, if something isn't going right or you feel like you need someone to help, you give me a call. I can't stop what's going to happen, but I want to help you if I can."

"Ray, you've always been a good friend. I'm sorry that there have been times I wasn't as candid as I should have been. I really appreciate your friendship." They stood and hugged, and Tony left.

Ray sat back down and ordered his second breakfast of the morning.

28

Justice For All

The wheels of justice turn slowly, but they do turn. Ray got back from his trip to Boston, retrieved the gun, went home, and slept for fourteen hours. He then called the head of the state police, an old buddy, and gave him the information and the gun. The police could sort out whose jurisdiction everything belonged in—Ray was tired of thinking about all of the people who had screwed up their lives because of lust or greed. He just wanted to spend time with his favorite person, Sue, and his best dog—actually, his only dog—Happy.

Ray and Sue sat at the kitchen table, drinking coffee and looking through information about San Francisco.

"What sort of life do you want to have?" he asked.

"What kind of stupid question is that?"

"Sue, it's not a stupid question. Do you want to travel, do you want to have lots of company, do you want to paint, do you want to write a book, or do you want to sleep till noon—it's not a stupid question at all."

"Something's bothering you, Ray. Just spit it out."

"Okay. I've been thinking that what I'd like to do is enter Big Jack's annual fishing tournament—you know I'm the reigning champion. I'd like to fish for a few weeks to get back into the right mind set and see if I could win again."

"You don't want to go to San Francisco do you?"

"I don't want to make you unhappy."

"You're so full of shit, Ray. Just say it: you don't want to go to San Francisco."

"Okay, I don't."

"Me either."

"What! What do you mean, 'me either'? It was your idea."

"Ray, I just thought you needed something else—something else for you to think about and plan. I'm perfectly happy at home. You're the one who's been grumping around, not me."

Ray wasn't completely sure why, but the whole conversation suddenly seemed funny to him and he started to laugh. Soon Sue was laughing. Happy stood up and began wagging his tail. It was a family breakdown of joy.

The phone rang. Sue pulled herself together and answered. She listened and then handed the phone to Ray.

"It's the governor's chief of staff."

"Ray Pacheco."

Ray listened, said 'okay' to something, and hung up.

"Governor wants to see me tomorrow morning. He wants a verbal report and some advice on what to do. Want to come along?"

"Sure."

Ray made arrangements with Tyee to watch Happy—Tyee and Big Jack both had keys to the cabin in case anything happened. Sue called and made a reservation at La Fonda.

They packed, then got in the Jeep and headed out. Ray immediately felt happy—because this time Sue was with him.

The drive to Santa Fe was uneventful, although it seemed like with every trip he made the roads became more crowded. The movement of cars between Santa Fe and Albuquerque was creating big city traffic problems out in the sticks. They made their way to the Plaza and used valet parking for Ray's beat up old Jeep. The attendant actually made a slight face when he got in, but Ray just chuckled. The Jeep was absolutely theft proof—nobody would want it.

Sue had reserved a suite, which turned out to be very attractive. The Spanish architecture of the building, with the old Mexico and New Mexico themed rooms, was a treat to the eye, with bright colors everywhere. They freshened up a bit, before going downstairs to the bar for a margarita. The bar had the same vivid colors, and there was background music that seemed to float in the air. They decided to sit at the bar rather than take a table, and were astonished at the size of the margaritas they were served. Ray was mostly a beer drinker, so he was going to have to be careful with this baby.

Sue had a sip and declared the drink to be perfection. After one and a half of these massive concoctions, they realized that it was a good thing they were staying at the hotel. Neither Ray nor Sue was feeling any pain. It had been a long time since Ray had really relaxed, and he was starting to feel like he wanted to sing.

Sue leaned over. "No singing Ray. I've seen that look in your eye before, and it was followed by singing—not here." She giggled.

"I like it when you giggle."

"I like it when you like it when I giggle." This conversation was at its end. It was either dinner or the room. They felt a little unsteady and decided to head to the room—they could eat in the morning.

Ray was up early and feeling great. He'd expected to have a headache, but it was just the opposite: he felt alert and ready to get the day started. He showered and dressed, then gave Sue a little nudge and a kiss to see if she was going to have breakfast. She woke up reluctantly, but soon was smiling. She was definitely interested in breakfast and said she would join him downstairs.

Once seated in the main eating area Ray had coffee and orange juice and began reading the Albuquerque newspaper. Most of the problems in the world seemed to be a lot like the problems that were reported every other day. He did notice an article about Lisa Collins—she had agreed to extradition and was currently in the Bernalillo County jail. He was sure there was a lot more to that story. He skipped everything else and concentrated on the sports page. He wasn't a sports nut, but it was safer than the other news. The stories generally didn't involve mayhem.

Sue joined Ray. She was looking great, and he felt a sense of pride in his beautiful wife. They ordered way too much food, but it was absolutely delicious. Having had no dinner meant they now had healthy—or at least robust—appetites.

Sue decided not to join Ray at the governor's office for their meeting. She was going to walk around the Plaza for a little while, then take a rest and wait for him to return. For his part, Ray decided that he'd walk to the appointment, so he left in plenty of time and began his trek. It was a glorious morning. One of the benefits of the high altitude was cool mornings—even when it was in the nineties during the afternoon, the mornings always started off very mild. It was a great time to walk in the lovely little city.

Ray let the Governor's secretary know he was there and took a seat to wait. Not a minute later, the governor opened the door and told him to get his ass inside.

"Ray that was one hell of a job you did getting all of that nonsense in Ruidoso straightened out. Son of a bitch! I'd never had guessed that Marino had been shot by his ex-wife. If that asshole Marino had nine lives like a cat, he'd still be dead—there were that many people and more who wanted that bastard permanently retired."

"No question governor, the guy was bad news. Probably not a good thing to say, but the world might be better off without Mr. Marino."

"That's a goddamn understatement. Ray, I wanted to talk to you about what to do with some of these people. You may or may not have heard this, but that Isabella person has been released from jail. I know she made a confession—actually, that was to you wasn't it? Well, I guess she changed her mind or something. She hired the top dog fuckin' lawyer in Albuquerque, and he got a judge to toss the confession because her rights hadn't been properly read to her—can you fuckin' believe that? Anyway, without the confession the prosecutor is saying he doesn't have a case. Anyone who could testify against her is dead. The only asshole alive is some moron name Tito, but the prosecutor says he never saw Isabella and only knew she was running things because all the dead SOB's told him so—so it's just hearsay, she walks."

"Sounds like I may have contributed to that little foul up. I should have asked if she'd been read her rights—my mistake. On the other hand, it may not be perfect justice but she's suffered a lot. I'm not sad that she won't have to serve time."

"What are you some kinda' fucking liberal? My god Ray, we need to put more people in jail, not less. Jeez! And now, for the next innocent murderess. Lisa Collins has also hired what looks like some kind of Harvard glee club or something. The prosecutor says he can make a circumstantial case, but without a witness or some other corroborating evidence the gun might not be enough to convict her—in his most humble opinion. The prosecutor thinks that if we push real hard and bring out the big threat of jail time, that we can get Kate Garcia to testify against her half-sister and then he thinks he can win. But— fuck, there's always a 'but,' isn't there? He says that the most likely outcome is a conviction on a lesser breed of murder, or even manslaughter. He says her attorneys have developed a pretty good case that she was suffering from diminished capacity and can't be held fully responsible for her actions. Isn't that somethin'? And guess who the prosecutor says would be a no-brainer to charge and convict: Kate Garcia, as an accessory. Her actions after the fact were clearly made with a clear mind and allowed Lisa to leave the state. What a bunch of bullshit."

"The law doesn't always get things right."

"Fuck, Ray, you're a philosopher. Well, I'm a philosopher too. I won't pursue a prosecution of Kate, because she got blindsided by her crazy half-sister and then tried to help her. Kate and Tony could have stayed quiet about the whole damn thing and we'd have never unraveled it. So you can tell Tony, nobody in the state of New Mexico will prosecute him or his wife. They can even come back here and vacation if they want—the crazy fuckin' governor won't arrest them."

"Tony will be very happy to hear that, governor."

"Yeah, the only people we can arrest and convict are penniless bastards who then live like fuckin' kings on the state's dime."

The governor really needed a bigger audience this morning—he was in rare form.

"As far as the sister goes, I had them offer manslaughter with a three to five year sentence—meaning she could be out in less than two years. With that many goddamn Harvard lawyers there's always a chance that they'll figure out some way that we actually owe her millions of dollars for our shitty attitude."

"Governor, I'm glad the people of Ruidoso can go back to more normal lives. And Sheriff James is an excellent sheriff— he'll do a great job and not bother you."

"You're on the ball Ray, 'cause that's what I want. Do your goddamn job and don't bother me. Ray, as soon as we get a new AG in place I want you and your lovely wife to visit us again so we can talk about some additional things we want your group to do for us. I want to personally thank you for a good job."

Ray thanked the governor and left. On his walk back to the hotel he thought about it and decided that, all in all, most things had worked out okay. The one exception was Dick Franklin. By all accounts he wasn't involved in anything, but he ended up being killed nonetheless. Ray was as close to sure as you could get without being completely certain that responsibility for his death lay with some of the goons who worked for Isabella's father. That was something that should never have happened. As Sue said, some people just had bad karma and nothing ever worked out for them.

The walk seemed shorter going back to the hotel than it had in the other direction. It was close to lunch time, and Ray was hungry again. He'd been told that the altitude gave everyone here a good appetite—he sure knew it worked on him.

Ray and Sue debated and finally settled on a salad. The large breakfast would probably give them enough calories for the day, but still they needed something. Ray gave Sue a recap of what the governor had said.

"Sounds like he's trying to be fair."

"It does in a way. One reason he's being fair, though, is there's some high-dollar legal talent on the other side who have forced the state into a corner. But even with his bluster, I kind of like the governor."

"Do you think Tony would ever come back to New Mexico?"

"Kind of doubt it. He and Kate will establish their life in Boston and New Mexico will just become a memory."

"How about Michael, do you think he'll visit?"

"Don't know that either. I had a feeling at the time that he might think about it. But when you have to take off and arrange to stop delivery for your paper and find someone to mow your lawn —I don't know, might just be too much trouble."

"I'm glad you got to talk to him."

"Yeah, me too."

29

Isabella Ortega Franklin

Tularosa, New Mexico

Isabella had always lived in isolation. Her family's hacienda in Tularosa was remote and well-guarded—no one accidently entered the compound. She seldom came into contact with strangers—the only people she saw were her tutors and the staff who maintained the residence and did the cooking. She knew no other kind of life and so wasn't aware of the things that were missing in her young life. Her companion, teacher, and best friend was her mother, Clara. Clara Ortega was Isabella's entire universe. She didn't resent Clara for this, she loved her—she knew nothing else.

Growing up, her father stayed away for weeks at a time—off doing battle with somebody. When he came home he was like a king, always yelling at her mother. Isabella hated it when he was there. She'd hide in her room and worry about her mother. He even hit her mother once and Isabella saw it—she swore that one day she'd kill the bastard.

When her father was gone, which was most of the time, Isabella and her mother were very happy. They lived in a protected world and enjoyed each other's company. As Isabella grew older, her mother would take her on trips. They usually were gone for only a few days, a week at most—visiting Albuquerque, El Paso, Phoenix, San Antonio, and Houston. On these trips they'd shop and go to museums, or see a movie or a play. Isabella was fascinated by the "outside" world, but also wary. Crowds bothered her and sometimes the noise of the big cities would give her headaches. She enjoyed the trips, and thought she learned a lot, but she was most comfortable at home.

"Mother, what do you think I will be when I grow up?"

"A princess, my dear. The most beautiful princess in the whole world."

Isabella often wondered what a princess in Tularosa, New Mexico, actually did. She decided that when the time was right her mother would tell her.

Her mother's most-often repeated advice was about Isabella's father, Andres Ortega. Her mother hated her father, and often told Isabella to be careful around him. She had told her young, impressionable daughter that her father was a violent, uncultured man who might do anything. Isabella was terrified of her father.

"You must learn to accept that you are a special person and you have responsibilities because of your upbringing. You must study and learn so that you will be ready when it is your time to act."

Her mother had said things like this to Isabella for as long as she could remember. It was never clear to her if her mother had some specific plan for her, or just a general idea that Isabella was important. Her mother had told her if they lived in Spain she'd be a princess and would be honored and adored.

Isabella did as she was told, practicing being a lady in a world she was never allowed to see. She had a strict schedule, and her only real companion was her mother. This made the encounters with her father even more frightening. He was big and loud and didn't seem to care much about anything other than yelling and drinking.

As Isabella became a young woman, she began taking on more responsibilities around the compound. Her parents were aging quickly. Her father had suffered a series of small strokes and had become withdrawn, mostly staying away from her and her mother. When Isabella did see him, he seemed to be a different man—her hatred of him didn't diminish, though, because of his waning strength.

"It is time that you go to university and get an education and find a husband. I have arranged for you to enter the University of New Mexico in Albuquerque. I know it is going to be difficult for you to leave, but it is vital that you establish your own life—while I am still alive."

"I will do as you say mother." Isabella was ecstatic. She wanted to jump up and down and scream for joy. On her own in Albuquerque. She was not worried or afraid, she was thrilled. She had no idea what to think about finding a husband, but she was ready to have some freedom. She worried about leaving her mother, but she'd be close at hand in case she was needed.

Isabella enrolled in the university and would stay in the freshman dorms for women. She was driven to Albuquerque by servants, who unloaded her belongings and then departed. Everyone stared at her as she entered the dorm. She decided that she liked the attention, and walked with a practiced elegance. She didn't have a roommate, even though it appeared everyone else did—something she suspected her mother had arranged. It didn't bother Isabella to be something special— it's what she'd been, and been trained for—her entire life.

School wasn't much of a challenge. While she lacked certain social skills, she'd been given an amazing education by her mother and a team of tutors. Every class was easy and Isabella excelled. During her first semester, she became aware of attention coming from one of her professors. He was a middle-aged, handsome man named Tim Baxter. Professor Baxter was very attentive towards Isabella, and had on several occasions asked her to coffee or for a beer—though she'd always declined. After some weeks she decided to accept and agreed to join him at a local bar for a drink. The evening ended with them at the professor's apartment and Isabella had her first sexual experience.

She enjoyed sex and wanted to learn more about love making. She moved in with the professor and had an intensive, two-week education. Isabella was intrigued. The poor professor was exhausted and madly in love. After two weeks, she told the professor she was moving back to the dorm and that he shouldn't bother her anymore. The professor went ballistic. He pleaded with her, he threatened her—she ignored him and moved out. The next night the professor made such a scene outside her dorm that he was arrested. He was fired the next day. Isabella went to class.

She was soon enjoying an active sex life with a different professor who was much younger than Professor Baxter, and in Isabella's opinion more stable. She spent the next two years enjoying sex while still landing on the dean's honor role for her academic achievements. But she knew it was time to find a husband—her mother's health was deteriorating.

Isabella married Dick Franklin, a nice man, though weak, because her mother insisted. She knew her mother wanted her out of the house and away from what was happening between her parents, and Clara worried that Isabella's father would hit her one day as well—she'd said as much to Isabella.

Isabella tried to do what her mother wanted. She found Dick and decided he was controllable and would give her protection from her father, mostly by taking her away. She endured Dick, even called him Richard—her personal joke—but she had no respect for him. He was the opposite of her father, kind and thoughtful, but also weak. She knew he'd do whatever she asked—she was the strong one. And then he began to challenge her. He shouldn't have done that, not ever.

After her mother died, Isabella knew she had to do something if she was going to be able to have her own life. She felt that her father was a constant threat and his behavior had become increasingly erratic. While her mother was alive there was at least some restraint on her father—her mother was someone he seemed almost to fear.

Isabella had observed much about her father's business over the years and had become acquainted with some of the leaders in Mexico. She decided that the path to her ultimate independence was money. Without her father's knowledge, she'd implemented a plan to bring drugs in from Mexico. She loved the irony of carrying out this illegal activity right under her husband's nose.

But now it was all coming to an end. It was time to start cleaning up the mess and to find a new life.

Isabella was going to be free. Her whole life had been controlled by people who had treated her like some kind of doll, a plaything, something attractive to own and put on display. Now she was her own person for the first time in her entire life. The only person she'd ever really cared about was her mother, Clara. She shared her mother's secrets regarding her father and what their life was really like.

She had planned for years how the end would come for her father, and she'd begun to implement the plan over the last few years. She'd used the drug money to make a variety of necessary arrangements, and now she was in the final stages.

The first matter to deal with was the suddenly righteous Dick Franklin. That moron Marino had told Dick that he should just keep his mouth shut about everything because the person responsible for all the drugs being run through the racetrack was his wife. Dick had returned home after his fight with Marino and accused his wife of being evil—he said he was going to turn her in to the sheriff or the police. She told Dick exactly what she thought of his threats, told him he was weak and not much of a man, and then left for Tularosa. And now she was returning to Ruidoso to confront him. She entered the house and found Dick at home. He began yelling at her almost immediately.

"Are you crazy? How could you get involved in drugs? Your whole damn family has always been crazy. I am leaving you, Isabella. You have almost ruined me as a person because of your strange, wicked ways. You're some kind of evil witch or something, I swear. I can't believe I loved you—I loved you so much—but now I see you for what you really are. You're disgusting. I never want to see you again."

She walked up to Dick and spat in his face, standing there with hatred in her eyes. Dick was stunned. Something seemed to snap and he hit her as hard as he could, screaming that she was evil and she'd have to die. He hit her again.

Isabella stumbled backwards, but never fell. She had several deep cuts and was bleeding freely, but there was a strange smile on her face. Dick seemed suddenly frozen in a confused daze, just staring at her.

Isabella calmly walked to Dick, pulled out the .38 special handgun from her jacket, and shot him in the head. He was dead before he hit the floor.

She arranged his body as best she could in order to make it look like suicide. She typed the suicide note and then left. She was free. Free of all of the men who wanted her as some kind of prize. She was released from all of them—their groping and vile man-handling. She was sick of being an object.

She returned to Tularosa, went immediately to her room, and tended to her cuts. She hadn't seen her father or anyone else on her way in. It was late, so she just went to bed.

The next day Isabella woke late in the morning and applied some makeup to hide her cuts and bruises. As she entered the main area of the house, she heard her father talking outside. She glanced out the side window and saw him speaking, in his usual hateful tone, to two men in a car who were surrounded by the guards. She couldn't make out what her father was saying.

He came back into the house.

"Who were those men father?"

"Goddamned cops or something. Said they worked for the fuckhead Governor. They were looking for you and your idiot husband. I told them to leave or I'd have them killed. They chose to leave." He spoke without any emotion, as if threating to kill people was an everyday occurrence.

"Where in the hell were you last night?"

"I went to Ruidoso and got home late and went straight to bed. Can I get you some tea?" Her father had become enamored of herbal tea and had a cup at hand most of the day.

"Yeah, do something useful for a change."

Isabella ignored the snide remark. With the governor's investigators coming around she had to implement her plan immediately. For that, she needed her father out of the way for a few hours. She fixed his tea and added a substantial amount of drugs—enough to put him out for some time. She brought him the tea and sat with him as he sipped. The drugs began acting quickly.

"I am unusually tired this morning. Believe I will go to my room and take a rest."

Isabella called a trucking company she had on stand-by and told them they should be at the house that evening. She ordered the household staff into a frenzy of activity boxing, wrapping, and crating up the paintings. There were many by her mother, as well as maybe fifty by other famous artists. Isabella estimated their value at something over twelve million dollars. The process was irritatingly slow—the household staff were so stupid.

She looked in on her father several times and found him sound asleep. She locked him in his room as a precaution, and also took his pistol from the bedside chest.

The truck arrived on time to pick up the load of paintings and take them to a beautiful house in Rancho Santa Fe, California. Isabella would be so happy to finally leave the family prison where she'd been held for so long. Once everything was loaded, she dismissed the staff and gave them their final checks. She explained that she and her father had decided to return to Mexico and would not need staff.

At that point she went and found the head of the household guards. Most people thought these people worked for her father, the famous drug lord, but they didn't—they worked for Isabella. She'd made a deal with the man that once the paintings she wanted were removed, he could have anything else in the house. There were additional paintings, plus all sorts of silverware and gold *objets d'art*. Isabella had no idea how much it was worth and didn't care. The deal stipulated that he and his gang would drive the trucks across the border into Mexico and sell the goods there. And there was one other package that he had to take into Mexico.

Isabella went to her father's room. She opened the door and looked at the old man asleep on the bed. Her hatred of him was palatable. She thought of her mother and how miserable this old man had made her. Life would have been so wonderful if he'd never been around. She pulled the gun from a pocket in her jacket and shot him in the head. The noise was terrible—but Isabella felt free.

The goon and two of his men rolled Andres Ortega, the once-powerful drug lord, into an old blanket and took him to the truck. They would dispose of the body in Mexico. As a precaution against these evil men trying to blackmail her in the future, Isabella would shortly contact the cartel, say that the guards had killed her father, and tell them of their destination in Mexico, adding that they had trucks full of valuables.

Isabella gave the man some money, as they'd agreed, and left, never looking back at her childhood home.

She drove to Albuquerque and went to the hospital—her cuts needed medical attention. She was finally allowed to just be Isabella, not a treasure to be owned by someone else.

She had a plan. She'd turn herself in to the Albuquerque police after a few days. She'd demand to see that T or C private investigator who had been nosing around on behalf of the Governor. They'd be so excited to get her story, they'd screw it up some way. She knew no one could tie her into the murders of her father and husband—she'd confess just to the drug business. Her plan was to get off on everything, but if she had to she'd serve a little time for the drug trafficking she knew now that she could survive anywhere, even prison.

30

Mr. Mayor

Truth or Consequences, New Mexico

"Well, if it's not the Mayor himself. Do we call you Mr. Mayor or just Mayor—or maybe Mayor Big Jack?"

"Very funny, Ray. I really don't give a shit what you call me, just don't call me on the goddamn phone. Did I promise hundreds of people a job with the city? I don't think so. They just keep calling saying I said this or that—or even that my girlfriend said they could have a job. The phone doesn't stop ringing. Not real sure I knew what I was signing up for as mayor."

"Maybe that's why the ex-mayor was always in such a bad mood. By the way, who's your girlfriend?"

"Ray, you must have taken a funny pill today. Why am I here anyway?"

"We're going to have a wrap-up meeting to finalize what happened on the Ruidoso case, plus talk about what we have coming up."

"Is it too early to drink beer?"

"Yes. Have you seen Tyee this morning?"

"Nope. He's probably out fishing. You know it's been a long time since he could enter the tournament—I think he's going to be hungry to win. Your butt is in trouble, Ray."

Tyee entered the room followed by Sue, Beverly, and Nancy. Big Jack made a face, or at least it looked like he made a face.

"Looks more like a party than a meeting."

"Please come in and have a seat. This is going to be a wrap-up meeting regarding our recent case in Ruidoso. I want to make sure everyone has the facts about how it all turned out, and I want to kind of review how we handled everything. Plus, I want to go over where we are regarding new projects and how that's going to be handled going forward."

"But first, I wanted to talk about some changes. Toward the end of the Ruidoso case I got pretty tired and grumpy. I think more than anything it was the driving all over the countryside and not being home. I even thought that maybe I just didn't want to do this anymore. I think as a team we are pretty damn good, and we are going to be offered a lot of additional work from the state. Also, I received a call from FBI Agent Crawford and they have several matters they'd like us to get involved in. Much of what they have involves computer work and analyzing reports prepared by field agents. So we're a little overburdened and now we're going to have even more work. I asked Nancy and Beverly to be here to discuss the possibility of them helping us with various functions in the office. I know they're doing the taco business, but I thought that—if they were interested—we could devise a schedule that would work for them and for us. And I know I probably should have brought this up in a different forum, but I thought it might be best to just get it out on the table and see what happened."

Nancy raised her hand.

"You can just speak up Nancy—we're pretty informal."

"When I left Albuquerque I was a paralegal and I think I was pretty good. I'd love to have some more income, so I'd be very interested in working with you all." Nancy looked at Tyee and blushed. Ray was mostly oblivious to the things going on under the surface.

Sue jumped in. "Ray sometimes just gets going without thinking about all of the ramifications. Beverly and Nancy, this is not a fair forum for Ray to ask you if you want to work at *P&C*. So you think about it, and you can tell us later."

"Well hell, I didn't mean to embarrass anyone."

Beverly spoke up. "I'd love to work here—just tell me what to do. I don't have Nancy's background, but I'm good on the phone."

Everyone started talking at once. Ray had done this all wrong, but it had turned out to be just right. In a matter of minutes he had a decision and people working together—something that could have taken days if he'd talked one-on-one with each of them.

"What I'd like to suggest is that Sue becomes the office manager. She can arrange everyone's schedules and duties."

That made sense to everyone.

"We'll work out a bonus schedule for everyone based on the performance of the company—if we have profits, we'll share them. I know we got into this business because we're friends, and I want that to be the priority—maintaining our friendships, all of our friendships."

Ray changed the subject and started reviewing the Ruidoso case. He gave them all of the facts he had, plus what the governor had said would be the outcomes of the legal issues. They were surprised that Isabella was being released. Everyone agreed that Tony and Kate, while they'd been in the wrong, shouldn't be prosecuted. They all felt bad about Dick Franklin, whom everyone agreed was probably the only completely innocent victim in the whole mess. No one cared much what happened to Tito.

"Ray, don't you think it's an amazing coincidence that the same people from Houston ended up interacting in Ruidoso and also that Marino was associated with Kate's fiancé and ended up marrying her sister in Miami? Seems almost impossible that all of that could be connected." Tyee was frowning, his disbelief showing through.

"Yeah, it all seemed so odd—what do you make of it?" Big Jack also looked puzzled.

"Well first, coincidences do happen. We don't like to admit it, but they happen. I don't have the facts to back this up, but I think most of this is tied to Marino. My guess is that there was some connection with the mob that brought Marino to Miami. Probably Marino had to get out of Houston in a hurry and knew someone in the mob in Miami. We know that Lisa's father—Kate's half-sister's father—was socializing with the mob. I don't know the details of how, but one way or another Marino made a connection with Lisa. She was in her rebellious phase and started using drugs, probably at the urging of the asshole Marino. We know all of that got bad and Marino had to leave before the father killed him. Now Marino needs a new place to go to. We haven't been able to identify who it is, but I do believe he had a cousin in Ruidoso. Once Marino started to think about heading out to New Mexico, maybe he did some research and he found out that Tony was the Attorney General. Again, I'm guessing on the details, but the bottom line is that I think he knew the AG would be a benefit in some way because of what Marino thought he knew about Tony's wife. He thought he could figure out an angle to blackmail the AG for his own gain. It's almost certainly one of the reasons he moved to New Mexico—he thought he had leverage against the top law enforcement official in the state. That had to be very enticing to a thug like Marino."

Ray paused to let that much sink in.

"The circumstances with Nelson being the make-believe police chief in Ruidoso were just chance. I don't see any way that Marino could have known about Nelson before coming to Ruidoso. I can't imagine any circumstances where Nelson would have sought out Marino in Miami—that was just bad luck for Nelson. I haven't been able to prove this, but my guess is that Nelson was probably taking kickbacks from Marino in Houston, or Marino knew about him taking kickbacks from someone else. When Marino bumped into Nelson in Ruidoso, he leveraged his knowledge about Nelson into a job in the sheriff's department. And then, once he had the job, proceeded to spread his usual misery."

"Of course, Nelson had already started his drug smuggling business before Marino showed up. When I talked to Nelson on the first trip to Ruidoso, his hatred of Marino was obviously real and intense. I should have known right then. That kind of hate isn't casual or recent—this was hate with a whole lot of history. He knew Marino was trouble, and I believe he was going to kill him but stopped when Tyee and I showed up in his office. Once again this is just speculation, but I think Nelson backed off of his plan to eliminate Marino because suddenly people were watching."

"Not sure there are any winners in this small-town drama—although I think the county ended up with a much better sheriff and sheriff's department. I guess all of the players contributed to their own downfall, but mostly it just seems sad to me that humans can be so easily attracted to evil."

"On a personal note. Sue and I are going to spend more time doing things that are not related to the PI business. We all need to decide how much time is enough for the business and how much we need for ourselves. We can work out schedules, pay, and other details so that you guys meet your goals as well. We're people first and I want us all to be happy."

At the mention of his name, Happy began wagging his tail. Everyone laughed, although it looked like Beverly and Sue were crying a little.

Sue pulled Ray aside afterward. "You are a good man Ray—maybe you should have been a priest."

"Can priests carry guns?"

"If a priest has a gun, who's going to take it away from him?"

"I was wrong not to consult Tyee and Big Jack about Nancy and Beverly before springing that on them. Sometimes things just don't register with me until it's too late, and it's almost always something to do with women."

"Don't worry about it—it'll work out. It almost always does."

"If I'm a priest, can you be a nun?"

"I don't think so, big boy."

Sue grabbed Ray's hand and they headed to the cabin with Happy following. It couldn't get any better than this.

31

San Juan County Sheriff

"The research on this San Juan County stuff is pretty amazing. If what I'm finding is right, the sheriff has managed to accumulate enough military hardware to start a pretty sizable war." Tyee mentioned this as Ray walked into the computer room.

"Pretty sure that's not going to make the governor happy."

"Looks like it's worse than just the governor being unhappy. I've tracked some of the travel of these military vehicles, and it appears they left the state and entered Colorado. I have no idea where this stuff went once it was inside Colorado, but I've checked and it definitely did not come back out of that state."

Ray was frowning. Not only was the wacko sheriff apparently accumulating old military hardware for his white supremacist take-over of God-knows-what, but he now had taken property of the state of New Mexico and moved it to Colorado. *How do these people get elected?*

"How much equipment do you think we're talking about?"

"Well, over the last eighteen months I can track twelve armored vehicles, some of them described as having mounted weapons. One tank and two armored troop carriers. Of course, I can't tell you what was inside the vehicles."

"Did you say tank?"

"Yep. Just what a sheriff's department needs—a tank, in case they're invaded by the Chamber of Commerce."

"The governor is going to shit. Why would they move all that equipment into Colorado?"

"All I can do is guess, but my first thought is that they have some kind of joint operation with like-minded morons in Colorado and they're combining forces for some kind of action."

"Action? What the hell would that be?" Ray knew Tyee didn't know—he was just yelling to blow off a little steam. They both knew he needed to call the governor and give him an update on the San Juan County military movements. Ray could hear the governor bellowing already—and his imaginary version of the reaction wasn't far off.

"What the fuck are you telling me Ray? The asshole San Juan sheriff is gathering an army in Colorado with New Mexico fucking equipment. Is the guy a complete moron? Is every sheriff in this state a goddamned idiot?"

Ray hadn't said much. The governor was asking some of the same rhetorical questions Ray had asked.

"Ray, you know I could send in the National Guard, but I can't order them to cross into Colorado. And that bastard of a governor in Colorado hates my ass and will gladly keep all of that stupid fuckin' equipment if he finds out. Do you really think this guy is going to mount some kind of operation with these weapons?"

"No, I don't. I know some of these people—they just want to dress up in their uniforms and play war. I think the only people actually at risk are the participants, with some chance that one of their fellow loonies will shoot them."

"Yeah, that sounds about right to me. But hell, I can't let him take New Mexico assets into Colorado and not do something about it. Ray, I know this is beyond the scope of what we initially talked about on this, but could you and some of your people just go up to Farmington and snoop around and find out what the hell's going on?"

"Sure, governor. We'll see what we can find out. It's a long drive to Farmington—any chance the state patrol or somebody would have a plane we could use?"

"Shit, Ray, I've got a plane. And I hate to fly. Consider it yours, along with two pilots. You now have an official air force to attack the loony sheriff's army." Ray sure hoped he was just being the oddball governor of New Mexico—he didn't want to go to war, with or without an air force.

Keep reading for a free preview of...

FOUR CORNERS WAR

Navajos, Apaches, militias, good sheriffs, and bad sheriffs are all drawn to a small town by millions in stolen money and a small army's worth of stolen military equipment. Is this the start of a Four Corners War? Nothing is as it should be as Ray Pacheco and Tyee Chino try to untangle the mix of greedy businessmen, corrupt politicians and a slightly unhinged sheriff—along with the usual dead bodies.

Farmington, New Mexico's unique mix of cultures is the backdrop for Ray and Tyee's most dangerous assignment to date from the bombastic Governor of New Mexico.

.

CHAPTER 1

Farmington, New Mexico

"Tyee, I can't force you to get on the plane, but it's a long drive to Farmington and if you don't want to fly you'll have to drive—*alone*."

Tyee was pouting, his expression that of a two-year-old—a very big two-year-old—about ready to have a tantrum. He kicked at the ground and gave Ray a dirty look.

"Okay, I understand. You're not comfortable in a small plane. But this," Ray pointed at the aircraft behind them, "is really a big plane, with two engines and two professional pilots. They know what they're doing."

"Bullshit Ray. This is the crazy governor's plane with two pilots who may or may not know what they're doing. You can fire me if you like, but I'm going to drive." Tyee's stubborn expression dared Ray to demand that he get on the plane.

"What are you two arguing about?" Sue had walked up while Ray and Tyee were frowning at one another.

"Tyee's afraid to fly."

Tyee's face got still darker. He crossed his arms and gave Ray a stare that was decidedly cold.

"Well if Tyee isn't flying, neither am I."

"What! Have you all lost your minds?" Ray stomped off in the other direction—toward nothing in particular. He seemed to be mumbling.

This was not going as planned. Sue was coming along for the ride, to offer moral support and to take a break from her routine. Big Jack was babysitting Happy, with help from his new girlfriend, Beverly. Happy liked staying at Big Jack's bait shop for reasons that only a dog could understand.

What was supposed to be an easy plane ride of an hour or so was turning into a civil war. Ray continued to stomp around in the dirt, watching as Sue and Tyee engaged in some kind of conversation.

"We go." Tyee made this statement in his infamous minimalist Indian-speak, then climbed aboard the plane.

"What did you say to him?"

"None of your business, Ray. Let's get on the plane before he changes his mind."

Sue and Ray boarded. Tyee was slumped in his seat, frowning out the window.

"If everyone will get buckled up we'll be taking off in just a minute or two." The pilot sealed the door as he gave them this information. It was reassuring that he sported a professional-looking uniform and had the classic look of a pilot from the movies—complete with a broad smile. Of course that didn't mean he knew how to fly a plane.

In a matter of minutes they were in the air and everyone relaxed a little. Tyee was still not speaking to Ray, but he did smile at Sue. Ray just sighed.

After what seemed like a short time, the pilot announced that they were about ten minutes from Farmington and that everyone should buckle up.

Flying into Farmington had put the fear of flying into many a seasoned traveler. The airstrip sat on top of a small mesa in the middle of the town. While the location was convenient once you landed, the visual coming in for a landing was more than a little disturbing. The approach made it seem as if the plane was headed directly into the side of the mesa. While common sense said that the pilots weren't going to crash into the side of the cliff, your eyes told you that was exactly what would happen. Especially on a windy day like today, with the plane tossing about from side to side and up and down. Tyee glanced from the window to Ray with a look that suggested Ray had condemned him to death. But then, just when disaster seemed imminent, the plane settled onto the runway, easily clearing the mesa wall. Sue applauded, Tyee actually smiled, and Ray let his breath out.

Ray had been to many areas where the locals described the landscape as rugged, but this had to be the very definition of rugged. The natural terrain was jagged, with no level ground. The rocky faces included a variety of different colors of stone, but only limited vegetation. There were hills everywhere, and everything seemed exposed. It was an odd place to locate a town. After they'd deplaned, the wind immediately caught their attention. It was cold and gusty, making the whole area seem doubly inhospitable.

"The governor says we're at your disposal for the next several days, Mr. Pacheco," the pilot said. "We're a little less than an hour away from our base in Santa Fe, so if you agree, we'll head back to Santa Fe and whenever you need us again, just give us a call and we'll head out immediately." With that, he gave Ray a card with several names and phone numbers.

"Sounds great, captain. Not sure about our schedule at this point, but I'd guess we'll want to head back to T or C in a day or two. I'll give you a call as soon as we know." They shook hands, and Ray headed off to the small terminal.

"Sheriff Pacheco, hello. I'm Chief Deputy Thad Trujillo—welcome to Farmington."

"Thanks, appreciate you meeting us."

"No problem. The governor and the AG made it clear we're to assist you in any way we can. Even without the big brass giving me orders, I'm very pleased to meet the famous sheriff from southern New Mexico."

"Well now Deputy Trujillo, I think you might be messing with me." Trujillo grinned in a mischievous way.

"Your associates have gone to the restrooms. Your luggage has been placed in the patrol car outside. That car is yours to use as you see fit. Sorry we didn't have an unmarked car available, but I imagine you're used to riding in a patrol car."

"Yes, I've done that some. Any word from Sheriff Jackson?"

"Nothing direct. One of his followers came into the office yesterday to tell us he thought the sheriff had gone off the deep end. This guy belonged to Americans For Liberty—that's the group the sheriff has been active with—and he said the sheriff told them they'd begin seceding from the country as of October first. The guy said he enjoyed all the rah-rah stuff and the military crap, but he didn't want to leave his country. Seems like the sheriff may have taken this guy's truck—he wanted to report it stolen."

"What do you know about the Americans for Liberty?"

"It's a long-term anti-government militia group. Been in existence for maybe ten or fifteen years. Never thought they'd cause any real harm—just a bunch of beer bellies pretending to be tougher and meaner than they really are. The sheriff got involved about five years ago and he seems to take it pretty seriously. Lot of the softer guys dropped out after he started making them exercise and do real training."

"Does Sheriff Jackson have a family?"

"He's married, although they've been separated for a couple of years. Wife's name is Barbara—she lives in an apartment downtown. Don't believe they ever got a divorce, but lots of bitterness between them. His wife is active in local politics and the sheriff wanted her to stop, but she said no and moved out."

"I'd like to talk to her. Could you get me an address and phone number?"

"Sure."

"Sheriff have any friends who might know what's going on?"

"Our sheriff was a loner. The only person I know that he was close to was his mother, who died some years ago. All he cared about was work and stuff to do with the militia."

"Did you think he was a good sheriff?"

"Well, that's kind of a loaded question. He was, or is, my boss. He's a difficult man to get to know. Not very friendly. But in terms of running the department, I'd say he did a good job. A lot of people didn't like him much, but I think that was mostly because he was just not very friendly. Some people thought he was a real asshole, but those were generally law-breakers or people who wanted a special favor and didn't get it. The sheriff didn't play politics and more or less treated every-one about the same—even if he was a little cold. Occasionally he would drink a bit too much, which could create problems—but that mostly had to do with his estranged wife."

"Deputy, do you know where he is right now?"

"Not for sure, sheriff. My guess is that he's in Colorado at the militia's base camp. I think it's close to Ignacio, but definitely in backwoods territory. The guy who came in to file the stolen vehicle charge said the headquarters were in a very remote part of La Plata County. That's a sparsely populated area with limited access. The guy also said they have more weapons and ammunition up there than you can imagine. He said it would be a bloodbath if anyone tried to get them out of that camp."

"How about the military surplus equipment? I under-stand that he took some of that stuff with him into Colorado?"

"Yeah, I have definitely gotten an earful from the gover-nor about that. Most of the equipment is missing from the armory where it was stored. I guess the sheriff and his people took it. Most of that old junk was useless. It's old army shit that I think they just wanted to unload on law enforcement. But it was all in bad shape and would cost a fortune to main-tain—even assuming you had a use for an armored troop car-rier. The sheriff loved that military crap, though. Almost ev-ery weekend he would have people out there from the militia, washing and oiling. But we never used any of it in the sheriff's department. It just took up space. I told the governor it was a waste of money and he should just let Colorado have it—turns out that wasn't the thing to say. The governor went nuts, telling me the goddamn governor of Colorado was not getting any of our shit. Then he hung up."

"Our governor and the governor of Colorado seemed to have their own little war going on."

"Well, what's our plan Ray?" Tyee had forgiven Ray for the plane ride, given that he'd survived.

"We'll get checked into the hotel and then go back to the sheriff's department and get the contact information for the sheriff's ex-wife. Might go talk to her and see if she knows anything about the sheriff's plans. Want to talk to Deputy Trujillo some more, but my first impression is that he has everything under control. If that's the case then I think the issue of the sheriff stealing equipment and then holing up in some remote part of Colorado with a small army is a problem for some federal agency, not anything to do with us. So once we're comfortable that Deputy Trujillo has everything handled in Farmington, we can report to the governor and go home." No one objected to that.

CHAPTER 2

Many Years Prior—Colorado

"Ladies and Gentlemen it is with great pleasure that I introduce my great friend and one of the best representatives this country has ever had, Congressman Jeremiah Johnson." There was thunderous applause—the event was being held to honor the Congressman, so you wouldn't expect any boos.

"Thank you, Senator Graham. Good to see you back in Colorado for a change. Tommy and I have known each other for many years and have generally had good things to say about each other—although I do have some stories I've been saving in case we ever become opponents—but I guess I'll just keep saving those little gems." Senator Graham smiled, but directed a suspicious eye toward his not-so-great friend.

"When I announced my intention not to run for reelection, I know some of you were surprised, maybe even a little upset, but I also know that many of you were happier than pigs in shit. Well, I'm going to make that crowd even happier. My wife Jane and I are moving to Las Cruces, New Mexico. I've enjoyed my time representing the great state of Colorado, but my old bones have requested that I move to a warmer clime. By the way, that was not a reference to my long-suffering wife." Jane looked pained, but continued to smile. Loving the old bastard took real fortitude and a great deal of patience.

The speech wasn't long, which was good, but he wasn't very kind. Congressman Johnson had a way of pissing people off—it was one of his most consistent qualities. He had been elected and then re-elected because he had a way of getting things done, but his skills were more those of a bully than a diplomat. Not many people would be sorry to see him leave, especially Senator Graham.

"You know it's not your job to make the senator angry."

"I know, Jane. I should learn to be more diplomatic. But if I did that I wouldn't be me, now would I?"

"No." Jane snuggled a little closer, giving him a quick hug and a little peck on the cheek.

"I don't deserve you, Jane."

"No, you don't." She smiled at her husband. "It was nice of the senator to come to your going away party."

"Well, I'm sure it was because of the *going away* part. He's nothing but an old crook dressed up in fancy clothes and hiding behind a law degree—if I could make his life more miserable, I would." The congressman's eyes narrowed.

Jane knew the look and tensed for what was about to come.

"Senator, mind if I have a few private words?"

"You know Jeremiah, there's no reason for us to be enemies—why don't we part as friends?"

"Tommy, you are the biggest bullshitter I've ever met. Plus you're a crook. Why the fuck would I want you as a friend?"

"Listen you dumb son-of-a-bitch, I've had it with your foul mouth and holier-than-thou attitude. Fuck you!" The senator turned to leave, an ugly expression on his face.

"I know what you and your lowlife brother are trying to do in Pueblo. I won't stand for it. I have documentation on who owns that land and what'll happen to its value if that road project you're pushing through actually happens. That road to nowhere is a boondoggle, designed for no reason except to line your pockets. Either drop the project or I'll expose you."

The senator stopped, turning slowly. His face was red, and he was starting to perspire. "You do anything like that, and I'll have you killed." He spat the words in Jeremiah's face.

"I would rethink that senator, you two-bit thug. Your little threat is on tape." He pulled a small recorder out of his pocket. "Now, unless you want to go back to Pueblo and work in your idiot brother's construction business, you better do what I told you." Jeremiah Johnson's first instinct was to punch the fat senator in his fat face, but he saw Jane staring at him in a familiar stop-whatever-you're-doing way, so he just walked off.

"You know my dear, I think it's time we move."

The next few months were full of activity. They sold their house in Colorado Springs and rented a house in Albuquerque. They'd decided to park in Albuquerque a while and get a feel for things, then decide if they wanted to buy a house in Albuquerque or Las Cruces.

But the congressman couldn't sit still. He got involved in Democratic Party activities in Albuquerque, and soon was being talked about as a potential state leader for the party. Jeremiah was happiest when discussing politics—it was his life. He hadn't been active in New Mexico politics for some time, but it was amazing how similar the issues were to Colorado.

Being an ex-congressman gave him status and respect that pushed him up the ranks in the party pretty quick, and his wit and his bombastic ways opened a lot of doors.

The congressman's family had been long-time residents of New Mexico and were considered one of the "noble" families in politics. The problem with that, though, was that every member of his famous family had been a Republican. Jeremiah had become the black sheep when he declared himself a Democrat. Might as well have declared himself the devil. And after all these years there were still certain family members who wouldn't talk to him.

After he and Jane had lived several years in Albuquerque, occupying the same rental house they'd originally moved into, they were still not sure if they were going to stay or move to Las Cruces. But they had firmly established themselves as active political beings in all things New Mexican.

The years moved along. The Johnsons were happy, and very active for people in their middle sixties. Senator Tommy Graham had just run for governor of Colorado and won. Jeremiah had debated with himself about offering some of his nasty tidbits to the senator's opponent, but had decided he didn't need the grief. Life was at the stage where it was good to be satisfied with your existence, and he and Jane were—why stir up old pain and anger?

Then tragedy struck. Driving home from the grocery store, Jane was rammed broadside in a busy intersection by a speeding police car. The cruiser was pursuing a car thief and wasn't using its siren. She died instantly.

Jeremiah withdrew from everything and became a recluse. He had his phone disconnected and would often not answer the door. There were days when he couldn't get out of bed. The man of action, full of piss and vinegar, had been defeated. He dreamed of being dead.

"Hey anybody home? Mr. Johnson this is the police—we need to make sure you're okay. Hello? If you can hear me, I need you to come to the door or we're going to break it in."

They banged on the door some more. The doorbell hadn't worked in months. Jeremiah lay on the couch listening to them. He hated the police. He knew it wasn't rational, but that didn't change how he felt. They'd killed his wife and now they were going to break into his house. Something snapped. He blinked very quickly several times and his mind began racing. What the fuck!

He threw open the door.

"You better stop pounding on my door you moron. Do you know who the fuck I am, you little piece of shit? I tell you who I am—I am an ex-congressman, I am friends with the mayor, I am friends with the police chief, I know the asshole governor. And I am pissed. You need to get off of my property and file your goddamn report saying that the old fart who lives at this address is alive and well. Now fuck off!"

Slam. The police left. Their report said the man living at the house was up, and apparently not in any physical danger, but they suspected that he might be crazy.

After that, he began attending political meetings again. It was hard. He moved out of the house that he and Jane had shared—the memory of her was too strong there. He moved into a small apartment in downtown Albuquerque. Sometimes he would go home to his apartment and cry—he'd never done anything like that before. After some time, he cried less.

The incumbent governor of New Mexico was a Republican. He was running for reelection unopposed by anyone in the Republican Party. He was a colorless man who talked a lot about money, mostly his, and about arts and culture. He was expected to win in a landslide.

The Democrats were having a difficult time finding a viable candidate who was willing to run—and most assuredly lose. In a why-the-hell-not moment, the party chair approached Jeremiah and asked if he would consider running.

"Lookin' for someone to get stomped on by that elitist asshole of a governor."

"I understand Jeremiah. More than likely the governor's going to be re-elected. It'll be his final term, though, which means that the next election will be an open election. All of our eager beavers want to wait and run in four years. We need someone who can run a good campaign and talk about Democratic values."

"And be willing to lose."

"Yeah, I guess that's the deal. Will you do it?"

"Hell yes, I'll do it. And I will beat that pompous ass!"

Jeremiah had been a politician his entire life. He knew every trick in the book. But there was something else. He wanted to do the right thing. Not that he'd ever *not* wanted to do what was best for the people, but there was just a new intensity to his drive to help people who were being stepped on by the assholes of the world—like the current governor.

He ran a populist campaign that came from the heart. He denounced the incumbent governor in words not often heard at public meetings, and the crowds began to grow. He was an overnight sensation. He held nothing back, saying whatever he wanted to say, and people loved it. The incumbent called him foul-mouthed, crazy, a communist, another Hitler—and people loved that, too.

They only had one head-to-head debate, and Jeremiah was in his element. His opponent—who had spent years saying almost nothing of substance and now found it impossible to shift gears—was not. By the end of the debate it almost seemed like even *he* had decided to vote for Jeremiah Johnson.

Jeremiah was elected in a landslide. Within months of taking office, he'd implemented most of his campaign promises. He became the most popular and colorful governor New Mexico had ever had. He lived a simple life and spent every day trying to make Jane proud.

CHAPTER 3

Present Day, 1989—Farmington, New Mexico

Chief Deputy Trujillo had made reservations for them at the Casa Blanca Inn, just a short distance from the airport and only a few blocks from the sheriff's offices. Check-in was easy, and they were pleasantly surprised by the southwestern charm of the building and the uniqueness of a hotel that was outside the usual national chains. The overall effect was cozy and romantic.

"Ray, this place is beautiful. Guess I wasn't expecting such Santa Fe charm in Farmington."

"Plus, it's about half the price of those Santa Fe joints."

"You're always so romantic."

Ray paused a minute to see if Sue was upset or just kidding him. From her expression, he couldn't be sure. He was still getting used to a lot of new things in his life, marriage being one of the larger areas demanding his attention. He couldn't have loved Sue any more than he did, but there were many times that he wasn't sure what she was thinking. At those times he felt like he didn't know her. He had a very reliable gut instinct about crooks, but much less of one about his wife.

"Man this place just screams romance. Maybe you two should stay and I should go down to the Holiday Inn." Tyee's scowl suggested he wasn't pleased with much of anything.

"Okay, look both of you. Let's just get on with the task at hand and enjoy a nice place to stay at the expense of the governor, then head home—okay?"

The biggest problem with that plan of action was that there didn't appear to actually be a specific task at hand. Sheriff Jackson's actions were beyond anything that Ray, or even the governor, could likely deal with. If anyone was going to do something, it would have to be federal guys from the FBI or ATF. It was also apparent that Chief Deputy Trujillo had everything under control. The obvious course was for the governor or his AG to simply appoint Trujillo acting sheriff, set a special election for a little while down the road, and then stand back and let the man do his job. End of assignment.

Sue smiled at Ray in a way that told him clearly that she wasn't angry and he should go do whatever he had to do.

"I think I'll hang around the hotel and have a leisurely lunch while you two go about your duties. See you later." She gave Ray a peck on the cheek along with a wink, then set off in the direction of their room.

"Listen Ray, I know I'm being a pain in the butt. Guess it was the plane ride, not real sure. But there's something else. I know this is going to sound silly, but ever since we landed I've had a feeling of foreboding. I know you're going to mock me for getting mystical, but I have a really powerful sense of danger."

Ray let out a deep breath. "Tyee, I trust your instincts. It's not silly. I feel on edge too for some reason. I think we need to be careful. The whole thing with Sheriff Jackson is strange, but right now I think the most important thing to do is to get as much information on Trujillo as we can so we can give the governor a heads-up on whether the deputy can take over the department until there's an election."

It was a short ride to the sheriff's downtown office. Ray and Tyee were both quiet—absorbed in their own thoughts.

FACTS IN THE FICTION

The Village of Ruidoso

Not everything in my books is fiction. I've lived in New Mexico and the Southwest for many years, so I've gotten to know a lot of real places that I use as part of my fiction. Sky High Stakes mostly takes place in Ruidoso, New Mexico, a real place that I've visited many times. First, let me point out that—as far as I can tell—none of the criminal mayhem described in the story has ever actually occurred in this lovely artistic community. The Billy the Kid part is true—but that was a long time ago.

The village has long had a reputation as home to a lot of hippies, who mostly enjoy smoking pot, but it has a lot of other facets as well. There's an active art community, with many galleries. And as I mention in the book, the high altitude seems to enhance appetites, which makes it fortunate that there are quite a few wonderful restaurants in Ruidoso. Some are owned by now-aging hippies, just like the one in the Sky High Stakes, Bud's Breakfast.

You can find out more about Ruidoso at www.ruidoso.net.

The Inn of the Mountain Gods

There really is an Inn of the Mountain Gods, too, and it's a world-class resort. Today it features casino gambling, and is even grander than it was during the period in the book. I first found out about the Inn when I was living in Oklahoma in the 1960s. I read an article about The Inn of the Mountain Gods, which sounded exotic and mysterious to me. Tucked away in the New Mexico mountains, it seemed both distant and nearby. My wife and I were young and just recently married and had no money—actually, less than no money—so going to the Inn of the Mountain Gods was as farfetched as a trip to Paris—or the moon. But for some reason it found a special place amongst those fantasy locations I wanted to see one day. A remote luxury resort located next to a 12,000-foot-high mountain named Sierra Blanca, owned and operated by the Mescalero Apache Indian tribe—you can't get much more exotic to a young man in Oklahoma than that.

Many, many years later, through a strange twist in my employment situation, we ended up in Las Cruces, New Mexico, only a couple of hours away from Ruidoso. But as time grows long and memory short, I'd forgotten about the Inn of the Mountain Gods. During my first months working in Cruces there was a business conference, and it was held at the Inn of the Mountain Gods. I hated the conference—something to do with extractive resources tax strategies (*ugh*)—but I loved the Inn. After that, my wife and I visited several times. I highly recommend a visit if you're ever in New Mexico.

The Inn's web site is at www.innofthemountaingods.com.

Ruidoso Downs Race Track

Another real-world feature of *Sky High Stakes* is the Ruidoso Downs Race Track. Horse racing and gambling have gone up and down in popularity in Ruidoso. Competition from other forms of gambling has caused the racetrack problems from time to time, but horse racing and Ruidoso have remained linked through many years of history. Today the racetrack has hedged it bets by adding slot machines in the Billy the Kid Casino.

My job and my business interests often took me to Ruidoso, and on many of these trips I was accompanied by a business associate who owned horses. He raced them at Ruidoso Downs and also in El Paso, Texas. He was a larger-than-life kind of guy who loved the adrenaline rush that went with horse racing and betting, and who also greatly enjoyed consuming beer—large quantities of beer. He could have been best friends with Big Jack. He and I spent many an enjoyable (or maybe wasted) afternoon at the racetrack during the season. On at least one occasion we were asked to leave when my friend expressed his displeasure with the race results in vivid, inappropriate language. His bombastic manner contributed to the Big Jack character, and played a part in the flamboyant governor's style as well.

The racing season runs from May to the first part of September—a glorious time to be in the mountains. During the summer months you can climb from White Sands, with a temperature approaching one hundred degrees Fahrenheit, to a cool high-altitude afternoon in the upper sixties or low seventies, all within forty-five minutes or so. From hot to comfortable with just a short drive up the mountain.

Find out more at www.raceruidoso.com.

The Lodge at Cloudcroft

Another nearby attraction was part of *Dog Gone Lies*—The Lodge at Cloudcroft, which is located in the same mountains as Ruidoso. The path to get to Ruidoso from Cloudcroft is not an easy trek—the most logical approach is actually to go *back* to Alamogordo and then to Ruidoso.

The Lodge has been in existence for over a hundred years. The accommodations are outstanding, with an upscale lodge-style building housing the rooms. Features include outbuildings for special occasions that can accommodate large groups in unique room settings, including antique decor.

While we were living in Las Cruces, my daughter got married and had her wedding at The Lodge. It was a beautiful wedding, and it was enhanced by the stunning scenery and background provided by the location. This is a place that's off the beaten track and can be the highlight of any trip.

More about The Lodge here: www.thelodgeresort.com.

White Sands National Monument
From Wikipedia:

> The White Sands National Monument is a U.S. National Monument located about 16 miles (26 km) southwest of Alamogordo in western Otero County and northeastern Doña Ana County in the state of New Mexico, at an elevation of 4,235 feet (1,291 m).

> The area is in the mountain-ringed Tularosa Basin and comprises the southern part of a 275 square miles (710 km²) field of white sand dunes composed of gypsum crystals. It is the largest gypsum dune field in the world.

White Sands National Monument really does exist—why would I make that up? It appears in this story when Ray and Tyee have to go out of their way each time they drive to Ruidoso from T or C. The path they'd take goes straight across the national monument area, but also the White Sands Missile Range, which restricts access to much of the surrounding land. The military takes this very seriously.

Conclusion

Writing a book of fiction gives any author great latitude in creating characters, locations, and events, but stories seem more real to me if they take place in a location that I know. Placing fictional characters in real locations—with all of the appropriate sights, textures, fragrances, and other details—just makes the characters seem more real and alive—and it often brings back good memories.

Ted Clifton

ABOUT THE AUTHOR

Ted Clifton has been a CPA, investment banker, artist, financial writer, business entrepreneur and a sometimes philosopher. He lives in Denver, Colorado, after many years in the New Mexico desert, with his wife and grandson.

Keep in touch

Once a month, I send my readers a newsletter with a little of everything in it: southwest US culture, be it art, recipes, or local sights; my thoughts on writing and reading; book recommendations; updates on my current writing project; and from time-to-time a short story.

To sign up, visit TedClifton.com and either wait for the pop-up window, or scroll to the bottom of the page. Everybody who signs up receives a mystery gift, with my compliments.

You can also learn more about me and my latest books by visiting TedClifton.com or emailing me at ask@tedclifton.com.

OTHER BOOKS BY TED CLIFTON

Pacheco & Chino #1: Dog Gone Lies

Sheriff Ray Pacheco returns from his introduction in *The Bootlegger's Legacy* to start a new chapter as a private investigator, along with his partners: Tyee Chino, often-drunk Apache fishing guide, and Big Jack, bait shop owner and philosopher.

Available from Amazon.com at:
www.amazon.com/gp/product/1927967651

Pacheco & Chino #2: Sky High Stakes

Lincoln County, New Mexico was best known as the site of The Lincoln County Wars, featuring the likes of Billy the Kid. Martin Marino, the acting sheriff, is also short in stature, just like The Kid—and no doubt also like The Kid, Marino is crazy. Lincoln County survived Billy the Kid, but Martin Marino might be a different matter.

Ray Pacheco and Tyee Chino have been asked by the state Attorney General to find out what the hell is going on in the Lincoln County Sheriff's department. Ray is sure there's some big trouble waiting for them and his gut is right: murder, lust, madness and greed are visiting the high country.

Pacheco & Chino #3: Four Corners War

Navajos, Apaches, militias, good sheriffs, and bad sheriffs are all drawn to a small town by millions in stolen money and a small army's worth of stolen military equipment. Is this the start of a Four Corners War? Nothing is as it should be as Ray Pacheco and Tyee Chino try to untangle the mix of greedy businessmen, corrupt politicians and a slightly unhinged sheriff—along with the usual dead bodies.

Farmington, New Mexico's unique mix of cultures is the backdrop for Ray and Tyee's most dangerous assignment to date from the bombastic Governor of New Mexico.

Coming in late 2016.

The Bootlegger's Legacy

When an old-time bootlegger dies and leaves his son Mike a cryptic letter hinting at millions in hidden cash, Mike and his friend Joe embark on a journey that takes them through three states and 50 years of history. What they find goes beyond money and transforms them both.

An action-packed adventure story that takes place in the late 1980s and the early 1950s. It all starts with a key, embossed with the letters CB, and a cryptic reference to Deep Deuce, a neighborhood once filled with hot jazz and gangs of bootleggers. Out of those threads is woven a tapestry of history, romance, drama, and mystery; connecting two generations and two families in the adventure of a lifetime.

Praise for *The Bootlegger's Legacy:*

"... superb character development ... vivid backdrops, brisk pacing, and meticulously researched ..." —*Kirkus Reviews*

"A rollicking good time." —*Self-Publishing Review*

"... interesting characters, true-to-life situations, and intriguing twists ..." —*Stanley Nelson, Senior Staff Writer, Chickasaw Press*

Where to find *The Bootlegger's Legacy:*

Available from Amazon.com at:
www.amazon.com/gp/product/B014TFC9AK

Or ask for it by name or ISBN at your favourite bookstore.